Forever K9

A K9 Mystery

Holly S Roberts

Wicked Story Telling

Contents

Chapter One

Part I

D ETECTIVES WORK BEST IN teams. It's that whole right brain, left brain scenario. In a good, well-established team, what one person misses, the other zeros in on. That's what I lost when my partner Tony died of cancer. It's been two years, and I still can't find someone who complements me—someone who pushes me to be a better detective, tolerates my moods, and doesn't scoff at my outside-the-box theories. Tony was always first to congratulate me when I was dead-on, even after making fun of my leap from evidence to outrageous. He also pointed out when I was wrong and made sure I remembered it, several times over.

The walls of our old precinct still seem to echo with his voice—his dry wit and that easy chuckle he'd let out when I was thinking too far ahead. His absence is like a constant shadow, lurking just beyond the periphery of my workday. And even though I keep moving forward, it feels like I'm just marking time, waiting for something to change. Waiting for that spark that most likely will never come. I'm a pessimist and an all around disgruntled cop and I like it that way.

My department has five detectives, and I'm the odd one out—or, in my case, the odd woman out. Out of thirty-two certified officers, I'm one of only three women, and the only female detective. I work in a man's world, and it shows. That was another reason Tony and I meshed so well. He didn't care that I was a woman. He cared about solving cases, plain and simple, and we were darn good at it. Together, we were a force. Now, it feels like I'm drifting, barely keeping afloat.

For the past two years, I've been coasting, making the motions but without the same sharpness, without the same urgency. I still solve cases—good ones—but not with the same rate of success Tony and I had. I've tried working with other detectives, cycling through partnerships in the hopes of finding someone who could even come close. But none of them fit. None of them challenged me the way Tony did.

Our relationship was never romantic. He was happily married to Beth, and Beth and I were close, too. After Tony passed, Beth and I stayed in touch for the first year, meeting for drinks every now and then. We'd reminisce about him, sharing memories that were as painful as they were sweet. But after a while, Beth began moving on. She started dating again, and when she sent me a "save the date" card for her upcoming wedding this fall, it felt like a punch to the gut.

Save the date—what a ridiculous concept. I didn't need a card to remind me that life was moving forward for everyone except Tony. It was just another reminder that the world keeps spinning, even when you're standing still, trapped in the past.

Beth's life without Tony had moved on. Mine? It was ending here today at a dog kennel.

Yes, an overdramatic statement, but in my opinion, accurate. After years of complaints from fellow officers and detectives, my sergeant, Lou Spence, finally stopped listening to my excuses. He decided to partner me with a dog. A trained K9. The so-called miracle partner—one who never files grievances, never challenges my mood swings, and most importantly, never questions my hunches.

Our first conversation on the subject was brief.

"How do you feel about dogs, Detective Jolett?" he asked, flipping through a stack of papers without even glancing up at me.

"I've dated a few," I replied, my tone dry. "They smell, they need a tight choke collar, and you have to throw them a bone every now and then to keep them from running off. It doesn't help much. They're still generally a nuisance." I paused, hoping to get some reaction out of him. Nothing.

Lou wasn't fazed. "Your training starts Monday at 0800. You'll be gone for eight weeks. Don't worry about your cases; they're being reassigned." He met my eyes finally, and the corners of his mouth twitched as if he might smile. For a second, I thought he would. "Don't call me, Laci—I'll call you." He used my first name, making it clear I had no choice in the matter.

"Sir, respectfully—" I never finished.

"Whatever canine you choose will be your new partner. There will be no complaining from him, threatening to quit if he doesn't like you, or being stubborn when his supervisor gives him or her an order. Do you understand what I'm saying, Detective Jolett?"

There was nothing to do. My Sergeant was behaving like a cold brick wall and I would not win this battle. The war was not over, and I didn't doubt I would be the ultimate victor. I didn't like dogs of the two- or four-legged variety and that wouldn't change.

Now, six weeks later, I'd gone through basic K9 training with different dogs used specifically for idiots like me. I was currently standing in a cold, industrial kennel with two more weeks of training left, about to pick my new "partner." Jack Mallory, the head of the Arizona Police K9 Reserve Program, was leading me down a long, dimly lit hallway, where the clamor of barking dogs echoed off the concrete walls. It smelled like bleach and wet fur, the sharp tang of disinfectant mixing with the earthy scent of kibble. Overhead, the fluorescent lights flickered, casting a harsh, sterile glow that made everything feel even more clinical.

The dogs here weren't pets—they were tools, highly trained, highly skilled, and most of them looked at me with disdain as I passed. German Shepherds, Belgian Malinois, even a Staffordshire terrier—all bred for precision, for work, for loyalty.

One of the Shepherds lunged at the bars as I walked by, snarling. I didn't flinch, even as he tried to take a bite out of my hand. I glared back at him, but my stare didn't intimidate him one bit. His growls echoed in the narrow corridor, the sound rattling in my chest. Jack, who had been quiet up to this point, gestured toward the dog.

"Cocamo's a good dog, but he'll take some adjustment time," Jack said, his tone calm, as if he hadn't just watched me nearly lose a hand.

"Not for me," I replied, already moving on. I wasn't interested in a challenge.

We kept walking. One of the Malinois caught my eye, so Jack brought him out of the cage. The dog moved with sleek precision, his fur shining under the cold fluorescent light.

"Sterling," Jack said, running a hand over the Malinois' back. "He's got a good disposition. Not too high-strung, but he's fierce when he needs to be. He likes to play during downtime. He's young, needs a lot of stimulation."

I barely paid attention to my own reflection in the mirror each morning, let alone anyone—or anything—else. Stimulation was the last thing I had to offer to a dog I didn't want. I was here to get Spence off my back, not to make friends.

Then I saw him—curled up in the far corner of a cage, barely moving, a black mass of fur. His head was turned away from us, disinterested in the commotion around him. I pointed. "Who's that?"

Jack followed my gaze and sighed, rubbing the back of his neck. "That's Suii. He's lazy, and he's getting up there in age.

Maybe two years left before he's retired. He's not the most enthusiastic worker, but he's got experience."

I liked the sound of that. We had something in common. "Bring him out."

Jack hesitated, then opened the cage. Suii lifted his head slowly, his big chocolate eyes meeting mine for a brief second before he let out a deep sigh, almost as if this entire ordeal was an inconvenience. He uncurled himself, stretching his massive body and lumbering toward Jack with a slow, deliberate gait. He sat down, slouching heavily beside Jack's leg.

Jack handed me the leash. "He's trained in German. You'll have two weeks to learn his commands."

I took the leash and gave it a firm tug. Suii didn't move. I tugged again, snapping my fingers. Slowly, ever so slowly, Suii shuffled over to me, his hulking frame moving with a kind of lazy grace. He sat at my feet, his massive head tilting as he looked up at me with those deep, weary eyes.

I crouched down, meeting his gaze. "I have a couch, a TV, and a small back patio. If you can handle that, we'll get along just fine."

Suii cocked his head slightly, his floppy ears twitching ever so slightly in acknowledgment. That was good enough for me.

"When can we leave?" I asked, not taking my eyes off the dog.

"We'll start the next phase of training right now. Suii's a bit of a handful," Jack said, his voice softening. "His handler was killed in the line of duty. Since then, Suii hasn't bonded with anyone. Don't get your hopes up."

Bonding wasn't something I needed. Suii and I would get along just fine.

Chapter Two

S UII WAS LAZY, STUBBORN, and perfect. From the moment we began our final two weeks of training, it was clear that this dog and I were cut from the same cloth. He performed every task with the least amount of effort possible, moving slowly, his tongue perpetually hanging out, dripping saliva all over the training grounds. His dark coat gleamed under the Tucson sun as he panted heavily, his breath sounding like the rhythmic hum of an engine after a long drive. Jack, the head of the K9 program, tried to hide his dismay, but I could see it in his eyes—he didn't think Suii and I were a good match.

But I didn't care. Suii was my kind of dog, and besides, this training wasn't about impressing anyone. It was about getting through it and heading back home to Northern Arizona, where the temperatures were cooler and the air less stifling. Jack had mentioned that Rottweilers weren't the best suited for service in warmer climates, as they didn't acclimate well to the heat. And Tucson, with its mid-spring desert heat, was a prime example. Every day, the sun beat down relentlessly on the training field, casting long shadows across the dry, cracked earth. Even though I was used to the Arizona sun, the heat was oppressive, but Suii made it his personal mission to find any sliver of shade within leash distance. He'd stretch his lead to its absolute limit, dragging me along until he could collapse into a patch of coolness, his massive body landing with a soft *thud* and a long, satisfied huff.

Suii's version of parade rest was more like parade lounge. He'd sprawl out on the ground, legs askew, eyes half-lidded, completely unbothered by the commands Jack barked at him. I secretly cheered him on when Jack wasn't looking. There was something endearing about Suii's refusal to play by the rules, and I appreciated his lack of enthusiasm. If nothing else, it was refreshing to see a dog that didn't try so hard to impress everyone. He wasn't here to win anyone's affection, and neither was I.

The last two weeks of training passed without incident, though I'd be lying if I said I didn't complain—just a little. Despite Jack's skepticism, I knew Suii was the right fit for me. He didn't need constant attention, didn't care about winning praise, and was perfectly content doing the bare minimum. That was something I could relate to.

On graduation day, I received Suii's documentation, and we made our way to my car. The heat was unforgiving, and the sun glinted off the hood of my green, unmarked patrol unit like a burning star. I opened the door to the back, revealing the K9 cage, and Suii jumped in without hesitation, giving his stub tail a quick wag before settling in.

I cranked the air conditioner to full blast, the cool air instantly filling the car and offering relief from the sweltering day. Suii stretched out in the back, his massive frame taking up nearly the entire cage, and within moments he was fast asleep, his deep, steady breaths a low hum over the sound of the air conditioning. I adjusted the radio to some upbeat pop station, not because I liked it, but because it was better than the static of silence.

As we crossed the desert and headed toward Pierce, the city limits sign came into view, and the familiar streets began to unfold before me like an old, worn map. The rolling hills of Northern Arizona, peppered with juniper trees and dry brush, were a welcome sight after weeks in the flat, sunbaked desert.

I turned the radio down and started talking to Suii, who had finally roused from his nap.

"I've got a neighbor for you to terrorize," I said, glancing at the rearview mirror to see Suii's head lift at the sound of my voice. "You do a good job, and there'll be treats in it for you. He's got this little rat of a dog—calls it a Shih Tzu. You can eat him if no one's looking."

Suii's ears perked up ever so slightly at the word "treat," but then his head flopped back down, his attention waning as quickly as it had sparked. I grinned. He was the perfect partner.

As we pulled into my neighborhood, the first thing I noticed was Mr. Knock-toes shuffling toward me, his pigeon-toed gait more exaggerated than ever. Tucked under his arm was Craptzu, the bane of my existence—a dog that didn't seem to understand the concept of boundaries, especially when it came to my five-by-ten strip of grass. Craptzu left his mark regularly, piles of poo and brown pee spots that peppered the small patch of green in front of my townhome. It didn't take a detective to figure out who the culprit was.

I parked the car and stepped out, already formulating a plan. With deliberate slowness, I made my way to the back, opening Suii's door. He blinked up at me lazily, not yet interested in the prospect of getting out. I clipped the leash onto his collar and made a subtle motion toward Mr. Knock-toes and Craptzu, who were now standing just a few feet away.

"Fass," I whispered in German.

Suii's transformation was immediate. The lazy, indifferent dog I'd been training with for weeks suddenly sprang to life, muscles coiling as he lunged forward, pulling me several feet before I regained control. His growls were deep and menacing, completely overwhelming the pathetic yips coming from Craptzu, who was now squirming in Mr. Knock-toes' arms.

"Nein, nein!" I shouted, fighting to keep my balance as Suii strained at the leash, his powerful body nearly yanking me off my feet.

Mr. Knock-toes' eyes widened in terror, and for a brief moment, I thought he might pass out. Craptzu was screeching now, a high-pitched wail that only added to the chaos. It was glorious. I didn't need to stick around to see if Mr. Knock-toes' pants were as soiled as my yard usually was. With a quick command—"Hier"—I called Suii back. He followed me obediently, still growling under his breath as we headed toward the front door.

Once inside, I shut the door behind us, leaning against it for a moment as laughter bubbled up inside me. "Good dog, Suii. What a good dog," I crooned, using the high-pitched play voice I'd learned during training. His tail wagged slowly, his big brown eyes looking up at me with what I could only describe as smug satisfaction.

I led him to the back door, opening it with a flourish. "Not much, but it's your kingdom," I said as he padded outside, his nose already twitching as he sniffed the air. "Mark your territory while I bring in our things."

As I unloaded the car, I glanced toward Mr. Knock-toes' yard. No sign of him. Smart man.

For the first time since Tony's death, I felt a sense of satisfaction—a small victory, maybe, but a victory nonetheless. And it made me happy.

Over the next few days, Suii and I settled into a comfortable routine. We worked together for two hours each day, running through commands and exercises that were necessary for his ongoing training. I meticulously logged everything into his training manual, ensuring that we hit all the required marks. But when we weren't working, we were lounging. Suii wasn't a fan of my kale chips, and I wasn't a fan of his dog biscuits, but we made it work.

At night, he took up his position in front of my bedroom door, a silent sentry who listened to my complaints without judgment or commentary. And for that, I was grateful.

Chapter Three

I AWOKE EARLY ON Wednesday, my first day back at work after eight long weeks away. Sunlight filtered through the half-closed blinds, casting soft rays across the room, and for the first time in a long while, I felt rested. As I stretched and climbed out of bed, I realized something surprising: I didn't feel the usual drag of exhaustion pulling me back under the covers. Maybe, just maybe, I'd needed this break more than I thought.

For the past two years, I had relied on an endless stream of coffee to keep my eyes open and my feet moving, using caffeine as a crutch to get through the grind. But today, with only one cup and Suii at my side, I was ready to go. The dog, already awake and alert, sat at attention near the door, his large, sleepy eyes now sharp and focused as if he knew today was a big day for us both. He gave me a sidelong glance, then let out a slow huff, the same kind of lazy sigh that had become a familiar sound in the weeks we'd spent together.

There was something about working with a dog that was different from the human partnerships I'd relied on before. Suii's aloofness, his indifference to my moods, had grown on me. His companionship, though wordless, was oddly comforting. Maybe this change wouldn't be so bad after all.

After getting dressed, I headed downstairs, Suii padding behind me with his massive paws making soft thuds on the hardwood floor. I grabbed my coffee, he grabbed a quick lap of water from his bowl, and we were ready to face the day. We both stopped to inspect the front yard before leaving—no crap and no sign of Craptzu, the pesky little Shih Tzu that had terrorized my small patch of grass for far too long. A small victory, but it set the tone for the day. So far, so good.

The ride to the department was short—less than ten minutes. The roads were quiet, the early morning sun casting a soft glow on the sleepy town. The temperature had dipped into the low sixties, a far cry from the brutal desert heat I'd endured during training, and I relished the cool breeze that filtered in through the cracked window. I pulled up to the department gate, entered my pin code, and waited as the large, metal fence rolled back with a mechanical hum. As soon as I was inside, I parked beneath the only tree in the lot, claiming the limited shade as my own. I made a mental note to let Sergeant Spence know this space was mine from now on.

The department building stood tall, its brick walls weathered by years of sun, rain, and wind. I glanced at Suii in the backseat, where he was sprawled out, already looking far too comfortable. His eyes were half-closed, but I knew better than to assume he wasn't paying attention.

"I'll be right back," I muttered to him, closing the car door quietly behind me. I took a few steps toward the squad room when a sudden, loud bark broke the morning silence. Half bark, half whine, Suii's voice rang out from the car.

"Nein. Phui," I snapped, using the German commands he knew so well. Shame. But instead of quieting down, Suii's noises only grew louder. His bark-whine evolved into a full-blown howl that echoed across the parking lot. The deep, mournful sound reverberated off the walls of the nearby buildings, drawing more than a few curious glances from the officers heading into work.

I groaned inwardly. This was embarrassing. For a dog who looked as tough as Suii, he sure was acting like a baby.

Turning on my heel, I marched back to the car, opened the door, and grabbed the leash. Suii immediately ceased his tantrum and sat there, head cocked to the side as if he'd just won a small battle. I clipped the leash to his collar and let him out. "Who's got who trained here, huh?" I muttered under my breath as I led him toward the squad room.

Inside, the atmosphere was typical for the early morning. The dull clatter of keyboards filled the air as officers sat at their desks, typing up reports or nursing cups of coffee. A few glanced up when I entered, but no one said anything. That was fine by me—I wasn't one for idle chit-chat, especially with Suii's hulking, muscular presence by my side. The sight of a 150-pound Rottweiler was enough to keep most people from trying to make small talk.

I made my way to Sergeant Spence's office, gave the door a quick knock, and stepped inside. Spence was sitting behind his desk, hunched over a mountain of paperwork, but his head popped up when he saw me.

"Detective Jolett and K9 Suii reporting for duty, sir," I said, my voice dripping with sarcasm.

Spence grinned, leaning back in his chair as he looked at the dog by my side. "Glad to have you back, and glad to meet our newest officer," he said, eyes glinting with amusement.

"This is Suii," I replied, resting a hand on the dog's head. "His disposition's about the same as mine, so naturally, we're getting along just fine. Got any work for me, or do I need to go cruise town and rustle up some deadbeats?"

Spence chuckled. "May I approach Suii?" he asked as he slowly stood, giving the dog a respectful nod.

"Bleib," I commanded. Stay. "Approach at your own risk," I added, flashing Spence a sly grin.

"You know, I was a handler for twenty years," Spence said as he walked around his desk. "It's good to see a K9 again. The department's been needing one for a while."

Suii, ever the slacker, didn't move. I handed Spence the leash, explaining, "He's trained in German."

Spence didn't miss a beat. "Heir." Come.

For a moment, Suii did nothing but shoot me a sideways glance as if to say, *Really? Him?*

"Pass auf," I muttered. Pay attention.

Suii let out a sigh, clearly annoyed by the whole ordeal, before he meandered over to Spence, his massive frame lumbering across the floor like a reluctant giant. He didn't sit, of course—no, that would be too much effort. Instead, he flopped down dramatically at Spence's feet, expelling a gust of air from his lungs as if to make it clear that he wasn't pleased.

"He's an embarrassment to the department," I muttered, shaking my head.

Spence laughed, bending down to run his hand through Suii's thick fur. "He's a darn fine dog. I talked to Jack Mallory, and he said you two did well together."

I bit back a snort. I had no idea how Spence managed to keep a straight face while saying that. My training with Suii had been less than stellar, with both of us doing the bare minimum to get by.

"May I have my fur bucket back?" I asked dryly. Before I even extended my hand for the leash, Suii was already up, plodding back over to me with a grunt.

Spence handed over the leash with a grin. "The two of you are bonding."

"Bonding my hind-end," I replied. "I hand out the cookies, and he knows it. Now, about those cases?"

"They're on your desk. Call dispatch and give them Suii's badge number. I'll send over an official order in the next hour."

As I turned to leave, I glanced over my shoulder. "And what is Suii's badge number?"

"David Sixteen," Spence called after me.

****

I sat at my desk, staring at the far wall of my office while Suii curled up at my feet, his steady breathing a comforting presence in the otherwise quiet room. D16—David Sixteen. The badge number echoed in my mind like a bell, each ring heavier than the last.

That had been Tony's badge number.

I felt a lump rise in my throat, my hand hovering over the phone as I contemplated calling dispatch. But I couldn't bring myself to do it. Not yet. The memories of Tony, the partnership we'd shared, the cases we'd cracked together—it all felt too close, too raw. I leaned back in my chair, closing my eyes for a moment.

A cold, wet nose nudged my hand, pulling me from my thoughts. I opened my eyes to find Suii standing beside the desk, his big brown eyes full of concern. Without warning, his massive tongue darted out and licked my hand, leaving a trail of slobber in its wake.

"Ugh, that's gross, you know?" I muttered, wiping my hand on my pants.

Suii let out a soft whine, the first real show of affection I'd seen from him. It wasn't much, but it was something. Maybe the big lug understood more than I gave him credit for.

I scratched behind his ears, rubbing the underside of his neck. "You'll never be half the partner Tony was, but I guess you can have his badge number."

With a sigh, I picked up the phone and dialed dispatch.

D14 and D16 were a team again.

Chapter Four

O THER THAN THE EVER-PRESENT pile of fur by my side each day, my first week back at work was uneventful. Suii had settled into his role as my constant companion, his hulking presence a deterrent for casual conversation. A few snide comments floated through the air, whispers about "the new female at the department," but I didn't care enough to correct them. Let them think what they want. If they'd been paying attention, they would've noticed that Suii, the so-called "new female," was a neutered male. The whispers were low, barely reaching my ears, and Suii's leash didn't extend far enough for me to do anything about it. Not that I would. Giving the attack command would be satisfying, but the paperwork would be a nightmare.

My fellow detectives showed more respect toward Suii than the gossipmongers. None of them could deny that I was a good detective—darn good—but I wasn't winning any Miss Congeniality awards, and I didn't care. Tony had been well-liked, his easy charm opening doors for me that I couldn't have opened on my own. He'd taught me to play nice, to engage in small talk and gossip, all the things that kept a police department humming along smoothly.

Blah, blah, and blah.

Tony was no longer around to smooth the edges, and without him, I found myself even further out of the loop. Suii's presence, with his large, powerful jaws and brooding eyes, put an even wider distance between me and the rest of the department. And I liked it that way. It was quieter. Simpler. Less fake.

The first day of my second week with Suii, however, changed everything.

It started out routine. I was heading to a woman's house to interview her about her car being stolen the week before. We'd already recovered the vehicle—her son had been the culprit, naturally. What bothered me was the fact that she'd failed to mention her son was living with her and had disappeared at the same time as the car. She'd wasted my time, and that was something I hated more than anything. Now, to make matters worse, she didn't want to press charges.

I was fuming as I neared her home, weighing whether or not I should file a felony complaint against her for obstruction. The streets were quiet, the neighborhood just starting to wake up, when a call came over the radio—a domestic in progress, a family fight. I recognized the address immediately, a familiar knot of frustration forming in my gut.

The couple who lived there had been on my radar for a long time. They had small children, and though their violent arguments had brought the cops out several times, we'd never been able to remove the kids from the home. No bruises, no outward signs of abuse, nothing the courts would act on. But anyone with half a brain could see those kids were suffering.

I pressed the button on my mic, my voice steady. "David Fourteen and Sixteen on scene. Please send backup patrol." I usually wouldn't enter a domestic situation without backup, but Suii changed things. He was more than just a deterrent—he was my safety net.

I parked two houses down, the sound of arguing already filtering through the air as I stepped out of the car. The tension was thick, the kind that made your skin prickle with anticipation. I grabbed my outer ballistic vest, tugging it over my head and securing the heavy-duty Velcro strips. The vest was laden with tools of the trade—a Taser, cuffs, rubber gloves, and a flashlight. I attached Suii's leash, and together we headed toward the front door.

Suii's low growl started before I even reached the door. His body tensed, every muscle coiled with energy as his growl deepened. That's when I heard it—a woman's scream, sharp and terrified, followed by the high-pitched wails of children.

Without hesitation, I turned the knob and found the door unlocked.

"Police," I called out, stepping into the entryway with my gun drawn and pointed down. The house was small, cluttered with the accumulation of family life—scattered toys, laundry that hadn't been folded, and the faint scent of something burnt lingering in the air. But what grabbed my attention immediately was the scene unfolding in the living room.

Daryl, the husband, had his wife, Melody, pinned to the floor, his fist raised as he pummeled her with savage, brutal strikes. He didn't even look up when I entered. The two kids were cowering in the hallway, wide-eyed and trembling. Melody had stopped screaming after the first punch I witnessed, and from the way her head lolled to the side, I knew she was unconscious.

"Back off!" I shouted, leveling my gun at Daryl. My voice was loud, authoritative, cutting through the chaos. But Daryl didn't look at the gun. His gaze shifted instead to Suii, whose growls had grown louder, more menacing. Daryl's eyes widened with fear, his fist hesitating in mid-air.

And then, in an act of sheer stupidity, he pulled his fist back to hit Melody again.

"Fass," I commanded, dropping Suii's lead.

Suii sprang into action, his massive body moving with terrifying speed. One hundred and fifty pounds of muscle and teeth crashed into Daryl, knocking him away from Melody. The man's scream echoed through the small house, louder than the children's cries, as Suii latched onto his arm, dragging him off his wife.

"Stop moving and he'll back off!" I shouted, repeating myself over the noise. Daryl's body went rigid, fear overtaking his instincts.

"Officer Franks behind you," came a voice from the doorway.

"Call an ambulance," I barked, moving quickly to check on Melody. Her eyelids fluttered, her breathing rapid and shallow. "You with me, Mel?" I asked, kneeling beside her.

"The kids," she whimpered, her voice barely audible over her sobs.

"They're safe," I reassured her, though their cries still pierced the air. I glanced toward the hallway, where the children were huddled together, staring wide-eyed at the chaos. Suii stood over Daryl, his jaws still locked around the man's arm, blood seeping through his fur.

"Call your dog off and I'll cuff him," Franks said, stepping forward.

"Suii, aus!" I ordered. Release.

With a final growl, Suii let go of Daryl's arm and padded back to my side, his eyes still locked on the man as if daring him to move. I clipped the leash back onto Suii's collar and gave him a quick pat.

"We've got an ambulance on the way, Melody. Stay down—you might have a concussion. Let me check on the kids," I said softly, though my voice was strained with adrenaline.

I approached the children, my mind still reeling from the violence I'd just witnessed. I wasn't thinking about how scared they must be—how terrifying it must have been to see a dog like Suii take down their father. But Suii knew. He slunk low to the ground, his belly brushing against the floor as he slowly crawled toward the kids. His growls had ceased, replaced by soft whines.

The children's eyes never left him, wide with fear and curiosity. I tugged gently on the leash, trying to pull Suii back, but he inched closer until he was within arm's reach of the older girl. Then, in a surprising display of empathy, Suii rolled onto his back, his massive belly exposed, whining softly.

The girl tentatively reached out a trembling hand and placed it on his belly. "He... he hurt my mom... mommy," she whispered, her voice trembling with fear and confusion.

For a moment, I thought she meant Suii, but I quickly realized she was talking about her father.

Before I could respond, the girl threw her arms around Suii's massive body, clinging to him as though he were her lifeline. Suii responded in kind, licking her tear-streaked face gently, his large tongue moving slowly as if he knew she needed comfort. The younger child, a boy of no more than two or three, hesitated for a moment before placing his small hand on Suii's belly, joining his sister in a quiet, tender moment that seemed to eclipse the violence of just a few minutes before.

I turned to Franks, who had already cuffed Daryl and was holding him by the shoulder, his expression one of stunned surprise. For a moment, we locked eyes, neither of us sure what to make of the scene before us. We had one man in custody, two calm children, and Melody following my orders by lying still on the floor, waiting for medical attention.

The ambulance crew arrived, their voices low as they surveyed the room. "Do we need to check the kids?" one of them asked, stepping toward me.

Suii growled softly, still lying on his back. It was a low, rumbling sound, but it was enough to freeze the EMT in his tracks. I held up a hand. "No, they're fine. Check on mom first—she was unconscious for a bit. Dad'll need a few puncture wounds tended before he's carted off to jail."

"I'm suing the entire department for what that dog did to me," Daryl spat through gritted teeth, his face twisted in a grimace as Franks tightened the cuffs.

I ignored him, turning my focus back to the children. Neither of them even glanced at their father as the EMTs worked. It was as though they'd already written him off, too accustomed to the violence and chaos that had filled their young lives. The older girl remained perched on top of Suii, her small fingers tangling in his fur as if holding onto him for dear life. The little boy had inched closer, his face now buried in Suii's soft belly.

It broke my heart to see kids so used to this kind of horror that they could find solace in a dog who had just taken down their father. I crouched down, keeping my voice low and steady. "Hey, how about we step outside? The ambulance crew needs to check on your mom, and Suii here could use some fresh air." I gestured toward the open front door, where the sunlight streamed in, golden and warm, a stark contrast to the cold violence we'd just witnessed.

The older girl looked up at me, her tear-streaked face showing a mixture of fear and confusion. "Is mommy gonna be okay?" she whispered.

I nodded, trying to convey a confidence I didn't entirely feel. "She's in good hands. Let's go outside and give the paramedics some room to help her. Suii will stay with you, okay? He needs some more love."

The girl sniffled, wiping her nose with the back of her hand before taking Suii's leash from me. "He's brave," she said with quiet conviction.

I smiled softly, my heart aching for her. "Yeah, he is."

The girl gave a slight tug on the leash, and Suii immediately got to his feet, following her toward the front door with a calm, gentle pace. I scooped up the younger boy, who didn't resist, and we made our way out into the fresh air. The sun felt like a balm against my skin, the weight of the situation lifting slightly as we stepped onto the porch.

Suii, always attuned to the needs of others, lowered himself back onto the ground as soon as we were outside, rolling over again onto his back. The girl wasted no time in resuming her position next to him, running her small hands over his belly while her brother joined in, their soft giggles filling the air as Suii's large tongue made quick work of cleaning their tear-streaked faces.

I stood at the edge of the porch, watching the scene unfold with a mixture of awe and sadness. How many times had these kids witnessed their father's violence? How many nights had they cried themselves to sleep, wishing for something—anything—to change? I knew the answer to those questions all too well. And I knew, too, that this wouldn't be the last time I'd be called out to this house unless something drastic happened.

I grabbed my mic and called into dispatch. "David Fourteen, request immediate CPS on scene. Two minors need assistance. Over."

"Copy, David Fourteen. CPS is en route. ETA ten minutes."

I clipped the mic back onto my vest and turned to check on the kids. Suii was doing what he did best—keeping them calm, distracting them with his playful nudges and gentle licks. I crouched down beside the girl, brushing a strand of hair from her face.

"Hey," I said softly. "I'm gonna stay with you until someone comes to help. They're gonna make sure you and your brother are okay, alright?"

The girl nodded, her grip on Suii's leash tightening slightly. "Are they gonna take us away?"

Her question hit me like a punch to the gut. I wanted to lie, to tell her everything would be fine and that she'd stay with her mom and everything would magically be better. But I couldn't. I wasn't sure what would happen next, and it wasn't in my power to make promises I couldn't keep.

"They're gonna make sure you're safe," I said, my voice firm. "That's the most important thing."

Behind me, the ambulance crew wheeled Melody out of the house, her face bruised and swollen, but her eyes open and alert. She looked over at her children, her expression a mix of relief and shame. As they loaded her into the ambulance, Daryl was escorted out in handcuffs, his arm bandaged and his face twisted in pain. He shot me a glare as he passed, his voice dripping with venom.

"I'll own this entire city if that dog hurts my kids," he spat.

I didn't bother responding. The man had already lost far more than he realized, and in that moment, he was nothing more than noise. The children, his own kids, hadn't even looked in his direction as he was led away. It was a sad, silent testament to how immune they had become to the chaos and violence he brought into their lives.

As Daryl disappeared from view, I made a silent vow. If Melody didn't find the strength to leave him, I would do everything in my power to ensure those children never had to face another day of fear in that house.

A few minutes later, the CPS worker arrived. She was a calm, soft-spoken woman with kind eyes, and as I introduced her to the children, I felt a small sense of relief. The kids would be in good hands tonight, at least. And for now, that was enough.

Suii, still basking in the attention of the children, rolled over one last time as they scratched his belly, their giggles filling the warm afternoon air.

The older girl looked up at me, her eyes clear for the first time that day. "He's a hero," she whispered, her voice full of wonder.

I smiled down at her, my hand resting on Suii's massive head. "Yeah," I said softly. "He really is."

Chapter Five

S UII WHINED SOFTLY FOR a full ten minutes after the children left with CPS, his big brown eyes following their retreat as if willing them to come back. His usual confident posture was gone, replaced with something almost vulnerable. I could tell the whole situation had affected him more than he'd let on during the chaos. I knelt down, resting a hand on his head, and his tongue darted out to lick my fingers in a comforting, albeit slobbery, gesture.

The street was quiet now, the aftermath of the domestic dispute already starting to fade into the background of a regular workday. Two more officers arrived, their patrol cars crunching softly over the gravel as they parked alongside mine. Their voices broke the stillness as they approached, casual and almost conversational—a far cry from the tense urgency of just an hour ago.

As I began taking pictures of the scene, documenting every detail for the report, I couldn't shake the lingering weight of the kids' faces, the way they clung to Suii as if he were the only solid thing in a world of uncertainty. I rarely ended up first on a scene like this, but for once, I was grateful it had been me. I could have easily handed off the report to Officer Franks, who was already wrapping up his side of things, but I wasn't going to. I wanted to lead this case. I needed to.

I glanced up from my camera as Franks made his way over. "That's a good K9 you've got there," he said, nodding toward Suii, who stood close by my side, ever-watchful.

A sense of pride swelled in my chest, and I found myself smiling. "Yes, he is," I replied, the words coming out with more warmth than I expected. The officers began chatting with me—something that rarely happened—and for once, I didn't immediately shut them down. I explained why I wanted the case, laying out my intentions to push for the kids' removal if their mother didn't make the right decision. It was strange, talking openly about my motives. Normally, I kept that kind of stuff to myself. But for some reason, today felt different.

Suii stood quietly beside me, his posture relaxed but alert. The other officers didn't try to pet him—there was an unspoken respect for the dog's role, and for mine as his handler. It wasn't lost on me that their attitude toward me had shifted ever so slightly. Maybe Suii had something to do with that.

"He's got a drug certification too, right?" Franks asked, curiosity in his voice.

I nodded. "Yes, he's dual trained."

Franks smiled, a mischievous glint in his eye. "So, would a call in the middle of the night bother you?" He hurried on before I could answer. "The drug task force works I-40 on weekends, and we're always short on K9s. We could really use you and Suii when we've got something big."

I considered it for a moment, then sighed. "If you can limit it to two or three times a month, I won't complain."

His grin widened, almost comical. I was known for complaining about just about everything. This would be a first.

Three hours later, I had my report finished—pictures attached, details logged, and the endless stack of paperwork that came with using K9 force. Most people had no idea just how much paperwork went into closing a police report, let alone one that involved a K9 apprehension. And on top of that, I had Suii's record book to fill out. It showed a successful apprehension with minimal injury to the suspect, which was about as good as it got.

Suii and I made our way to Sergeant Spence's office. The precinct was quieter now, the hustle of the morning giving way to the slower rhythm of midday. Lou was on the phone when I entered, so I took a seat at his desk, resting my feet on the chair's edge as I waited. Years of working with Lou had taught me that if he wanted privacy, he'd shut the door. For now, I was content to sit and wait.

Lou caught sight of Suii standing obediently by my side and snapped his fingers. Without hesitation, I released the leash, and Suii trotted over to Lou, accepting the affection with a contented huff as Lou scratched behind his ears.

"Call me back when you've got an answer," Lou said into the phone before hanging up and turning his full attention to me. "Two weeks back on the job, and not a single complaint against you. I'm impressed."

I raised an eyebrow. "You're exaggerating," I said, crossing my arms. "I average about one complaint a month, if you don't count the verbal grumbles from the rest of the department."

Lou grinned. "You're unaware of half of the complaints I take from the department because I rarely wanted to tangle with you myself." He gave Suii a final pat on the head before looking back at me. "Seriously, though, he's a great dog."

"I think so too," I said, my voice softening as I glanced down at Suii. He let out a small, appreciative whine, as if he understood the compliment.

"All these years, and no one figured out that your only real problem is a dislike of people," Lou said, shaking his head with a chuckle.

I shrugged, leaning back in the chair. "I liked Tony."

It was the first time I'd initiated a conversation about my old partner, and the significance of that wasn't lost on me. The words came out easier than I thought they would. I hadn't realized it until that moment, but it was time to start moving on with my life.

Lou's face softened, his smile tinged with a hint of sadness. "We all liked Tony. He made you tolerable to be around," he said with a wink. "Looks like Suii's having the same effect. I'm glad it's working out."

I wasn't quite ready to thank Lou for pairing me with Suii, so instead, I handed over the report, the use of K9 force document sitting on top. Lou flipped through the paperwork, his brow furrowed in concentration.

"Good job, Suii," he muttered as he reached into his desk drawer and pulled out a box of dog biscuits. He held one out, and Suii accepted it with a wag of his tail, crunching the treat contentedly.

I fought back a smile. If I wasn't careful, Sergeant Spence would win over Suii's trust, and I'd be back to square one. Still, seeing them bond was surprisingly... nice.

After Lou signed off on the report, I made my way over to the district attorney's office to hand-deliver a copy. I wanted Daryl in jail until I was sure the kids were safe, and my mood improved significantly when the DA agreed. It wasn't often that I walked out of the DA's office feeling like I'd accomplished something, but today, I did.

After my shift, Suii and I headed to the park. The late afternoon sun was still warm, but a gentle breeze rustled the leaves in the trees, cooling the air just enough to make it comfortable. We worked on commands—sit, stay, heel—but truth be told, I needed the practice more than Suii did.

It felt good to have something to do, something productive, rather than heading home to eat a microwave dinner and zone out in front of the TV. My life had been predictable and stagnant for too long, but now, because of this exceptional dog, everything was changing. I could feel it.

The next morning, I woke up with Suii lying at the foot of my bed. His large frame stretched across the blanket, and I had to wiggle my toes just to get him to move over. "You know, if I ever get married, this won't work, right?" I said, yawning.

Suii barked, a single sharp sound that I took as his approval of the current arrangement.

"As long as we're clear," I muttered, swinging my legs out of bed and heading into the kitchen. Suii followed at my heels, his ears perked up, waiting patiently for his morning kibbles. I poured myself a cup of coffee and found myself, surprisingly, looking forward to what the day might hold. Life had started to feel... lighter.

Each morning for the next week, I found Suii inching farther up the bed. By the end of the week, his massive head rested on the pillow beside mine. I scratched his neck and belly before getting up to fetch my coffee, shaking my head with a smile. Who needed a husband when you had a dog like Suii?

On the one-month anniversary of having Suii, we made a trip to Tony's grave. The cemetery was quiet, the soft rustle of the wind the only sound as I walked through the rows of headstones. The sadness was still there, but more distant now, like a shadow fading in the late afternoon sun.

I stood at the foot of Tony's grave and spoke to the green grass that covered his coffin, introducing him to Suii. The dog sat quietly beside me, his usual energy subdued, as if he understood the solemnity of the moment. I told Tony about the cases I was working on, just like I used to when we were partners. The silence stretched on, but it was a peaceful feeling.

I told Tony about the cases I was working on, just like I used to when we were partners. The silence stretched on, but it was a peaceful silence. No replies from either of them—Tony or Suii. They had that in common. As I stood there, I felt a sense of calm settle over me. Maybe it was the finality of speaking to Tony, of acknowledging that chapter of my life. Maybe it was Suii's quiet presence, a living reminder that life moves forward, even when you think it's standing still.

After a few minutes, I gave a small tug on Suii's leash and turned to leave. But just as I took my first step, I stopped in stunned disbelief.

Suii, my loyal, well-trained K9, had trotted over to Tony's grave and, with all the dignity of a king, raised his hind leg and peed on it.

It took a few seconds for the shock to wear off before laughter bubbled up from deep inside me. I laughed until tears streamed down my face, the kind of deep, uncontrollable laughter that you can't hold back. And as ridiculous as it was, I knew Tony was laughing with me, wherever he was. If there was ever a competition between the two of them, Suii had just won it—hands down.

The laughter turned to tears, but they were healing tears, the kind that washed away some of the weight that had been pressing on my heart for so long. I wiped my eyes, still chuckling as I looked down at Suii, who seemed completely unfazed by his actions, wagging his stubby tail with pride.

I knelt down beside him, scratching behind his ears. "You'd win a peeing contest between you and Tony any day, buddy."

Suii tilted his head as if he understood, his big brown eyes full of mischief and loyalty.

With a final glance back at Tony's grave, I stood up, feeling lighter than I had in years. It was time to move on. Time to live my life, just as Tony would have wanted. I had a job to do, and I wasn't going to waste another second standing still.

"Come on, partner," I said, giving Suii's leash a gentle tug. "We've got work to do."

As we walked back to the car, Suii's tail wagged the whole way, and for the first time in a long time, I felt like I was exactly where I was supposed to be.

Chapter Six

I T WASN'T UNTIL THE end of our second month together that I finally got around to calling Jack Mallory and asking more questions about Suii's history. I'd meant to reach out earlier, but time slipped by faster than I expected. Between adjusting to life with a K9 partner and getting back into the rhythm of work, the days blended together in a blur. But now, with two months under my belt and Suii having fully integrated into my life, I felt ready to learn more.

When Jack's gruff voice came over the line, I smiled instinctively feeling a sense of warmth that I hadn't noticed while we worked on getting me adjusted.

"I expected this call within two weeks of you leaving here, not two months," he said, his tone teasing but warm.

"You think I'm giving him back, don't you?" I replied, leaning back in my chair with a smirk.

He chuckled, and the sound was so rich it sent a ripple of goosebumps across my arms. "No, but I figured you'd want more information about your K9."

Jack was a smart man. He knew exactly what I was calling for. Suii was mine now, no question about it, but there were still pieces of his story I didn't know. "Life's been interesting with him, to say the least. What can you tell me?"

Jack didn't waste any time. "Suii was with his handler, Officer Bradly, for four years. Bradly was one of the best—solid cop, great guy, and Suii was an exemplary K9 under his care.

They lived together—Bradly, his wife Tina, and their two kids. After Bradly's death, Tina tried to adopt Suii, but rules are rules. Only certified officers can handle active K9s. So, Suii ended up back here at the center."

That explained a lot—Suii's love for kids, the quiet sadness I sometimes caught in his eyes. My heart broke a little for Tina and her children, for what they lost. And it broke for Suii too. He had lost more than a handler. He'd lost his family.

"Suii went into a heavy state of depression after Bradly's death," Jack continued, his voice softening as he spoke. "Don't give me any crap either. Dogs suffer just like humans do—maybe even worse. You can't explain to a dog why their world's been turned upside down. One day their handler's there, the next he's not. It messes with them, same as it does with us."

I nodded, though Jack couldn't see it. The truth of his words hung heavy in the air.

"I take it you and Suii are getting along?" he asked, his tone lightening.

I smiled, the warmth of it reaching all the way to my chest. "He's one of the best partners I've ever had."

Jack let out a low, pleased laugh. "I knew he was the dog for you before you ever saw him. Took him home myself when the last guy came to pick a dog because Suii was waiting for his forever team and I couldn't let him down."

My grin widened. "You knew, huh?"

"I always know," Jack said with certainty.

That admission made me happier than I expected. "I've been meaning to ask—how did he get the name Suii?"

Jack's chuckle rumbled through the phone. "You didn't read his paperwork?"

I sighed, scratching the back of my neck. "No, I didn't think to look. Does it explain it?"

"Suii is short for Suicide. The story goes that anyone who goes up against that dog is committing suicide. He'll tear you apart if he needs to."

I glanced over at Suii, who was watching me with those big, soulful eyes, his head slightly tilted as if waiting for me to say something. I smiled and reached out to give him a loving pat on his massive head. "Well, he hasn't torn me apart yet," I said, laughing softly.

Jack and I spent a little longer on the phone, our conversation drifting into small talk, something that didn't bother me nearly as much as it usually would. There was something comforting about Jack's voice, the familiarity of it. Too bad he lived so far away. Jack struck me as the kind of man who wouldn't mind sharing a bed with a dog that hogged all the pillow space.

After we hung up, I sat in silence for a moment, contemplating everything I'd learned. Then, feeling a tug of curiosity, I started doing some research. A couple of phone calls later, I had scheduled an appointment for Saturday.

That Saturday morning, I climbed into my old four-wheel-drive truck, the one I used for non-work-related driving. Suii immediately took his spot at the back window, where he could hang his head out as we drove, his ears flapping in the wind. The sliding back window was the perfect spot for him, and I was thankful it kept the slobber off my upholstery.

As we drew closer to our destination, Suii began to whine, a low, excited sound that grew more insistent with every mile. By the time I parked the truck, he was practically vibrating with anticipation, his massive body pulling at the leash as I stepped out. He didn't even give me a chance to straighten fully before he dragged me to the front door.

"Suii!" two boys yelled in unison as the door flew open.

This was Suii's family—his real family. The moment Tina stepped out onto the porch and threw her arms around him, I felt a lump form in my throat. Her tears came fast, and before I knew it, I was crying too. The boys were hugging and petting Suii, and Suii was licking their faces like it was the happiest moment of his life. It probably was.

We stood there for several minutes, letting the emotions wash over us, before Tina finally invited me inside. We sat at the kitchen table, the same one I imagined Bradly had sat at with his family, while the boys took Suii out back to play ball. I could hear the thump of the ball bouncing and the sound of their laughter filtering in through the open window. Suii knew this routine well. He was home.

"Thank you for bringing him," Tina said, handing me a tissue as she wiped her own eyes. "You don't know what this means to us."

I took the tissue gratefully, dabbing at my cheeks. "You might not be thanking me when it's time to leave. I had no idea how hard this would be."

The thought of dragging Suii out of here after such a joyful reunion made my heart ache. I could already picture him crying all the way home, his big, sad eyes watching the house fade in the distance. And the boys—they'd be heartbroken all over again.

Tina smiled, her eyes still wet but filled with hope. "It would be easier if you agree to bring him back again."

"You'll have trouble keeping us away," I replied, and I meant it.

We spent the next two hours talking—about her husband, the boys, and Suii. It was easy, natural, like catching up with an old friend. But when it was time to leave, it was just as hard as I'd imagined. Suii looked at me with confusion, his body hesitating at the door. I explained to him the entire drive home that I'd bring him back, my voice soft and reassuring as he finally settled down. He licked my hand before sticking his head out the window again, the wind ruffling his fur.

He understood.

In the months that followed, my case-solved ratio returned to what it had been when Tony was alive. The other detectives started requesting K9s of their own, a silent nod of respect toward me and Suii. Unfortunately, the sergeant didn't oblige. My relationship with the department changed, too—there was an ease to it now, a quiet camaraderie that I hadn't felt in years. I was back in the fold.

Beth's wedding loomed closer, and I finally returned the RSVP card. It had taken me longer than I thought to check the 'plus one' box, but I did it. Tony would have wanted Beth to be happy, and I wanted that for her too.

When the day of the wedding arrived, I stepped out of my truck wearing a cream blouse and flowing brown pants. I wasn't exactly an expert in wedding attire, so I'd gone to a nearby boutique and asked the clerk for advice. She'd done a decent job, though I still felt slightly out of place. But it wasn't my outfit that caught attention—it was Suii.

I'd found a white bow tie at a thrift store, attached it to a piece of black elastic, and fastened it around Suii's neck. He was my plus one, after all. As we walked up to the ceremony, heads turned, but no one seemed to mind. Beth smiled warmly when she saw us, and her new husband gave me a nod of approval. Suii remained on his best behavior, sitting quietly by my side as the vows were exchanged.

Life moved on, as it always did. And so did love.

I reached over and scratched Suii under his chin, feeling the smooth warmth of his fur beneath my fingers. He turned to look at me for a moment, his eyes full of understanding, before shifting his attention back to the ceremony. He knew, just as I did, that weddings were important.

And as the ceremony continued, I knew that I was exactly where I needed to be.

Chapter Seven

AFTER THE NEW YEAR, we had a string of burglaries that were driving us crazy. Downtown businesses were being hit about once a week, on random nights, without any discernible pattern. No rhyme or reason that we could figure out. Patrols were increased in the area, but it didn't seem to matter. Whoever was behind the burglaries was smart, slipping through our fingers every time. It was starting to get under everyone's skin.

We knew we had at least two suspects, thanks to the two distinct sets of shoe prints left behind at several scenes. What really got to me, though, was the amount of cash these business owners were leaving out—everything from the soda money collected from employees to hundreds of dollars stashed in office cabinets and drawers. It was like these guys were just daring someone to rob them. The bad guys were quick, smart, and had a knack for getting in and out before anyone knew what hit them.

The city council wasn't happy. They complained to the chief of police, and the chief in turn leaned on Sergeant Spence. The pressure trickled down to us, and no one was feeling good about it. Detective units were put on stakeout duty—my least favorite job in the world. Hours of sitting, waiting, and doing nothing but letting your mind wander. Boredom was practically guaranteed, and the graveyard shifts didn't help.

We were taking four-hour rotations for the stakeouts, working our regular day shifts in addition. It was exhausting, but we didn't have a choice. Something had to give. I spent my four hours on Saturday night doing what I did best—complaining. And as usual, Suii was my only audience. He sat beside me, silent and alert, as I vented. "They're getting smarter," I grumbled, shifting in my seat. "Last night they hit between four and five in the morning, right under our noses."

It was maddening. We couldn't cover the entire downtown area, not with the resources we had. And we knew they were on foot, which only made it worse. Every time we followed their tracks, they led us in different directions—no pattern, no consistency. No vehicle lights to track either. It sucked.

"Next weekend, I'll take you to see Tina and the boys," I promised, reaching over to scratch behind Suii's ears. We made the trip every two weeks, and while it had been hard at first, it was getting easier to leave every time.

Suii gave a near-silent bark, knowing instinctively to keep quiet but also acknowledging that he understood what I said. By this point, I'd stopped questioning what Suii did and didn't understand. The dog knew every word I spoke. That was just a fact.

Then, suddenly, a low rumbling growl escaped from him. It wasn't his usual sound—a warning, more primal. My heart rate quickened as I peered into the dark, waiting, listening. I lowered my window just an inch, and a few minutes later, the faint but unmistakable sound of glass breaking reached my ears.

They'd hit last night, and now, they were back, thinking they were safe.

I glanced at Suii. His body had gone tense, his muscles coiled, ready. I decided to check things out before calling it in. If a patrol officer happened to be in the vicinity, the flashing lights might tip our guys off before we could make a move. Quietly, I opened my door, then moved around to open Suii's.

The interior lights of my vehicle had been disconnected for stakeouts like this, so we wouldn't give away our presence.

Suii was all business. He didn't whine, didn't fidget. His focus was on the task, just like mine.

I held my gun in my right hand and a small flashlight in my left, though I hadn't turned it on yet. I kept Suii's leash tight in my grip. His hearing was sharper than mine, so I relied on him to lead. "Voran," I whispered. Take the lead.

Suii obeyed without hesitation, moving silently ahead of me as we rounded the front corner of the saddle and leather shop. There was a narrow alley on the far side, the perfect place for someone to slip into without being seen. I heard the crunch of glass underfoot, and Suii let out another low growl.

My pulse pounded in my ears as I followed him around the corner. Two men were there—one clearing glass from a shattered window, the other standing watch.

Crap. I should've called dispatch.

I brought up my gun. "Stop right there. Police!" I shouted, my voice echoing off the narrow walls of the alley. As I gave the command, Suii's growl grew louder, more menacing.

Both men froze.

I kept my flashlight off, my thumb pressed against the button that would keep it on only as long as I held it down. I didn't dare twist it to lock the light in place—not while Suii was pulling at the leash, ready to spring into action.

"Bleib," I ordered. Hold.

Suii stopped straining against the leash, but his growl didn't cease. I could feel the tension radiating off him.

"Put your hands where I can see them," I said, stepping closer as both men slowly lifted their arms. The guy I'd seen climb out of the window was fidgeting, shifting on his feet. I knew that look. He was about to run.

Sure enough, he turned and bolted.

"Fass!" I shouted, releasing Suii's leash.

Suii was on him in seconds, the man's scream tearing through the still night air as Suii took him down. Meanwhile, the second guy, the one still standing, started to lower his hands, looking antsy.

"Hands up!" I snapped, my voice sharp as I clicked on the mic to my radio. "Backup needed in the alley next to the saddle shop."

Protocol said I should've given my badge number, but everyone knew who was on stakeout tonight. There was no time for formalities.

"Get him off! Get him off!" The guy Suii had pinned was screaming now, thrashing beneath the weight of the Rottweiler.

The second man turned his back to me, hands lowering further. I knew he was about to make a break for it. I couldn't shoot him in the back, and my Taser was my next best option. I holstered my gun and grabbed the Taser, but everything seemed to slow down as he turned.

The flash of a gun caught the corner of my vision a split second before he fired.

Instinct took over. I dove to the ground, my heart pounding so hard I couldn't tell if I'd been hit. My hands were already moving, transferring my Taser to my left hand while my right reached for my gun. But I knew it was too late. There was no way I could get a shot off in time. I heard the blast from another round.

One hundred and fifty pounds of muscle and fury slammed into the man's chest. Suii had saved me. The gun flew from his hand, clattering several feet away as Suii pinned him to the ground, growls echoing through the narrow alley.

I whipped my head toward the other guy, the one Suii had already taken down. He was rolling on the ground, moaning in pain, but I had no idea if he was armed. My training kicked in. Where there's one gun, there's usually two.

"Don't move!" I shouted, my gun trained on him as I struggled to keep my focus on both men.

Out of the corner of my eye, I saw Suii, still growling, his jaws clamped down on the man who had fired at me. The man beneath him struggled, but Suii wasn't letting go. Not until I said so.

Seconds later, two patrol cars arrived, their lights cutting through the dark alley, casting everything in a harsh, flashing glow.

"Cover this guy! He might be armed!" I yelled, motioning toward the first suspect as I ran to Suii.

I kicked the gun a few feet farther away from the man beneath Suii, just to be safe. "Suii. Aus." Let go.

Suii released the man instantly, but instead of standing tall, he slumped onto the ground beside him.

That's when I saw it. The dark, wet stain spreading across his side.

"No, no, no," I whispered, my throat tightening as I fell to my knees beside him. My hands pressed against the sticky wetness, desperate to stop the bleeding. "No, Suii, please."

His breathing was shallow, labored, and his big dark eyes looked up at me, full of the loyalty and love I'd come to know so well. He lifted his paw weakly, placing it on my arm, and I choked back a sob. I could feel the weight of him slipping away from me.

With one final breath, the air left his chest, and his eyes glazed over.

Suii was gone.

Chapter Eight

WHEN A POLICE K9 dies in the line of duty, the handler is the one who plans the funeral. I'd been to a few K9 funerals before—solemn, respectful ceremonies that honored the fallen dogs who'd given their lives in service. But nothing prepared me for planning one for my own partner. I couldn't have done it without the help of the other detectives and officers. Suii's death left me in a place I hadn't been since Tony's passing. It was a dark, hollow feeling, one that settled in the pit of my stomach and refused to leave.

Tony had battled cancer for a year, and his death, while heartbreaking, was expected. The department had rallied around his wife, Tina, as they should have. She had taken center stage when it came to support from the force, and I had stayed in the background, grieving in my own way. But this time, it was different. This time, I was the one center stage. Suii had died saving my life, and that fact weighed on me like a boulder pressing down on my chest. I grumbled a little, complained a lot, but in the end, I accepted the help.

One of the female officers, Justine, insisted on staying with me at my place until after the funeral. It was completely over the top, and I knew Sergeant Spence had something to do with it. Justine didn't give me a second of alone time. As much as I protested, deep down, I knew I needed someone around, even if I wasn't ready to admit it to myself. The house felt too empty without Suii, and the silence was deafening.

The day of the funeral was cold and windy. The kind of bone-chilling wind that made everything feel harsher, like the world itself was mourning. The local newspaper had written a huge article about Suii, splashing his story across the front page and making it the biggest news in the county. Sergeant Spence had told me to expect a packed house, and he wasn't kidding.

The moment I stepped out of Lou's vehicle, the sorrowful sounds of bagpipes filled the air. They were playing "Going Home," and it hit me hard. The bagpipes always got me, but this time, the sound was like a punch to the gut. I wiped at my eyes, trying to pull myself together before the ceremony. My crisp dress uniform was stiff, uncomfortable, yet strangely comforting. It felt like a shield, a layer of protection between me and the overwhelming grief that threatened to swallow me whole.

We were early, but the bagpipes had already begun. Their mournful wail carried on the wind as we walked toward the auditorium. Several officers were waiting inside, their faces somber as they greeted me with tight hugs, offering their support. The weight of their shared grief was palpable, but somehow, it didn't make things easier.

Lou gently steered me up to the front, where a picture of me and Suii sat on a high table. I remembered that day vividly. Someone had snapped the photo while I was showing off Suii's abilities, and half the department had gathered in the parking lot to watch. In the picture, Suii was standing tall beside me, his chest puffed out with pride. It was one of my favorite photos of us.

Next to the picture sat a wooden urn, polished and smooth, holding Suii's ashes. I'd picked it out with Justine's help. There was a silver plate on top, engraved with words that had been haunting me since the moment I read them:

The heart and soul of a K9 lives forever. His four paws enjoy the path of endless walks. His food bowl is always full. His fearless sacrifice never forgotten. Rest in peace, Suii.

My fingertips traced the inscription as my tears flowed freely. I'd missed him every second since that night, the emptiness gnawing at me. I needed him so badly. His presence had filled a void I didn't even know existed, and now, that void had grown into a chasm.

A hand rested gently on my back, and I turned to see Tina standing beside me. Her boys were with her, all three of them crying. My heart broke all over again. I dropped to my knees and wrapped the boys in a tight hug, feeling their small bodies tremble against mine. They had already lost their father, and now, this. How much more could they endure?

"He saved my life," I whispered, my voice choked with emotion. I needed them to know that. Suii had been a hero, just like their dad.

Tina gave me a long hug, her arms strong yet soft, offering comfort that I didn't know how to accept. "Thank you for bringing him to see us so often," she said, her voice thick with tears.

Suii had needed it as much as Tina and the boys did. "I'm so glad you came," was all I could manage to say. The words stuck in my throat, and my tears kept me from speaking further.

I glanced around, realizing for the first time that the auditorium was nearly full. People had come from all over to pay their respects. I hadn't expected such a turnout, but it seemed like everyone whose life had been touched by Suii wanted to be here. The front double doors swung open, and handlers with their K9s began filing in, one after the other. The sight was overwhelming, a line of officers and their dogs, standing in solidarity for one of their own.

Behind them came Jack Mallory. Our eyes met across the room, and I felt a wave of relief wash over me as he approached. His strong arms circled around me in a tight embrace, and for a moment, I let myself lean into him, drawing strength from his quiet presence.

We took our seats in the front row as the service began. Officer Franks was the first to speak, telling the story of how Suii had successfully apprehended a suspect during a domestic dispute. His words were simple, but they carried a weight that settled deep in my chest. One by one, officers came forward, each sharing stories about Suii's short time with the department. Their words wrapped around me like a blanket, offering warmth in the coldness of my grief.

With Jack on one side and Tina and her boys on the other, I let myself cry for my friend and partner. The tears came hard and fast, but I didn't try to stop them. I'd spent too long bottling everything up, and now, it was time to let go.

Sergeant Spence spoke last. He told the story of how Suii had saved my life, giving his own in the process. His voice cracked more than once, and when he finished, he picked up Suii's urn from the table. I stood on shaky legs and walked forward to meet him. Lou placed the urn in my arms, and I cradled it against my chest, the weight of it both comforting and devastating. This was all I had left of him now.

Slowly, we made our way outside for the final call. The cold wind bit at my cheeks, but I barely felt it. We turned on our radios, and the dispatcher from the night of Suii's death spoke over the airwaves. Her voice wavered, thick with emotion, as she called out, "K9 Officer David Sixteen."

She took a deep breath, her sobs audible between the words. "K9 Officer David Sixteen, last call." Another pause. "K9 Officer David Sixteen out of service."

The silence that followed was deafening. The weight of her words hung in the air, final and unbreakable. It was over. I had lost another partner.

So many people came forward to offer their condolences. I shook their hands, barely registering their words as I moved through the motions. The K9 handlers waited until the last person had walked away, their dogs standing at attention by their sides. My heart broke a little more at the sight. Jack guided me over, and together we walked down the line, shaking hands with each handler.

"Can I drive you home?" Jack asked when we were done.

"Sounds good," I replied, my voice hollow. "Let me tell my sergeant."

I walked over to Lou, who pulled me into a quick hug. "I expect you at work tomorrow," he said, his voice low and firm. He knew me well enough to understand that I needed the structure, the routine. Grief didn't stop the job.

Back in Jack's car, the drive was quiet. He looked sharp in his state police dress uniform, though it hadn't really registered with me until now. What a job it must be, working with K9s and their handlers every day. He hadn't just trained Suii, he'd known him in a way that most couldn't.

"How are you doing?" he asked, his eyes soft with concern.

I couldn't stop myself from running my fingers over the top of the urn, tracing the edges. "I'll be okay... someday."

"You're a great handler. When that day comes, you call me, and we'll find you another dog," Jack said, his voice steady and sure.

The words cut deep. "I don't think so," I whispered, the idea of replacing Suii too painful to bear.

"I know so," Jack replied gently. "But we don't have to worry about that now."

When we pulled up to my townhouse, I hesitated before unbuckling my seatbelt. The weight of the urn in my lap was heavier than it should have been, like it was tethering me to the car, to this moment. I didn't want to get out. Going inside meant facing the emptiness of my home, the silence that would greet me where Suii should have been. It was a stark reality I wasn't ready to deal with yet.

"Do you want to come in?" I asked, my voice soft, unsure if I really wanted company or if I was just trying to postpone being alone for a little while longer.

Jack shook his head, offering me a small, understanding smile. "I need to head back to Tucson. But will you be okay alone?"

I glanced out the window and noticed Mr. Knock-toes standing outside his place, Craptzu tucked under his arm like always. He wasn't moving—just standing there, watching me with a solemn expression. It occurred to me that he was waiting for me to get out of the car, probably unsure how to approach.

Turning back to Jack, I forced a small smile. "I'll survive. Thank you for the ride."

Jack gave a nod and placed a hand on my arm, a silent gesture of support before I stepped out of the car. As he pulled away, I waved him off, feeling the strange weight of everyone's concern settle over me. I appreciated it, but it was exhausting. Everyone wanted to know how I was holding up, but all I wanted was to disappear for a little while and pretend that none of this was happening.

I didn't make it two steps toward my front door before Mr. Knock-toes called out to me. "I read about you and your dog in the paper," he said, his voice quieter than usual. "I'm very sorry."

I swallowed hard, nodding in acknowledgment. "Thank you, I appreciate it."

For a moment, we just stood there, the silence stretching out between us. Even Craptzu seemed subdued, his little ears drooping as he looked up at me. Then, unexpectedly, the small dog let out a soft whine and squirmed in his owner's arms, reaching out toward me with his tiny paws. Without thinking, I extended my hand and scratched beneath his chin. To my surprise, the usual irritation I felt toward the little Shih Tzu wasn't there.

Mr. Knock-toes shifted awkwardly on his feet, his pigeon-toed stance even more pronounced than usual. He cleared his throat, his voice tentative. "Would you like some company? Maybe a cup of tea or something?"

I looked at him for a long moment, considering. The truth was, I didn't want to be alone. Not tonight. And as strange as it seemed, the idea of sitting down with my irritating neighbor and his dog didn't sound so bad.

"I've got tea," I said, then added with a faint smile, "And something stronger if you'd prefer."

His face broke into a small grin, the first I'd ever seen from him. "Stronger sounds good."

I led the way inside, the urn still clutched tightly in my hands as I stepped over the threshold. My townhouse was quiet, almost too quiet. But tonight, with Mr. Knock-toes and Craptzu in tow, maybe it wouldn't feel so empty.

And maybe, just maybe, that was enough for now.

Chapter Nine

THE FIRST FEW MONTHS were the hardest. Grief sat heavy on my chest, like a dull weight that wouldn't lift no matter how much time passed. There was a hollow space in my life, one that I couldn't quite fill, not with work, not with anything. But this time, my fellow officers weren't letting me retreat into my usual standoff routine. It was different now, and I wasn't sure if it was them being more persistent or if, somehow, Suii had softened me. Maybe it was both. Whatever the reason, it worked. The walls I'd built up over the years—walls meant to protect me from the kind of hurt that came with loss—were gone.

That didn't mean I was willing to be partnered up again. I refused, flat out. The thought of working alongside another human or K9 was too much. I wasn't ready to let anyone or anything get that close again. Surprisingly, Lou gave in with little more than a shake of his head. He didn't push it, didn't ask questions. He understood.

I threw myself back into the thick of things, diving into cases with a single-minded focus that felt almost like therapy. It was easier to lose myself in work, to pour all my energy into solving cases and catching bad guys. And while I drove around town, I found myself talking to Tony and Suii, just like I used to. Their spirits were with me in those moments, though they still weren't answering back. Speaking out loud helped me connect the dots, helped me make sense of the chaos around me. They might be gone, but they were still a part of my process.

A little over six months after Suii's death, I was nearing the end of my shift when my cell phone rang. The number on the screen made my heart skip a beat.

"Detective Jolett speaking," I said, trying to keep my voice steady.

"It's Jack."

Just the sound of his voice was enough to stir something inside me, something I wasn't quite ready to acknowledge. "Hi," I replied, my breath catching in my throat. I probably sounded like a fool, but I couldn't help it.

"I spoke to your sergeant," Jack continued, his tone calm and matter-of-fact. "He wants you driving here first thing in the morning to look at a dog."

The words hit me like a punch to the gut. Crap. I wasn't ready for this. "I can't, Jack," I said, the panic rising in my chest. The idea of taking on another K9, of putting myself through that kind of emotional attachment again, terrified me.

"You don't have a choice. I just want you to have a look," Jack insisted, his voice firm but gentle. "No pressure."

No pressure? Yeah, right. There was plenty of pressure. "It's a waste of time. I'm not taking on a new K9," I argued, though the words felt hollow even to me.

"I'll expect you here at ten," he said, and before I could protest any further, he hung up.

The line went dead in my hand, and I stared at the phone for a long moment, torn between anger and something I didn't want to admit—hope.

The next morning, I left my house at seven, the drive to the K9 center stretching out in front of me like an emotional gauntlet. My emotions swung wildly between sadness and anger. How could Jack do this to me? Didn't he understand that I was the bad-luck partner? That everyone who got close to me ended up dead? The weight of that thought hung heavy as I drove, and by the time I pulled into the kennel, I was in a full-on snit, my nerves frayed and raw.

"I worried you'd disobey a direct order," Jack said, rising from where he'd been changing out a water dish in one of the kennels. His easy smile should have lightened my mood, but I wasn't in the frame of mind for it to work.

"The last thing I need is my pay docked," I snapped, folding my arms across my chest. "So, I'm here. Show me the darned dog."

Jack's smile didn't falter, and despite myself, I felt a small thrill run through me. He looked good. Too good for my current mood. "Come meet Mika," he said, walking me over to a row of kennels.

He stopped in front of a pen and opened the door. Out stepped a German Shepherd—sleek, muscular, the kind of dog that looked every inch the perfect police dog. "He's new, but a darn fine K9," Jack said, his voice full of admiration.

And yet, when I looked at Mika, my heart sank. He wasn't the one. I could feel it immediately, a deep, gut-level certainty that there was no connection between us. I'd sworn to myself that I didn't want another dog, that I couldn't go through that kind of bond again. But now, standing here, I knew it was a lie. I did want another dog. I just didn't want *this* dog. Mika wasn't Suii, and he never would be.

I gave the German Shepherd a quick scratch behind the ears, more out of politeness than anything else, and stepped away from the pen. "I've got a long drive back," I muttered. "No point in dragging this out."

As I turned to leave, something caught my eye—a black ball of fur curled up in the back of the next cage. The dog's coat was sleek, shining even in the dim light of the kennel.

"Don't even look," Jack warned, his tone almost playful. "Her disposition is horrible."

I raised an eyebrow, glancing at the dog. "It's a Lab. Just how bad can she be?"

"You'll be sorry," Jack said with a smirk, but he stepped over to the pen and opened the door anyway.

The black dog unfolded herself slowly, rising to her feet with the grace of a creature much too large to be that quiet. Dark brown eyes met mine, and in that moment, I felt it—the connection I hadn't felt with Mika. She walked over to me, her steps unhurried, and gently pressed her head against my legs. I knelt down without thinking, my fingers immediately finding the soft spot behind her ears. She sighed, a soft, contented sound, and leaned into me.

"What's her name?" I asked, my voice softer than it had been all morning.

"Bell," Jack said, standing behind me with his arms crossed. "Short for Belladonna. As in the poison."

I looked into her deep brown eyes, feeling a pull I hadn't expected. "This is the dog you wanted me to see, isn't it?" I asked, already knowing the answer.

Jack smiled then, a full, wide grin that sent my heart skipping a beat. "She's your dog. I knew it from the moment she came in. Did you pack a bag for two weeks of training?"

I hated to admit it, but I had. "Yeah," I muttered, feeling both foolish and relieved.

"Good," Jack said, his smile widening. "We'll get started right now. Bell can be a little lazy, and she needs a strong hand."

I looked back at Bell, who was now sitting quietly beside me, her head tilted up as if waiting for my next move. "My kind of dog," I said, a small smile tugging at the corners of my mouth.

It was happening. Whether I liked it or not, Bell was already mine.

Chapter Ten

Part II

A TECHNO RENDITION OF Beethoven's 5th Symphony suddenly blared through the quiet of my bedroom, the sharp notes of "Da da da daaaaa" cutting through the darkness like an alarm. I groaned, rolling over to silence the offending noise, but my hand fumbled for the phone, knocking it off the nightstand. "Crap!" I muttered, my groggily whispered curse barely audible over the electronic chorus.

I blinked against the too-bright screen as the numbers 03:22 burned into my retinas. Saturday morning. My usual sleep-in day.

A half-mumbled, "Yeah?" into the receiver was the best I could manage before sunrise and caffeine.

Bell, my K9 partner—full name Belladonna—was curled up at the foot of the bed, her big black lab form almost invisible in the dim light. She let out a soft growl, clearly displeased at being woken up. She was stubborn that way, but I couldn't really blame her. Sleeping on my bed was a habit I should've broken, but when it came to Bell, I was a softy. Always had been, always would be.

On the other end of the line, the dispatcher's voice was disgustingly chipper, far too awake for this ungodly hour. "Officer Franks is requesting a detective at a death scene, and you're up," she announced, like I should be thrilled to be part of the action. Ugh. I wasn't feeling it.

Of course, it had to be my weekend rotation. I had made homicide detective a year ago, and while I loved it, I hadn't been planning on an early morning wake-up call. Our town was midsized, so our detective unit was small. Before homicide, I'd been a street detective, handling thefts, burglaries, domestic disputes, and the occasional sex crime. Homicide, though—that was the meat of the department, and I'd been happy to take the promotion.

Still, I wasn't happy about 3 a.m. callouts.

"Okay," I mumbled, my brain struggling to catch up to the conversation. "Who's dead?"

"Out-of-towner. Female guest at the motel."

I was awake now. Not a local, which was interesting. "I'll be there in fifteen," I said before hanging up.

With a sigh, I pushed myself up and swung my legs over the edge of the bed. "Come on, Bell, you need to do your business before we go to work," I said, the words falling out more automatically than anything else. No growl from her this time, though. Bell knew the word "work" as well as I did. We'd been partners for two years, and sometimes it felt like we were so in sync, we could read each other's minds.

"There's a death at the motel," I muttered, as I grabbed my holstered gun from the nightstand and secured it at my hip. "I really need sleep right now," I added, glancing at Bell as if expecting sympathy. She was already on her feet, ears perked, her entire body alert.

She didn't answer—because she's a dog, of course—but if she could, I knew exactly what she'd say: *Get over it.* Bell was good like that. No nonsense, no complaints, just ready for action.

I let her out through the back door while I focused on gathering what I needed. My basic evidence kit was already in the trunk of my car, but my larger duffel—packed with the more specialized equipment—was back at the office. I grabbed my cold-weather bag from the closet. Winter in Northern Arizona wasn't exactly forgiving, and this time of year, I kept a bag packed with essentials—energy bars, bottled water, extra gloves, and a hat. At the bottom, my bulletproof vest lay folded, ready for action.

Bell was waiting by the back door when I returned, her breath visible in the cold morning air. I hooked her harness and leash, feeling the familiar tug as she tried to bounce with excitement. "Bell, sit. Stay," I ordered, though it wasn't really necessary. Bell was highly trained, certified, and an awesome partner. But she had been bored lately. Homicide work didn't offer the kind of action that kept her sharp.

"Sorry, girl, no bombs to sniff out tonight," I said under my breath as I grabbed my coat from the hook by the door. Bell was cross-trained for explosives detection and personal protection. Her job was to give her life for mine, or for any of our officers, and the thought of that sat heavy in my chest. Suii, had done exactly that.

My eyes flicked to the mantel above the electric fireplace. Suii's ashes were contained in a wooden box with an inscription. The words tugged at me, as they always did. Suii had been irreplaceable, and there was a time when I thought no dog could fill the void he left behind. But Bell had. Slowly, surely, she'd filled that emptiness, though it had taken time for me to admit it.

"Come on, partner," I whispered to Bell as I clipped the leash to her harness. "Let's get to work."

The cold hit me as soon as we stepped outside, but I was thankful there hadn't been any snow overnight. The last thing I needed was to scrape ice off the windows of my new police-issued SUV at 3:30 a.m. Bell hopped into the backseat without hesitation, her tail wagging as I patted her head. She licked my hand, and for a moment, the world felt right. With a solid slam, I closed the hatch and climbed behind the wheel.

The SUV's engine growled to life as I pulled out of the driveway, heading for the cheapest motel in town. It wasn't the first time I'd been called there, and I doubted it would be the last. The place was a magnet for trouble. There were two nicer hotels on the east side, but they didn't attract the same crowd. The motel, on the other hand, was a hotbed for seasonal workers, truckers passing through, and, more often than not, drug users and dealers. It was the kind of place that saw its fair share of crime.

The streets were deserted, the cold holding the town in a quiet, still grip. It only took about ten minutes to get to the motel with no traffic, and as I turned into the far west entrance, I could see Officer Leo Franks standing next to his patrol vehicle, the red and blue LED lights casting long shadows in the empty parking lot.

Leo was a good cop—one of the best we had. He came out of the drug task force a few years ago, and I'd worked with him on several cases since then. Tall, dark-haired, and serious when he needed to be, Leo had a way of intimidating suspects without ever raising his voice. He was also one of the few people in the department who genuinely loved my dog, which automatically earned him points in my book.

I parked next to his vehicle, my eyes adjusting to the flashing lights as I stepped out. Leo's face was hard to read, but his posture told me everything I needed to know—this wasn't going to be a simple case of an accidental overdose. There was something more going on here.

I glanced at the backseat of his patrol car and saw a head resting against the window. Someone was already in custody. So much for my hopes of a quiet night.

Bell hopped out of the SUV, her tail wagging slightly as she sniffed the air. I gave her leash a gentle tug, my mind already shifting into work mode. Whatever was waiting for us, it wasn't going to be pretty. I could feel it in my gut.

"Come on, girl," I muttered as we approached Leo. "We've got work to do."

Chapter Eleven

LEO SAUNTERED TOWARD ME in that distinctive cop swagger, his movements deliberate and purposeful. He had the kind of walk that screamed authority—steady, confident, and just slow enough to signal control. I shifted slightly, positioning myself behind my SUV, ensuring we'd be out of earshot of Leo's passenger. The flashing patrol lights flickered shadows across the ground, giving the scene an eerie glow as the cold air clung to us.

"Whatcha got?" I asked, offering a quick handshake.

Leo nodded toward the hotel room door in front of his vehicle, the headlights from his cruiser casting a harsh light on the chipped paint. "I was called out around three," he began, his tone low but steady. "Mr. Ledmen," he inclined his head toward his vehicle, "called 9-1-1 because his forty-five-year-old wife wasn't breathing. Said he didn't know how long she'd been dead. When I got here, I checked her pulse. Rigor mortis was setting in, so my best guess is she's been dead for about two to four hours." He paused, his eyes narrowing slightly. "Found something that didn't sit right, so I had dispatch call you. Ledmen said his wife was drinking last night and passed out on the floor—"

I held up my hand, palm out, cutting him off. "Don't feed me your suspicions yet." Leo's observations were usually solid, but I wanted to see the scene through my own eyes before being influenced. Whatever he found, I needed to discover it independently. It was crucial to keep my perspective sharp. "Did you mess with my crime scene?" I asked, my voice tight, though I already knew the answer. Leo knew better, but I liked reminding everyone that I ran a tight ship.

His lips twitched into a half-grin, his hands going up in mock surrender. "Touched the body to check for a pulse, lifted one arm to confirm rigor. Other than that, I didn't touch anything. I had Ledmen step outside the room while I walked through it. I gloved up and didn't disturb a thing."

This was why I liked working with Leo. He respected the process, knew the importance of preserving the integrity of the scene. I gave a brief nod of approval, glancing around the parking lot. It was still quiet, a handful of cars scattered across the lot, their windows fogged with the chill of the early morning air.

"You're taking second on this," I informed him, my voice firm. "Write your initial report, and I'll take it from there. Who's got the shift after you?"

"Denise," he replied, his posture straightening slightly.

"Good. Call her out early. I want her sitting with Ledmen at the station. We need him out of here. I'll talk to him first, but I want him gone before we start processing the scene." My mind was already ticking through the steps ahead, compartmentalizing each task. "Did you notify Sergeant Spence?"

Leo shook his head. "No, he's out of town. Figured you'd want to call the chief yourself. I'll get Denise en route. Do you need anyone else?"

I paused, thinking. "No, not until we know what we're dealing with. I'm sick of rumors leaking from the department. Cops with flappy lips aren't my thing." I gave him a meaningful look, knowing he understood exactly what I meant. "Glad you're my cop on duty for this one." I added, "Have Denise swing by my office before heading over and grab the large evidence bag from the corner behind my desk."

Leo grimaced slightly, the first part of my statement hitting home. We'd both dealt with the fallout of leaked information before. In a small town like ours, secrets didn't stay buried for long. Cops talked to their spouses, and their spouses talked to friends. Within hours, the whole town would be buzzing with half-truths, and by then, the story would be so twisted, we'd be chasing rumors instead of facts. I had no patience for that kind of headache.

Pulling out my phone, I scrolled through my contacts and hit the chief's number. It went straight to voicemail, just as I'd expected. I left a message, covering my bases by notifying the chain of command. Next, I dialed Sergeant Spence, but his phone also went to voicemail. Finally, I called Gabe Macky, the department's other homicide detective.

"Hey, Gabe," I said when the line clicked over to his voicemail. "Sorry to put a dent in your time off, but I've got a suspicious death at the motel. Leo's second on the scene. If it turns into a homicide, I'll keep you in the loop. Call me when you get a chance."

I hung up and exhaled, sliding the phone back into my pocket. Gabe would get back to me when he could, but for now, it was my scene to work. Bell stayed close as I moved to the back of my SUV, retrieving my small evidence bag and slinging it over my shoulder. With a nod toward Leo, I headed toward the motel room door, my boots scuffing lightly against the cement. The cold air made every sound sharper, more pronounced in the quiet.

"Denise is on her way," Leo said as I knelt down, placing the bag on the ground by the door.

"Good," I replied. "Before the town stirs, turn off your top lights. The less attention we draw, the better." I paused, thinking through the next steps. "Once he's gone, run crime scene tape from pillar to pillar in front of the room to define the inner perimeter. Then run another line about twenty-five feet out to create the outer perimeter. No one crosses either without my say-so. Got it?"

Leo nodded, already turning toward his vehicle. I flipped the switch on my digital recorder, placing it in my left hand as I walked toward the back of Leo's patrol car. The last thing I wanted was for Ledmen to hear us talking about the case before I had the chance to assess the scene. Thankfully, Leo hadn't put the man in handcuffs, something I appreciated. If Ledmen had killed his wife, I didn't want him knowing we suspected it. But I trusted Leo's instincts, and if he thought something was off, I knew I needed to pay attention.

I crouched slightly to get a better look at Mr. Ledmen through the window. His eyes were red, wet streaks marking his cheeks. Tears didn't tell me much. People react to grief in all sorts of ways—some cry, some don't. It wasn't an indicator of guilt or innocence. What mattered was the evidence.

Mr. Ledmen's medium build and neat appearance stood out. He was wiry, no gut, fit for his age. Short blond hair, green eyes that flicked up to meet mine as I approached. His expression was a mix of confusion and exhaustion, the kind that came from either shock or something more sinister. Most women would probably find him attractive, but right now, all I saw was a potential suspect.

I extended my hand, my voice steady. "I'm Detective Laci Jolett. I'm sorry we're meeting under these circumstances." His grip was firm as he shook my hand, though his eyes drifted downward as if the weight of the moment was too much.

"Carl Ledmen," he replied softly, his voice almost a whisper.

"What's your wife's name?" I asked, keeping my tone as gentle as possible.

"Mary. Mary Ledmen," he answered, his gaze dropping to his lap again.

"I'll be handling your wife's case," I said. "I'll need to take your full statement, but first I need to assess the scene." I glanced over my shoulder as another squad car pulled into the lot. Denise had arrived, right on schedule. "Officer Bullock will be driving you to the police department. It's warmer there, and you'll be more comfortable while we get things sorted out. We can provide coffee and food if you need it."

Ledmen's eyes lifted slightly, his voice barely audible. "I know this doesn't look good. We had a fight last night. I can't believe she's dead. I need to call my family, but my phone's in the room. I don't have any numbers without it."

My mind was already working, filing away the details of our conversation into neat little folders in my brain. "I can't remove anything from the room right now, but if possible, I'll bring your phone to the station."

Out of the corner of my eye, I saw Denise exit her vehicle. I turned to face her, discretely turning off my recorder as I did. She was in full uniform, and I silently cursed myself for not having her dress down. Uniforms intimidated people, and Ledmen didn't need to feel more pressure than he already did.

As I approached her, I asked, "Are you ready for this?"

Denise nodded, her bright eyes shining with enthusiasm. She was fresh out of the academy, just six months into the job. This would be her first death investigation, and I could tell she was eager. Her red hair was cut short and neat, a far cry from the long waves she'd had when I met her before she joined the force. At just five-one, she had a pixie-like quality, all freckles and wide eyes. I didn't know if it was her height or her youthful appearance, but at this hour, she looked way too perky.

I really needed coffee.

"You might not like me after this assignment," I told her honestly, bracing her for what was likely to be a long, uncomfortable day. "I need you to sit with Mr. Ledmen at the station. I'll be here processing the scene, starting the investigation. Make him comfortable, but don't ask him anything. Let him talk if he wants, but don't press him. And, Denise," I added, leaning in a little closer, "no rumors. If any details of this case leak out, you'll never work another one with me."

Her face grew serious, her earlier enthusiasm tempered by the gravity of my words. "Understood," she said, and I handed her the digital recorder.

"It's set on auto. It'll start recording if anyone speaks. If he says anything, anything at all, it'll be on record. But remember, everything you say is admissible in court, so choose your words carefully."

She gave me a sharp nod, looking directly into my eyes. "Yes, ma'am." She shrugged slightly. "If anyone calls, I'll tell them I know nothing. Which, well... I actually know nothing."

I smiled despite myself. "Good. And remember, Mr. Ledmen isn't under arrest. He's just a person of interest at this point. Keep things casual. Don't make him feel like he's being detained but watch your back. I don't know what I have yet, and if it is a homicide, he's the only suspect we have for now. He should see this as us helping him, not accusing him. Also, don't call me ma'am in front of him. It'll make him feel even more formal."

She blushed slightly, clearly realizing how automatic that "ma'am" had become. "Yes—uh, I mean, got it."

Together, we walked back to Leo's vehicle, where Carl Ledmen sat hunched in the backseat. His shoulders were tense, his hands folded in his lap. His eyes lifted when we approached, wide and anxious. I made the introductions, keeping my tone calm and professional. Denise, to her credit, played her part perfectly, offering him a soft, reassuring smile. She opened the passenger door and helped him out, guiding him toward her car.

"You'll need to search him before he rides with you," I said, mostly for Ledmen's benefit. "It's standard procedure for civilian transport. Just to make sure we're all safe."

He nodded, too distracted to protest. I was sure Leo had already given him a cursory pat-down, but I wasn't taking any chances. Denise conducted a quick search, keeping her movements professional and nonthreatening. When she was done, she nodded to me, signaling that he was clean.

Ledmen stood about six feet tall, which made my five-three frame feel even smaller as I glanced up at him. His eyes were an unsettling shade of blue—clear but vacant, like someone who'd seen too much too fast. They gave nothing away. I wasn't getting anything from him, at least not yet.

Once Ledmen was situated in the front seat of Denise's car, I watched as they pulled away, the soft glow of the headlights fading into the distance. He sat in the front like a friendly, hopefully relaxing some. I had a feeling I needed him as calm as possible.

Let's get the crime scene secured," I said, my mind already shifting gears. "Run the tape. I don't want anyone getting too close."

Chapter Twelve

MOTELS ARE ONE OF the few places where I'm not required to obtain a search warrant. As long as there's no suspicion that the hotel owners or employees are involved, I can investigate a crime scene freely. This case didn't appear to have any such complication, and besides, I knew the owners well. They were usually the ones who called first when there was trouble. I'd worked with them before and had no reason to suspect they had any part in what happened, and they needed to know what was going on.

I placed Bell in the back of my SUV, her eyes sad and accusatory at being left behind. I had a non-threatening crime scene, and it was time for me to do my detective gig without her. The manager's office first.

Sveta and Feodor Ivanov were Ukrainian transplants. How they ended up owning the motel in this dusty Arizona town was anyone's guess, but I'd never bothered to ask. Feodor had an accent so thick it was difficult to understand him most of the time. His wife, Sveta, spoke better English and handled most of the communication. She was the one in charge, no question about it. She kept the place running like clockwork, while Feodor mostly stayed in the background, grumbling about guests and fixing whatever needed fixing.

As I stepped into the front office, a small bell chimed above the door, signaling my arrival. I knew the buzzer in their living quarters would be going off, alerting them that someone had entered the office. The room smelled like every other cheap motel I'd ever been in—stale coffee, faint cigarette smoke, and the lingering scent of industrial cleaners that didn't quite mask the years of wear and tear. The walls were decorated with faded pictures of Arizona landscapes, and the front desk was cluttered with brochures and a half-empty bowl of mints. A small sign near the counter advertised vacancy, but only for short stays.

I heard Feodor's heavy footsteps first, and sure enough, he appeared from the back room, pulling a jacket over his wrinkled shirt. His balding head gleamed under the fluorescent lights, and his round belly strained against the zipper of his coat. He saw me and didn't say a word, simply turned on his heel and disappeared back through the door. A moment later, Sveta emerged, her long gray hair pulled back into its usual bun. Even though it was still early, and she'd clearly just woken up, she greeted me with a warm smile.

"Detective Jolett," she said in her heavily accented English. "You have a problem I can help you with?"

I explained, giving her minimal details, but enough so I had her cooperation. I saw her concern and I waited as she explained to her husband.

"We will help you, please," she said.

"Thank you. For now, I need information." I replied, keeping my tone even. I explained that I might need to lock the room and return at some point. "I'll leave an officer here to make sure no one enters the room if that happens," I added.

Sveta nodded as I spoke, then turned to relay more information to Feodor. He grunted in response, though whether that was in agreement or just his usual grumpiness, I couldn't tell.

"I'll need the names and personal information of all the guests who stayed here last night," I said, watching as Sveta moved to the computer behind the desk. Her fingers moved quickly across the keyboard, pulling up the records I'd requested.

As she worked, I asked, "How long have the Ledmens been staying here?"

"Months," Sveta replied without looking up from the screen. "He works at the power plant."

I nodded. It didn't surprise me. Power plant employees traveled all over the country, often staying in one place for six months or more. They were steady customers for motels like this one, in towns like ours—hardworking, transient, and generally kept to themselves.

I was eager to look inside the room, but I couldn't rush things. Sveta printed out a list of the current guests and handed it to me. The list had all the personal information I needed, minus credit card numbers. I'd follow up with interviews later, but for now, I needed to focus on the scene and what made Leo itchy.

It was still dark outside as I stepped back into the cold, the double perimeter crime scene tape Leo had put up flapping slightly in the wind. The motel was quiet, only a few cars in the lot, their windows fogged over from the early morning chill. A few vehicles passed by on the highway, heading toward the power plant for the early shift, but the town was mostly still asleep.

I spotted Leo by his patrol car and made my way over. "Park your vehicle in the back," I said, gesturing toward the rear of the motel. "I want to keep this as low-key as possible. If we can keep people from noticing the tape for a little while longer, we'll avoid half the town showing up to gawk."

Leo nodded, pulling his keys from his pocket. "Where do you want me stationed?"

"At the door. Watch for guests trying to leave. If anyone can't wait for me, get basic info—did they hear anything last night? Notice anything strange in the past week? I'm treating this as a homicide until I know for sure what we're dealing with."

After moving to homicide, I had spent six grueling months earning my advanced certification in DNA and evidence collection. The training had been intense, but it paid off in situations like this. We didn't always have the luxury of waiting for the state forensic team, especially on smaller cases. In a midsized department like ours, cross-training was essential.

I took a few deep breaths, mentally reviewing the checklist I'd run through a hundred times before. Everything was in place. It was time to look at the scene with my detective eyes.

Leo had taken my large evidence bag from Denise and placed it by the door earlier, next to my smaller bag. I reached inside and pulled out a plastic bag containing hair covers, carefully tucking my hair inside one of them. Next came the gloves. I pulled out a fresh box and hooked my finger inside one of the rubber loops, sliding it over my hand without contaminating the outside. It was a tedious process, but crucial. One slip, and my DNA could end up mixed with the victim's, making the lab's job a nightmare. Once the first pair was on, I slid another pair over them. Double-gloving was always a good idea in crime scenes.

After getting partially geared up, I pulled my flashlight from my pocket and directed the beam toward the window. There were no signs of forced entry. The dusty metal frame hadn't been disturbed, and the glass was coated in a layer of grime that suggested it hadn't been touched in months. Given the cold weather, I wasn't surprised.

I checked the door handle, finding no immediate signs of tampering. The motel didn't have electronic keycards, just good old-fashioned metal keys. That, at least, made things simpler.

"I'm ready to go in," I told Leo as I finished putting on my shoe covers and mask. "Keep things mellow out here."

Leo gave a quick nod and moved into position by the door as I turned the handle and pushed it open.

The motel room was dimly lit, the only light coming from a small lamp on the bedside table. The air was heavy, almost oppressive, with that faint musty scent motels often have—stale smoke, cleaning chemicals, and too many people passing through over the years. Mrs. Ledmen's body lay on the bed, her form barely illuminated by the dull glow of the lamp.

I stepped inside cautiously, my boots making soft clicks on the worn tile floor. Bell stayed by my side, her dark eyes tracking every move I made, though she remained quiet. This wasn't a scene for her; there were no explosives or threats here, just the cold reality of death.

Mrs. Ledmen was lying on her side, her gray nightshirt wrinkled, the covers pushed to the foot of the bed. Her purple boxer shorts clung awkwardly to her body, as if she'd tossed and turned before dying. The first instinct for any detective is to go straight to the body, to examine the victim up close. But I resisted that urge. I needed to see the whole room first, to get a feel for the scene before I touched anything.

I took a slow breath, my eyes scanning the space. The room was lived in, clearly the home of a couple staying long term. Boxes of food and supplies were stacked neatly in the corner, and an extra clothing rack—likely brought in by the Ledmens—stood by the bed. The dresser along the wall was cluttered with everyday items: a hairbrush, a water glass, a pile of clean clothes. It all fit the profile of a long-term stay.

Two plates with half-eaten meals sat on the small table in front of the window, alongside two empty glasses. A sink at the back of the room held more food containers stacked beneath it, and an open closet area by the sink held additional clothes. A mini-fridge sat next to the clothes, topped by a microwave and an electric hot plate. None of that was out of the ordinary for someone living in a motel room for months on end.

But then my flashlight caught on something directly inside the bathroom door—a white toaster, lying on its side on the floor. The cord wasn't plugged into the wall, but it lay close to an extension cord running from the sink into the dark bathroom.

I crouched down, careful not to let my knees touch the floor, and took a closer look. That's when I saw it—a small, eight-inch pool of water seeping from inside the toaster.

Well, if detective training taught us anything, this was what we called a clue.

Chapter Thirteen

After scanning the bathroom one more time and finding nothing out of place, I retraced my steps back to the body. As I stood there, Leo cleared his throat from the doorway, drawing my attention.

"Yes, I saw the toaster," I said dryly. "You should be a detective."

He cocked his head with mock offense. "And go around with crap covering my gorgeous hair and face? No, thank you!"

We both stifled the urge to laugh, knowing better than to smile or joke too much at a crime scene. Still, I fought back a grin. Looks had never been part of my job, but then again, I wasn't an Italian man like Leo.

I turned my attention to the victim. Mrs. Ledmen was much smaller than her husband. She lay on her side, her legs partially drawn up to her chest, hands curled in tight. The room was oddly quiet, save for the faint buzz of the heater's fan. Despite the dry appearance of Mrs. Ledmen's body, the bedding beneath her seemed damp. I couldn't detect any strong smell of urine, but it would be unusual if her bladder hadn't released upon death. Rolling her over would reveal more, but for now, I made a mental note to check for bladder or bowel leakage when I was ready.

My eyes swept over the bed, searching for anything out of place, but nothing stood out. I decided it was time to document the scene and grabbed my camera to start taking still photos. As I moved into position, Leo's phone rang, drawing his attention away.

"Yeah?" Leo answered in his typical morning monotone. "No, Detective Jolett is here." A brief pause. "No, she's not requesting additional help."

It didn't take a genius to figure out who was on the other end of the call. Officer Stanley Conners—the personal thorn in my side. His father was on the city council, and Stanley thought that gave him a free pass to involve himself in everyone's business, especially mine. And I wasn't on his good list.

"No," Leo continued. "We don't need traffic control. There's no problem, but I'll call if Detective Jolett needs any-thing." He pocketed his phone with a wry expression. I'd bet Stanley had hung up on him. So it begins.

I stepped outside the room, the cool morning air hitting me as I removed my shoe covers and outer gloves, grabbing my camera from the SUV. The tedious part of the job had begun, but it was a necessary step. I retrieved the photo log from the evidence bag and handed it to Leo.

"I'll give you the picture number and what I'm shooting," I instructed. "Slow me down or correct me if I mess up. You'll need to stay near the door in case anyone approaches." There was no need to mention Stanley—both of us knew I was working on borrowed time before the inevitable interrup-tions. Stanley's father would call the chief, and the chief would call me.

I walked to the edge of the parking lot, passing the outer crime scene tape, and began photographing the area, softly calling out what I was documenting. I captured shots of the parking lot, the motel's exterior, and each vehicle, their li-cense plates, and finally, the door to the crime scene.

"Number thirty-one, outside motel room door," I called out. "Number thirty-two, looking into the motel room."

Before stepping back inside, I donned a fresh pair of gloves and new shoe covers, then resumed photographing the room and the victim. One hundred and sixty-two still shots later, I stood at the doorway again, careful not to step outside and risk contamination.

"Call Brett and get him out of bed," I told Leo. "I want him keeping people back. I need you in here with me."

Brett was our part-time animal control officer, and though he had a reputation for being moody and preferring animals over people, he had stood guard for me before. Most importantly, Brett was trustworthy, which meant he wouldn't leak anything about the scene to anyone.

While Leo made the call, I switched my camera to video mode and panned the room, capturing a full sweep of the crime scene. As I finished, Brett's diesel engine rumbled outside the motel. The sun was starting to rise, casting a faint glow over the horizon. Across the street, I noticed two people outside a convenience store, pointing in our direction.

"Tell Brett to park his vehicle parallel to the front door," I said, "block the view of the room. I don't want anyone seeing the body."

"Yes, ma'am," Leo replied with a smirk. It was his Italian heritage showing, a trait he shared with Tony, my old partner. I missed Tony more than I liked to admit. Losing him had thrown me into my darkest days, until Suii gave me hope again. Now, Bell was my partner, and as I glanced at my SUV, I knew I'd need to give her a break soon. She'd wait as long as needed, but I hated making her sit for too long.

Brett and Leo approached after Brett had repositioned his vehicle.

"Hi, Brett. Thanks for coming," I greeted him. "I need you to hold the scene."

"No problem," Brett replied, turning his back to us without further comment. He was a man of few words, and I appreciated that.

I turned to Leo. "Too bad I have to ruin those good looks. Glove up, mask, and booties—you need to look as good as me."

Leo sighed. "You know if someone sees me like this, it'll ruin my reputation."

"I'll be sure to snap a picture and send it to the local paper." I rolled my eyes, moving on. "I'll take pictures inside the drawers, cabinets, and the fridge before we tackle the body."

"You've got to be kidding," Leo muttered.

"Nope. If this case goes unsolved, another detective will look at the file years from now and thank me. Let's get to work."

Once Leo suited up, we got back to it. I opened each drawer, snapping pictures while Leo logged everything. He did his best to avoid groaning as we worked through the room. When the time came to examine the body, I began by photographing Mrs. Ledmen as thoroughly as possible before moving on to more hands-on work.

"Help me roll her over," I instructed Leo. With no space to maneuver, I braced my knees on the bed. Something wet soaked through my jeans—whatever it was, I didn't want to know. Not now, anyway. It would be hours before I had the chance to change. Together, Leo and I shifted Mrs. Ledmen onto her back, her stiff, curled hands sticking up awkwardly.

A sizable burn on her right hand caught my eye. Her fingers were curled inward, almost like she was gripping something. I'd seen burns before, but this one looked severe. Electrocution cases weren't common around here. In fact, I wasn't sure we'd ever had one.

Leo's eyes widened above his mask, and I couldn't help myself. "Death by toaster."

Leo's eyes grew even larger. "You said I was second on this one, right?"

I nodded.

"Good. This case interests me. If you need help after my report, let me know."

Before I could respond, my phone buzzed. The word "Chief" flashed on the screen, and I showed Leo the caller ID. I peeled off my gloves, making sure not to touch the phone until I was free of any contaminants. The last thing I needed was evidence—or worse, body fluids—on my phone.

"Good morning, sir," I answered. "Glad you called." And I was. I liked the chief, and I knew this call wasn't just about my earlier message. Stanley's father had likely paid him a visit.

The chief got straight to the point. "Councilman Conners just left my house. Thank you for the heads-up. I had him sit down and excused myself to check my phone in the bathroom."

That meant Stanley hadn't been able to feed his father inside information. "What did you tell him?"

"I told him you were on-scene and had everything under control. He wants an update in two hours, but I refused to discuss an open investigation. Don't be surprised if he shows up there. If he does, arrest him. Who's with you?"

I updated him on Leo, Brett, and our progress. The chief listened silently, offering no advice—he knew I didn't need it. We ended the call, and I waved Leo over.

I beckoned Brett, who came to the door. "Let me know the second Officer or Councilman Conners shows up. They're not allowed near this scene, and I'll deal with them personally."

Brett nodded. "If you say they can't come in, they're not getting in."

"Thanks, Brett. That's why I called you. Add your time here to your hours this week—the chief will make sure you get paid."

Brett gave a brief nod and returned to his post.

"I'm not scared of the Conners," Leo said. "The old man hated me after I went on the task force and his son didn't. Funny how that keeps happening."

I gave him a look. "You're taking all the fun out of my day. I was really hoping to arrest the councilman."

Leo smirked. "If we get the chance, we'll flip for it."

With that settled, I returned to the task at hand. Slipping my mask back on, I donned a fresh pair of gloves, grabbed two brown lunch bags, and walked over to Mrs. Ledmen's body. I slipped the bags over her hands and taped them securely at her wrists. Her hands would be crucial evidence. As I continued my examination, I noticed bruises on her legs and a small one on her chest, exposed by her pulled-up shirt. The medical examiner would strip her body, and we'd get a clearer picture, but for now, the details were stacking up.

I shifted my focus to her feet. Blood oozed from a wound on the top of her right foot, sizable enough to raise questions. We'd get a closer look during the autopsy.

When I stepped back, I noticed the dark, wet spot on my knee and the soaked bedding beneath Mrs. Ledmen. My stomach churned, but I kept my expression neutral. When I looked up, Leo was eyeing my jeans.

"This is exactly why I prefer traffic duty," he said, a little too smugly.

I raised an eyebrow. "You've handled plenty of bodies at accident scenes."

"Yeah, but those bodies don't pee on me."

He was pushing his luck now. "Just make sure you wash that uniform."

His face paled as he glanced at his sleeves, realizing he'd scratched his arm with the same glove that had touched the body.

"I'll do that," he muttered.

Chapter Fourteen

T HE EARLY MORNING SUN had made its full appearance by the time Brett called from outside the door. Its pale light cast long shadows across the parking lot, turning the damp pavement into a shimmering patchwork.

"There's a man from the room next door packing up his vehicle," Brett announced, his voice steady and low as always.

"Stall him for a few. I'll be right out," I replied, glancing at Mrs. Ledmen's body one last time before I peeled off my protective gear. Each motion felt deliberate, like shedding a layer of the investigation itself. With gloves, shoe and hair covers, and mask discarded, I hurried outside, feeling the crisp bite of the morning air hit my face. It was sharp, refreshing—a reminder that life went on despite the grim scene inside.

I rummaged through my small evidence bag, fingers brushing past various tools until they landed on my backup recorder. I hit the switch, but no green light appeared. My patience, always thin in the early hours, wavered. After more digging, I found the double-A batteries I needed and replaced them. A soft, comforting click followed as the recorder sprang to life.

Brett stood nearby, his broad shoulders a solid silhouette against the pale light, and he gave me a subtle nod toward the west, where the neighboring motel room sat. Before I could knock on the door, a man exited with a small duffel bag slung over his shoulder, heading to his car without even noticing me. He moved slowly, like someone in no particular rush, a stark contrast to the tension roiling inside me.

I approached as he opened the car door, his movements casual as he stowed the bag behind the driver's seat. "Hi, I'm Detective Jolett. I need to speak with you for a moment."

The man turned, revealing short, graying hair that contrasted with the deep lines of his face. Despite his age—fifties, I guessed—he wore an easy smile. It was a jarring sight given the circumstances.

"Sure, Detective. What's going on?" he asked, his voice calm but slightly curious.

"We've had a situation in the room next to yours, and I have a few questions." My words were neutral, leaving enough space for him to reveal something. I watched him closely, the way his brows furrowed slightly, his gaze shifting towards the door to the Ledmen room.

"Is she seriously hurt?" His tone was too casual, but his body language told a different story—stiff, a little uneasy.

His question cracked the case open a little wider. Why would he assume someone was hurt?

"Can you tell me why you think she might be hurt?" I kept my voice level, careful not to hint at what I knew. Silence hung between us, a heavy pause filled with potential.

He ran a hand through his graying hair, a classic nervous tic. I'd seen it a hundred times—people wanting to help but unsure if they should. It was a tug-of-war between staying uninvolved and doing the right thing. I could drag him down to the station, question him more thoroughly, but it was always better when they decided to help on their own.

He finally sighed, a sound that seemed to release some of the tension in his shoulders. "I got in yesterday around three in the afternoon. I've got a long drive home, about ten hours, and I wanted to push through but knew I wouldn't make it."

He paused again, this time glancing around the parking lot as if the mundane setting would give him an excuse not to say more. But I stayed silent, knowing full well people often feel the need to fill the void.

"I heard a man and woman arguing around six yesterday evening. It got pretty heated—I almost asked to change rooms, but then it quieted down, so I stayed put. Didn't hear anything else until around nine."

I nodded slightly, letting him continue at his own pace. "When you heard them arguing, did you catch what they were saying?"

"A lot of yelling. The woman was crying, but I couldn't make out most of it. Then she shouted, 'Stop, you're hurting me.'" His hand went back to his hair, combing through it again. "I should've done something."

There was guilt there, deep and unsettling, but that wasn't my job to address. "What happened at nine?"

His face tightened, the lines deepening as he relived the memory. "Just a thump against the wall. After that, nothing."

"How long did the argument last when she yelled out?" I pressed gently, watching the gears turn in his mind.

"Maybe ten minutes," he said, uncertainty creeping into his voice.

I moved on quickly. "Did you ever see either of the people in the room next door?"

He leaned back against his car, arms crossed in a posture that suggested defensiveness. "No. I heard the door open and close a few times earlier in the day, and the ice machine went off, but that was it. After the argument, it was just that thump."

"Could you tell what the argument was about?" I asked, though I already suspected the answer.

"I couldn't make out what the man was saying, no," he admitted before his expression shifted. "Is she dead?"

I couldn't confirm that, not yet. The last thing I needed was for him to spill this to a local diner, and within hours the whole town would be buzzing with rumors. "No. I just need your driver's license and phone number for my report. In case I have more questions later."

People's memories had a funny way of revealing details after the fact, and I had a feeling something else might pop into his head once he started his long drive home. I jotted down his license information and phone number in my notepad, then handed him one of my cards.

"If anything else comes to mind, give me a call."

"May I leave now?"

"Yes. Drive safe. Thanks for your help." I extended my hand, and he shook it briefly before sliding into his car and driving away, leaving the parking lot eerily quiet once again.

"Thanks, Brett," I said, turning back toward my SUV. He gave a short nod as I popped the hatch open. "Down, stay," I commanded Bell. She perked up, eyes fixed on Brett. A small whine escaped her throat—he was one of the few people she actually liked.

"Go ahead," I said, giving her the green light. Bell leaped from the car, her muscles coiled like a spring, and bounded to Brett's side. He dropped to one knee, giving her the attention she craved.

"What a pretty girl you are," he said, his deep voice softening as he scratched behind her ears. "So beautiful."

Brett hadn't been around when I had Suii, my first K9 partner. His part-time job was dependent on the city budget, and whenever funding was tight, the animal control position was cut. I hated those years. The department ran smoother when Brett handled the calls that came in—he was reliable, good with both animals and people, even if the latter didn't interest him as much.

After a moment, Bell gave a soft bark, her signal that she was ready for more action. I clipped her leash to the strap at the back of her neck. "Come on, girl. Time to do your business, and then back to the hatch for some slumber. I promise you an extra-long playdate later." I led her to a small patch of grass by the side of the motel.

Bell sniffed around, circling a few spots as if she was solving a mystery of her own. I always marveled at her thoroughness, the way she carefully selected the perfect place to squat. I'd asked her about it a few times, but she wasn't one to share trade secrets. When she finished, I scratched the scruff of her neck and whispered, "Good girl." Bell didn't complain as I led her back to the SUV, and I knew she understood her job—to rest, to wait, and to be ready for whatever came next.

Once Bell was settled, I re-geared, grabbing a pack of sticky notes and a black Sharpie. The weight of my camera slung over my shoulder was familiar, a tool I'd used countless times to document the darkest parts of life. I stepped back into the room, the smell of the crime scene now less jarring but still present—dampness, faint hints of decay, and the sterile scent of latex gloves and forensic equipment.

"Have an interesting conversation with Mrs. Ledmen? Solve my case while I was gone?" I asked Leo, deadpan. He stood at the window, his face partially illuminated by the sun's glow.

"You're hilarious," he replied, glancing over his shoulder. "But no, she hasn't uttered a word. Making your job harder, huh?"

"Too bad. I could use some answers." I moved toward the bathroom, something gnawing at me from earlier. As I stepped inside, I scanned the porcelain surfaces, the walls, the fixtures. I stretched the shower curtain, inspecting its folds, feeling the cool fabric between my gloved fingers.

Nothing was wet.

I glanced down at the toaster again, the pool of water next to it still undisturbed.

If someone had been electrocuted using that toaster, there would need to be more water. The tub was dry, too dry. I stepped out and checked the sink outside the bathroom. Dry as well. I moved deeper into the small space, eyes scanning the only other possible water source.

The toilet.

The water sat still in the bowl, its surface undisturbed.

More questions.

I didn't voice my thoughts to Leo yet. There was evidence to collect first. Striding past him, I grabbed swabs and boxes from my small evidence bag, then handed him my camera. "Change your gloves before touching my equipment. Also, grab the evidence log from my bag."

"Yes, ma'am," Leo said, giving me a mock salute but careful not to touch his face with his germy gloves. Ignoring his sarcasm, I returned to the bathroom.

I had yellow plastic evidence markers but inside, I preferred sticky notes. I used the Sharpie to number the notes, carefully tagging each potential piece of evidence. Sticky note number 1 went next to the pool of water on the floor, number 2 on the toaster, number 3 on the toilet seat. I tagged the shower and curtain as well. These might seem like small details, but sitting in a courtroom being asked why I didn't do these things was not a time I looked forward to.

"I need close-ups of each tagged item," I said to Leo. He muttered something under his breath but complied, carefully snapping photos of each marked location.

When he finished, he lowered the camera, looking puzzled. "Why are you tagging the shower, curtain, and toilet?"

I sighed. "I want to figure out where the water came from. The shower's bone dry, so I'm going to swab it with saline just in case. There's a tiny bit of dampness on the inside fold of the curtain, but my gut tells me the water came from the toilet."

His eyes widened in disbelief. "You're kidding, right?"

"I wish I was." I shook my head, trying not to dwell on the implications.

Without another word, I headed back to the door to grab the saline ampules, then paused to check outside.

Brett gave a quick chin nod in the direction of the small store across the street. "A few people were starting to gather, trying to catch a look."

Brett's broad figure stood firmly by his vehicle, arms crossed. He might be a softy with animals, but he was a wall of intimidation when it came to people. No one would get past him.

"Thanks, Brett. Keep it up. I'll close the door and leave you to it."

I closed the door behind me and returned to the bathroom. Using the saline ampules, I began swabbing the surfaces, working methodically. Leo held the boxes, marking each with the corresponding sticky note number. He logged the time for each sample, meticulously recording every detail.

It took us another thirty minutes to finish collecting samples from the bathroom and another hour to process the rest of the room. When all the evidence was bagged and labeled, I finally made the call to have Mrs. Ledmen's body picked up by the coroner.

The next step was speaking with Mr. Ledmen, and I had a feeling that conversation wouldn't go smoothly.

Chapter Fifteen

B Y THE TIME I walked into the station, the clock had just ticked past eight in the morning. The air outside had warmed up quickly, a reminder that fall hadn't shaken off summer's attitude. I'd spoken with Denise an hour earlier, and she'd mentioned that Mr. Ledmen had been quiet and cooperative during his stay in the holding room. She also mentioned, in passing, that he'd cried a few times. Not surprising given the circumstances, but it could mean many things.

Leo had already headed home to catch up on sleep. Poor guy had gone a few hours past his shift and he was wiped.

While Bell did her business outside the station, I talked to her softly, a habit I'd formed with Tony and then Suii. "This is a strange one, girl. If you have any ideas, toss them my way like a good partner, will you?" Bell kept her thoughts to herself, though her giant brown eyes tracked my every word. She had no problem offering a slobbery lick in response, which I wiped off on her fur. I gave her a quick pat on the head. "Let's go inside and solve this case." Her tail wagged, as if she understood every word, and like Suii, I believed she did.

Once inside, I headed through the squad room, ready to prep the interview room before I sat down with Mr. Ledmen. Bell was eager to follow, but I guided her toward my office instead. She deserved some downtime after waiting patiently in the SUV during the morning hours. I gave her a chew bone to occupy her while I worked, though she gave me a side glance that told me she'd rather be with me. "Soon, girl," I whispered, knowing I needed to focus.

With Bell settled, I grabbed the evidence from my car and made my way to the evidence lockers, logging each item carefully to establish the chain of custody. There was no way I was letting this case slip because of sloppy paperwork or protocol violations. Each piece had its place and timestamp, so I could show it hadn't just been sitting in my car. Satisfied everything was in order, I moved to the interview room.

The interview room itself was basic—a small table, two chairs, and a shelf at the back holding the breathalyzer machine. The room had seen countless drunks come through, some of them barely able to sit in the chair without sliding off. Back when I was on patrol, I'd often seen people hit the floor, look up with dazed eyes, and try to figure out what had just happened. Those cases were always easier to prosecute in court with the video footage that showed them toppling over mid-sentence.

Video was just as critical now that I was a detective. Sometimes the camera would catch expressions or body language I missed in the moment, subtle things that could break a case wide open when rewatched. I picked up a crumpled tissue from the corner of the table and tossed it into the garbage, giving the room a final once-over. Satisfied, I placed Mr. Ledmen's phone—a key piece of evidence—on the table where I wanted him to sit.

I made a quick detour to my office, checking the small green light on the camera recording equipment. Everything was set to capture every second of the interview. It was time.

When I entered the front records office, I found Mr. Ledmen sitting on the couch, flipping through a magazine. He looked distant, distracted, a man lost in the fog of recent events. Denise, sitting next to him, was glued to her phone—typical twenty-something behavior. I took a breath, readying myself for the interview ahead.

"Hi, Mr. Ledmen, I'm sorry it took me so long to get here," I said, trying to ease into the conversation. "I stayed until your wife was picked up." That wasn't a lie. I had stayed, overseeing everything until Mrs. Ledmen was taken away. I couldn't say she was at the morgue yet, but she was in a secured, refrigerated room, waiting for her trip to the medical examiner's office.

"Where is my wife?" he asked, his voice low and worn.

"She's at the mortuary," I replied truthfully, though I left out the details of her current state. There was no need to mention that right now.

He nodded slightly, a sadness hanging over him like a shroud. "My phone. I need to call my son."

The mention of his son made my chest tighten. "How old is your son?" I asked gently.

"He's nineteen. He's actually my stepson, but I've been his dad for seventeen years, so he's my son." There was pride in his voice despite the pain.

"Your cell is in the interview room," I said. "If you can give me just a little more time for some questions before calling him, I'll get you out of here sooner." I needed to get his side of the story before he made those calls. Unless Mr. Ledmen confessed to killing his wife in this room, he'd be walking out today. Without concrete evidence, I couldn't hold him, and until the autopsy came back, I was in a gray area. There was always the possibility Mrs. Ledmen had tried to kill herself by placing the toaster in the toilet. At this point, I didn't know what I had, but this interview would help clear some of the fog.

"I need to call my boss too," Mr. Ledmen added. "I'm sure he's been calling nonstop. I never miss work, and I've never been late."

I could see the nervousness building in him, and I didn't want to push too hard. If I made him feel cornered, he might shut down completely. "You can make your calls soon. I promise. Let's head to the interview room first." I motioned for him to follow. "Bring your water if you'd like."

Once inside the room, I took the chair in the back, leaving the chair with his phone in front of it for him. He sat down, immediately clicking the screen to check for messages. I'd already seen the notifications when I bagged the phone earlier—several missed calls, all from his boss. His wife's phone, however, was still in evidence, and I hoped he wouldn't ask for it just yet.

"If you can give me a few minutes for questions, I'll let you make your calls in here," I offered, keeping my tone as calm as possible.

He put the phone down, looking resigned. "Sure."

Since he wasn't in custody and was free to leave, I didn't bother reading him his Miranda rights. I needed him to talk, to open up and share his version of events. "It might be easier if you start from yesterday and walk me through the day."

He linked his fingers together on the table, staring down at them for a moment before speaking. "I went to work at six and got home around six-thirty." He paused, glancing up briefly before continuing. "Mary had dinner ready, but she wasn't in a good mood. She started in on me as soon as I walked through the door. She was drinking." His voice cracked slightly. "She hates it here. Says there's nothing for her to do all day. I told her that before we moved, but she insisted on coming."

He trailed off, his eyes distant as if reliving the scene. Something flickered in his gaze, maybe a memory he wasn't ready to share yet. "We argued. She stopped drinking around eight, took her sleep meds, and went to bed."

I recalled the meds I had packaged earlier—antidepressants, anti-anxiety pills, and a few others I didn't recognize right away. It wasn't uncommon to see such a cocktail these days.

"What happened after that?" I asked, keeping my voice soft.

His red, swollen eyes closed briefly, and when they re-opened, his shoulders sagged as though a weight had settled on him. "She went into the bathroom. I fell asleep. The next thing I know, I heard a noise and found her passed out in front of the sink." His words were rushed now, like he needed to get them out. "I dragged her onto the bed. I think she hit the side wall with her hip or leg. I wasn't gentle. I was angry she passed out again."

His voice broke slightly, and he looked at me, his eyes pleading. "This looks bad, doesn't it?"

His version of events lined up with what I'd seen at the scene—the bruises on her body could've come from him dragging her onto the bed while she was still alive. If she'd been dead already, the bruises wouldn't have formed the same way. But that didn't mean it wasn't something else entirely. Only time—and the autopsy—would tell.

I decided to probe a little deeper. "Did you see the toaster on the bathroom floor?"

His head jerked slightly, a flash of surprise crossing his face before he met my gaze again. "I saw it there, but it wasn't plugged in."

I made a mental note of his reaction. "Have you ever phys-ically hurt your wife?"

He shook his head slowly. "No, I've never hit her or any-thing like that. When she's drunk, she sometimes pushes me or slaps my arm, but it never hurt." His voice softened as he looked down, tears starting to well up in his eyes. "I guess none of that matters now."

"Did you ever report it when she hit you?" I asked, trying to keep him talking.

He shook his head again. "No. She never hurt me. It was just when she drank too much." Tears began streaming down his cheeks. "I didn't hurt her last night. I might have bumped her when I carried her, but I didn't mean to. I swear."

I pushed a box of tissues toward him, giving him a moment. "I'm truly sorry for your loss, Mr. Ledmen," I said softly. "Your room at the motel won't be available for a few more hours—maybe not until tomorrow. I'll need an electrician to look at some things before I release it."

He nodded weakly, his eyes still swimming with grief. "May I leave?"

"Of course. I just need your phone number so I can call you as soon as the room is released."

He read off his number, and I jotted it down in my notepad. "What about her body?" he asked, his voice breaking. "We live in Texas. She would want to be buried there."

"I don't know why your wife died," I explained carefully, "so I've ordered an autopsy. I'll be there with her during it." His face twisted in discomfort, but I continued. "I know you don't know me, but I have compassion for you and your wife. Part of my job is to keep her safe now, and that includes her body."

He nodded, clearly torn between grief and the grim reality of the situation. "Thank you."

"I'll know more by the end of the day," I added. "Would you like to make your calls here before you go? Denise can drop you wherever you need to go. A hotel if you'd prefer."

He shook his head. "I have a friend who can pick me up. I usually stay with him when we're here. I only got the room because of Mary. I can't go back to Texas without her."

"I understand," I said, standing. "Make your calls, and then you can wait in the front office for your friend. We'll leave you alone until you're ready."

I walked out, heading over to Denise. I gave her a quick signal to follow me into my office. Bell was still in her spot, chewing her bone, though her ears perked up when we entered.

"Bell, stay," I commanded, holding up my hand. Denise edged her way inside, keeping a wary distance from Bell. Most of the department knew what Bell was capable of, and Denise was no exception. The sight of Bell untethered made her nervous, even though I trusted my partner completely.

Denise's eyes darted between Bell and me. "Does Mr. Ledmen know you're recording him?"

"He didn't ask, and I didn't volunteer the information."

I turned up the volume on the recording as Mr. Ledmen made his calls. The first one was to his son. He cried through most of the conversation, apologizing over and over. "I'm sorry, son. I'm so sorry." His voice cracked repeatedly, the pain raw and undeniable.

The second call to his boss was equally emotional, though he managed to hold it together a bit better. Finally, he called his friend, the man who would pick him up. By the time his friend answered, Mr. Ledmen had regained some composure, explaining that Mary had died and asking if he could stay with him.

The whole process took about ten minutes, each one filled with varying degrees of grief and guilt.

Denise leaned forward, whispering, "You're going to let him go?"

I couldn't help but smile slightly at her innocence. To be a rookie again. "I have no choice. I don't have enough evidence to hold anyone, and I need to do some more legwork before I can figure out what happened. For now, I'm treating this as a homicide until I can prove it isn't. And remember, you didn't hear or see anything today. Got it?"

"Got it." She stood up, looking relieved. "If you don't need me, I've got some reports to finish."

"That works. Thanks for sticking with Mr. Ledmen earlier. I know it wasn't fun, but it helped me a lot."

"He was okay," she said, heading toward the door. "Just... sad."

Sad. Sad that his wife was gone, or sad that he had a hand in it? Time would tell, and it was my job to make sure the truth came out. The problem with people was they often acted in different ways for many reasons, and it was my job to figure out which one had driven him.

Chapter Sixteen

I FED BELL FROM her stash in my office and grabbed a protein bar for myself. My emergency bag, now safely inside from the car, sat by the door, always ready but rarely touched. Bell followed me as we made our way into the evidence room. The door clicked shut behind us, sealing us off from the noise of the station. It was just me and my partner, like always. Bell wasn't just a tool for protection or explosives detection—she was the one I bounced ideas off, the one who let me talk through my thoughts until something clicked.

As I started processing the evidence, I spoke aloud, a habit that had grown even more since Bell. "Everything points to her being killed by the toaster. The bruises on her body could've come from hitting the wall before death, or maybe while she was still alive."

Bell, having finished her food, sauntered over and plopped down on her blanket. She had a kennel here, but we almost never used it. The blanket was more her style—comfortable, familiar, and always within earshot of me. She yawned, utterly uninterested in my analysis.

"I need to look up more about death by toaster. It's one of those things you hear about but never think you'll actually deal with," I muttered. Bell rolled over, unconcerned, her eyes drooping. "You just lie there and contemplate what I've said while I give Sam a call."

Samantha Anderson, the assistant county attorney, handled all the felony cases. She was sharp, efficient, and, frankly, I didn't know how she balanced her job with raising kids. She'd dealt with enough of my cases to know they often came with twists, and this one was no different.

I dialed her number, and after the third ring, she picked up. "I have a strange one to run past you," I said, skipping pleasantries.

"Go ahead. Shoot." Her voice was a little lighter than usual.

I ran through the case details, outlining everything we had so far, ending with, "Bell's fresh out of ideas. I need an electrician, and she's not exactly well-connected."

Sam chuckled on the other end. "My brother's an electrician. I'll call him and have someone trustworthy sent over. I'd rather not involve him directly in the case, though. Conflicts of interest and all that."

She anticipated my concerns before I even had the chance to voice them. She was right, of course—having family involved in a potential homicide case was a complication we didn't need. "Good call. Can you think of anything I've missed?"

"Not right now. But death by toaster? That's going to make headlines."

"I'll do my best to keep it under wraps," I said, already knowing the councilman had his nose too deep in my investigation. "Councilman Conners has already called the chief."

"Figures. Have fun with that."

"Always." I hung up, glancing at Bell. Her ears perked up, as if sensing something was about to happen.

"We'll get in some K9 work after I call the medical examiner to set up the autopsy," I told her. Her tail started thumping against the floor, and I knew she understood exactly what that meant—time to work.

Suii, my old partner, never had a tail, so I hadn't had to deal with the constant thumping. Bell's, on the other hand, was a continual presence—knocking things over, wagging with excitement. It took a few days after she'd first come into my life for me to realize I needed to move my water glass to the center of the coffee table to protect it from her tail. Partners come with quirks, and Bell's twelve-inch-long whip was just one of them.

I dialed the medical examiner and scheduled the autopsy for the next afternoon. No sooner had I hung up than my phone rang again. Samantha was on the line.

"An electrician will meet you at the motel in two hours," she said.

Perfect. Enough time for a solid K9 training session. I left Bell in the office for a moment and headed back to the evidence room. There, in a special locker, I kept small amounts of inert explosives for training. I grabbed a baggy and set off to hide the items in strategic places around the squad room.

Before long, Denise spotted me moving around. "I'm bringing Bell through for some training," I said, giving her a heads-up. "Just stay where you are, and you'll be fine."

Denise smiled slightly, but I knew she wasn't completely at ease around Bell. Most of the department felt the same. Bell had a way of picking her favorites, and Denise wasn't one of them—at least, not yet. It had taken Bell a few months to warm up to Leo, but once she did, they'd become fast friends. Brett, on the other hand, had won her over quickly. Sugarplum, my neighbor's little yapper, was another favorite of Bell's. Ed, the neighbor? Not so much.

Suii had never been one for small dogs, and I'd often joked about letting him "eat" Sugarplum when we'd first met the little thing. After Suii's death, me and Sugarplum had become buddies. Ed had never thrown my bad behavior back at me, though I wasn't the nicest person back then. He'd been devastated when Suii died. Now, Ed watched my place when I wasn't home, and I knew he took the job seriously.

Once I'd hidden all the items, I retrieved Bell from my office and attached her leash. "Time to work," I told her, and she gave a full-body shake of excitement. Bell always loved working, and that enthusiasm never waned. We headed into the squad room, starting at one end. Bell's nose was down immediately, and before long, she barked sharply—her signal that she'd found what she was trained to detect.

"Stay. Guard," I instructed. Bell turned her back to the small blasting cap hidden in the corner and scanned the room, growling softly.

"Good girl. Release," I said, and her tail wagged wildly. I marked her success in my training log, and we continued, finding all the items I'd hidden.

"You're a good girl," I told her when we finished. "Let's play."

Bell jumped up, twisting her body mid-air with a small whine of excitement. "Let's grab your toy."

Her favorite toy was a thick rope, orange and purple stripes running along its length. I had three of them—one in the office, one at home, and one in the car. She loved it because it symbolized her reward for a job well done. We headed outside to the fenced-off lunch area behind the department. It was empty on weekends, the perfect spot for us to play.

I unclipped her leash and threw the rope. Bell pounced, growling and shaking the rope in her mouth as if she were taking down a wild animal. She tossed it in the air, catching it again with a snap of her teeth. I laughed softly, giving her a few minutes to enjoy herself before calling her over to me. I tugged the rope from her mouth and threw it again.

Watching her play like this reminded me of the shift that had happened in my life. When I partnered with Suii, I hadn't been a dog person. I'd barely tolerated them, if I was being honest. But now, with Bell, everything had changed. She was my life, just as Suii had been. That burning anger and sadness I'd carried after Tony's death had finally softened into something I could live with, though the ache of losing him never fully went away. Tony had been special, and I knew he would have loved Bell and Suii. He would've been happy to see that I'd found something that made me smile again.

After thirty minutes of playing, I brought Bell some water. She drank noisily, splashing it around before I loaded her back into my SUV. We were both ready for the next phase of the day.

Arriving at the motel, I found Brett still standing guard. He gave me a nod as I approached.

"If you can stick around a bit longer, I'd appreciate it," I told him. "I'm meeting someone soon, and after that, I should be able to release the room."

"You got it," Brett replied, his usual concise answer.

Before he'd even finished speaking, a van with *Daily Electric* plastered on the side pulled up beside his animal control truck. The driver cut the engine, and I waved him over.

Introductions were quick. The electrician, Malcolm, was an older man, at least sixty, with shaggy gray hair and a matching beard. His eyes, bright blue, sparkled beneath all that hair.

"I don't understand much about electricity," I began, leading him toward the room, "but I need to know if it's possible to tell if someone was electrocuted based on the wiring."

Malcolm didn't say much, just nodded as he set his toolbox down on the carpet. "Circuit would blow," he said simply.

"Okay. Can you check the circuits?"

"Yep. Any specific one you want me to look at?"

"All of them," I said, not entirely sure which ones mattered most.

"Yep," he said again, moving toward the first outlet beneath the front window.

I watched as he moved efficiently from one receptacle to the next, examining each carefully. "I need to know if any circuits are blown, and if so, how many."

"No safety circuit," Malcolm muttered, mostly to himself. "Usually in the bathroom, but some rooms have more than one. Gotta be sure."

When he reached the outlet near the sink, he pointed. "It's a GFCI outlet. And it's blown."

"What does that mean?" I asked, stepping closer.

Malcolm pulled out a screwdriver and began unscrewing the plate. "Shouldn't you turn off the power first?" I asked, worried.

He grunted in response, as if the question was ridiculous. When he pulled the plate away, I saw that the inside was blackened. Malcolm stuck his finger into the wires, pulling it back to show me. "Someone had quite the party with this."

"How would that happen?" I asked.

"Too much for the circuit to handle. Could be any-thing—multiple extension cords, a faulty cord, or even a bad appliance. Sometimes circuits just wear out."

I wanted to ask the question burning in my mind: *Could a toaster in the toilet do this?* But I stopped myself. Instead, I asked, "Is this the only blown circuit in the room?"

"I think so. Let me double-check the rest."

It took Malcolm about thirty minutes to inspect every out-let. None of the others had damage. Once he was done, he packed up and left, leaving me with more questions than an-swers. At least now, if this case went to trial, I knew Malcolm could testify about the circuits and outlets. I didn't need to understand all the technical details—just enough to get by. Watching him fiddle with live wires was not my idea of fun, and it confirmed that I didn't want his job.

Brett helped me remove the crime scene tape before head-ing out. I returned the room key to Sveta and Feodor, the motel owners. Sveta translated for Feodor, and both of them assured me they hadn't noticed anything unusual about the Ledmens.

"You can rent the room out again, but the bed needs replacing," I informed them. "The body leaked on it. Whatever it was, it wasn't good."

Sveta grimaced but thanked me politely. I left the office and called the chief, surprised when he answered on the first ring.

"Councilman Conners has called three times," he said, his voice tinged with irritation.

"This is an active investigation. You'd think he'd understand that by now."

The chief chuckled. "He's like a dog with a bone. He won't give up."

"My team knows to keep quiet. The only one I'm talking to is Detective Macky."

"It'll get out eventually," the chief said. "But keep doing what you're doing."

"I will. I've got a lot of work ahead of me, so the longer I can keep things quiet, the better."

"I'll deal with Conners," the chief promised. "Sergeant Spence will be back in town on Wednesday. Report your findings to him, and I'll be out of the loop."

"Thanks. I'm heading home to sleep. The autopsy's tomorrow, first thing."

"You're doing good work, Jolett."

We ended the call, and I couldn't help but reflect on how far I'd come. I'd been a huge pain in the ass for a long time after Tony died, and the chief had put up with a lot from me. I wasn't sure if I'd ever fully get back into his good graces, but it felt like I was on the right path.

"Hear that, Bell?" I said, glancing at her as I slid into the driver's seat. "I'm doing a good job."

Bell stared at me with those big brown eyes, her tail thumping gently against the backseat.

"Even with a possible death by toaster, you'd still want Detective Jolett on your case."

As usual, Bell didn't respond. But the lack of objection told me all I needed to know.

Chapter Seventeen

T HE NEXT MORNING, AFTER a sleepless night of tossing and turning, I left Bell behind when I headed out to the medical examiner's office. As much as I hated leaving her, I knew it was for the best. If I took her, I'd have to keep the SUV running for the entire autopsy, and if something interesting came up, it could take hours.

Before heading to bed last night, I had called Ed, my neighbor. He has a key to my place and promised to check in on Bell if anything seemed off. Bell also had her dog door, something I had installed after she'd been trapped inside once for twelve hours. That memory still gnawed at me. She hadn't gone to the bathroom on the carpet, bless her, but the guilt from leaving her to suffer for so long had eaten away at me. The pet door had been my way of apologizing, and Bell had accepted it after an initial battle with the rubber flap that seemed to insult her ego every time it slapped her on the butt. Now, if I was home, she wouldn't touch the dog door. I could swear she enjoyed watching me open and close the door for her a hundred times a day. A little game to see how well I stayed trained.

As I moved around the house, getting ready, Bell followed close on my heels, her soft whines letting me know she wasn't happy about being left behind. She didn't need words to convey her feelings—those big brown eyes said it all.

"I'm sorry you can't go, girl," I told her, genuinely meaning it. "You'd be bored the whole time." Her expression didn't change, though, and she plopped down at my feet with a dramatic huff.

"I'll take you hiking next weekend," I promised, knowing full well her trust in me was conditional. Her tail thumped twice, as if to say, *I'll believe it when I see it.* She knew better than to get her hopes up for something so far away.

Before leaving, I gave her one of her favorite treats, watching her gnaw on it as I slipped out the door. I was running a bit early, not wanting to leave anything to chance. It was the weekend, so traffic would likely be light, but you never knew in this city. The entire ride over, I mentally reviewed everything I had, turning it over and over in my mind. I was hoping the autopsy would give me the answers I needed—or at least point me in the right direction.

The medical examiner's office sat next to the trauma center, a hulking structure of glass and steel. It was the best facility in the state, which is why I had bodies sent here. Dr. Thomas, the ME on duty, greeted me with a smile that didn't quite reach his tired eyes.

"Detective Jolett. Your name popped up on the schedule this morning, so I'm hoping you've got something good for me."

By "good," he meant interesting. I had a habit of bringing him the strangest cases, and today wouldn't disappoint. "Death by toaster," I said, watching his expression.

He blinked, momentarily startled, then chuckled. "You're kidding."

"Look it up. Google 'death by toaster,' I dare you," I shot back with a grin.

His amusement faded, replaced by a weariness I understood all too well. "Come into my office, and let's talk about this case."

We sat down, and I filled him in on everything, from the crime scene to the small details that didn't quite add up. I left out the burns on Mrs. Ledmen's hand and foot, wanting his unbiased reaction when he saw them for himself. As I talked, the corners of his mouth twitched, but he waited until I finished to say anything.

"You really think a toaster killed this woman?" he asked finally.

"I'm hoping, if it was murder, that it was her husband and not the toaster," I said dryly. "Because prosecuting a toaster won't be easy."

"You're killing me," he groaned, half-laughing. "Let's gear up and take a look."

We left his office, walking in tandem down the long hallway. When we reached the autopsy area, Dr. Thomas used his fingerprint to unlock the door. I peeled off into the side room to gown up. The routine was second nature by now—mask, gloves, and eye protection in place before stepping out into the sterile, cold air of the autopsy room.

Mrs. Ledmen's body was wheeled in on a cart, her skin pale under the harsh lights. I had my camera ready, as did the assistant. The ME's office would send me their pictures, but I preferred to have my own. I'd learned early in my career that it was always better to have everything in hand rather than wait around.

Dr. Thomas started his examination at the head, checking her eyes before moving methodically down her body. He straightened her left arm first, then the right, speaking into his recorder about the burn marks on her fingers, though he didn't look up at me as he noted it.

Then he moved to her feet, pausing when he saw the burn on her foot. He raised his head and met my gaze, shaking his head slightly. "You may have a death by toaster."

I didn't smile. This wasn't a joke, and the headline wouldn't be a good one.

A loud *zap* filled the room as the giant fly zapper in the corner sparked to life. I jumped, my nerves shot for a moment, and both Dr. Thomas and his assistant laughed. Everyone but the regular staff jumped when the zapper went off. As much as I hated the thing, it was better than dealing with maggots.

An hour later, I was back on the road. The toxicology results would take a week, maybe ten days if the lab was backed up. Besides the burns on her hand and foot, the autopsy revealed nothing new beyond the bruises I'd already noted. Samples of Mrs. Ledmen's heart, liver, and kidneys were sent off for further analysis, and Dr. Thomas mentioned there might be evidence of electrical shock in her blood and muscle tissue due to seizures or muscle constriction. It wasn't much, but it was something. Still, if I had to wait two weeks for the autopsy results, Mr. Ledmen could very well be long gone by then.

Frustration simmered beneath the surface as I drove straight to the station, only to run into Detective Macky just as I stepped out of my car. His easy smile greeted me.

"Jolett," he called out. "Rumor has it you've got a live one."

"Oh really?" I said, raising an eyebrow. "They speculating, or has someone got a loose lip that's about to lose a job?"

Macky grinned. "I've got your back. Officer Conners has been running his mouth. He tried to hit me up for info, but I didn't even have to lie."

That got a smile out of me. "Let's head to my office. I need another pair of eyes on this, and Bell's been coming up short."

"Bell's the best detective I know," Macky joked. "Maybe it's time she got herself a new partner."

"Fill out the paperwork, and someone might take pity on you," I shot back. It felt good to banter again, a far cry from the anger I'd carried with me for so long after Tony.

"If you teach me how to be as disgruntled as you used to be, maybe I'll get my own K9," he teased.

I ignored his jab, and we made our way into my office. Once inside, I tore down the entire case for him, going over everything, including the limited thoughts Dr. Thomas had shared with me.

Just as we finished, my office phone rang. I held up a finger to Macky and picked it up. "Detective Jolett speaking."

"Dispatch. We have a man on the line who wants to speak with you about his deceased mother."

I gave Macky a thumbs-up. "Put him through."

A young voice came over the line, shaky and uncertain. "Hello, Detective Jolett?"

"This is Detective Jolett," I confirmed, keeping my tone calm.

"My name is Gary," he said, his breath catching. "My mother died last night, and my father said you're the detective on the case."

"That's right," I said gently. There was a pause, and I could hear the emotion rising in his voice.

"She..." He stopped, taking in a deep breath before continuing. "She told me if she ever died under strange circumstances, I should tell the police it was my father. My stepfather."

That was the last thing I expected to hear. "When did she tell you this, Gary?" I pulled my notepad from my pocket, jotting down the details.

"About a year ago," he said, his voice shaky. "I asked her if he was hurting her, and she said no. She just said I should be aware that he might kill her if something bad ever happened."

"What did you think when she told you that?"

"I told her Dad would never hurt her. I thought she was being dramatic. She told me to remember it, and after that, we never talked about it again." He paused, breathing heavily, clearly struggling with what he was saying. "My dad said she died in her sleep. She's not old enough to die in her sleep."

Technically, that wasn't true. "I'm treating this as a homicide, but right now, I don't have enough evidence to suggest anything other than an accidental death."

"I'm giving you a reason," he said, his voice breaking again.

I hesitated for a moment, then asked, "Did your mother ever call the police on your father for any reason?"

"Not that I know of," he said, his tone calmer now. "I moved out after high school, but I don't think she ever reported him. I know this sounds crazy, but I just feel like my dad is responsible."

He started crying again, and I waited patiently before ending the conversation, promising to call him if there were any updates.

When I hung up, I turned to Macky. "Son says his mom warned him that her husband might kill her. I need to find out if Mrs. Ledmen was having an affair at that motel or if Mr. Ledmen had someone on the side. It'd give us a better motive than just a fight."

"If it's a homicide, it could've just been the fight," Macky pointed out.

We both knew that all too well. "Then why leave the toaster on the floor with water coming out of it?" I didn't wait for him to answer. "I didn't see the water at first. Mr. Ledmen said he saw the toaster on the floor. None of this adds up. And why would you put a toaster in the toilet and not fill the tub first?"

I paused, thinking out loud. "If you really wanted to electrocute someone, you'd force them into the tub, drop the toaster in, and it'd be over. To do it in the toilet? That's messy. It feels personal—like there's an underlying hatred."

"What about suicide?"

I had considered it. "I'll need to do a full interview with the son to gather more details. Her doctor's name is on her medication, so I'll subpoena her medical records, too."

Macky smirked. "Sounds like you don't need me."

"Nope, don't need you at all. I've got my trusty partner Bell, who comes up with better suggestions than you," I teased. "Besides, I need to get home and spend time with her before she files a transfer request."

Macky stood up, grinning. "If she does, I'll snap her up. You've been warned."

Chapter Eighteen

O N DAY THREE OF the investigation, I called each person who stayed at the motel the night of Mrs. Ledmen's death. The room on the other side of the Ledmens' was empty, which led me to Sveta again. She ran the motel, so she would've seen if anyone was hanging around during the day when Mr. Ledmen was at work. But when I called, she had nothing new to add—no strange men lurking or visiting Mrs. Ledmen. I combed through my photos from the crime scene and rewatched the recorded interview with Mr. Ledmen. Unfortunately, nothing jumped out as a glaring clue. The pieces were still scattered, and I wasn't any closer to finding that one detail that would tie it all together.

Bell watched the interview from her blanket, her head resting on her paws, and offered no wisdom either. Her quiet company was enough, though. Sometimes, even a good detective needed to think in silence.

I jotted down a list of questions for Gary, Mrs. Ledmen's son, and decided it was time to call him again. I needed more background, more insight. When Gary answered, his voice cracked, the kind of sound that let me know he'd been crying recently.

"I don't have anything new," I started, trying to keep my tone gentle. "But I do have some questions that might help me in the investigation. Is this a good time?"

There was a brief sniffle on the other end before he spoke. "I'll tell you anything I can to help."

"Does your father—" I corrected myself quickly, "—does your stepfather know you're speaking to me?"

"No, and I'd rather you call him my stepfather," Gary said, his words weighted with distrust. It was clear he really believed his stepfather was responsible for his mother's death.

"I will, Gary," I reassured him. "Do you know if your mother ever spoke to anyone else about her fears regarding your stepfather?"

"She didn't really have friends. My stepdad traveled a lot for work, and she hated being alone. She wasn't one for group activities or going out. She worked on crafts sometimes, but that was it. I was glad she was excited about this trip."

I scribbled a note, trying to imagine her life—isolated, lonely. "Do you know if your stepfather was ever arrested for anything violent?"

"He got into a bar fight once, maybe five years ago. He was arrested for being drunk and disorderly. My mom was furious, but that's all I know of."

That bar fight would show up on the criminal history report, but I'd double-check just to be sure. I hesitated before asking the next question, knowing it could shut Gary down. "Did your mother suffer from depression?"

Gary didn't hesitate. "Yeah, she did. Maybe her whole life, really. It was more like she was just sad all the time. My dad and I both hated seeing her like that."

He'd slipped. He said "dad," not "stepdad." That told me a lot—Gary still had some love for the man, even if he suspected him now. You don't just stop caring for someone overnight.

"Do you know if she ever tried to commit suicide?" I asked carefully.

Gary was quiet for a moment. "Once. She used pills. That's the only time I know of, and she was hospitalized."

"How long ago?"

"About three years," Gary answered. "But she promised me she'd never do it again. And I believed her. She mostly got sad when my dad was away."

It was the kind of history that couldn't be ignored, but I pressed on. "Did your parents argue a lot?"

"Almost never."

"Did they have a happy marriage, in your opinion?"

"My mom loved him, and I thought he loved her." His voice broke, and I could hear him trying to hold back tears.

"Is there any reason you can think of—any reason at all—that your stepfather might have harmed your mother?"

There was a pause before Gary spoke again, his voice quiet. "Life insurance. That's all I could think about last night."

That was it—motive. My pulse quickened. "Do you know how much life insurance?"

"They'd had the same policy for years, but a few months ago, my mom had to get a physical for a new one. She told me my dad wanted to make sure she'd be taken care of if anything happened to him. She wanted a joint policy so he'd be taken care of too. It was for a million dollars."

Bingo.

I steered Gary away from the topic of life insurance, hoping it wouldn't fester in his mind too much after we ended the call. He promised to reach out if he thought of anything else, and I hung up, my thoughts spinning.

"Bell," I said, looking over at her, "I'm pretty sure we have a homicide." Bell blinked a few times before resting her head back on her paws. She knew when I had paperwork to do, and she was giving me the space to catch up. Always considerate, that dog.

I needed to move quickly. If Mr. Ledmen caught wind of what was coming, he could leave town before I had enough to arrest him. I ran a background check on both Mary and her husband, and while I was at it, I ran Gary's too. Mr. Ledmen's bar fight popped up, and aside from a traffic ticket, Gary and Mary were clean.

I wrote up my initial report, documenting the interview with Mr. Ledmen. The second report covered the autopsy, and the third was my conversation with Gary. All of it was now ready to be reviewed. Once I was satisfied, I called Samantha at the county attorney's office.

"I want to go back to the motel room," I told her. "I think I might have enough for an arrest warrant, but I'm still not sure exactly how the murder was committed. I want to run everything past you first."

"Do you have your report written up?" she asked. Nothing happened without paperwork, after all. No warrants, no arrests, no searches.

"In hand and ready to go. I can drop it off at your office and drive you to the motel."

"I like how you think," she said, her voice brightening. "Give me fifteen minutes, and I'll be ready."

Exactly fifteen minutes later, I pulled up outside her office. Samantha was waiting, having shed her suit jacket. Despite her graying hair, which was perfectly styled, she was in her forties, a force to be reckoned with in court.

"You still working with that psycho dog?" she teased as she climbed into the passenger seat.

"Bell has her moments, but she's not psycho," I replied, smiling as I pulled away from the curb.

"I once saw her take down grown men in training at the park," Samantha said with a laugh. "She only responds to you. No one else. She's your dog, through and through."

I could easily imagine Samantha as the kind of person who would have a house full of cats once she retired, and I told her so which only made her grin widen.

"No offense taken," I said, laughing. "Bell knows her job." I didn't add that Bell was a complete softy around Sugarplum, the mop-like dog next door. Samantha's image of Bell as a tough, take-no-prisoners K9 was better left unchallenged.

We arrived at the motel, and I grabbed the key from Sveta, who had been holding the room for us. She mentioned she still needed to get the electrical problem fixed, but otherwise, the room was ready. Once inside, the first thing I noticed was the smell—a sharp, antiseptic scent clung to the air. The bed had been remade, the room given a surface-level clean.

"She was in the bed," I told Samantha, pointing to the right side of the mattress where Mrs. Ledmen had been found.

"You said the bedding was wet?"

I nodded, staring at the bed. "It was. Her clothes were damp, too. I got some on the knee of my pants. I figured it was urine, but I never smelled any."

Samantha wrinkled her nose. "Your knee?"

"To roll the body, I had to get on the bed. That's how I ended up in the wet spot. But I never smelled urine or anything else."

"Is it possible she died in the bathroom and was carried to the bed?" she asked, glancing toward the bathroom.

"It's possible. But the tub was dry, and the only source of water in the bathroom was the toilet. Unless he cleaned everything up after tossing a toaster in the tub, it doesn't make sense."

"It could've gone down that way," Samantha suggested. "But why leave the toaster on the floor, leaking water?"

"Homicides never add up perfectly," I muttered, frustrated. "There are always loose ends."

We both knew that was true. Real life wasn't like the movies—cases were messy, complicated. It was rare for everything to tie up neatly. When it looked too perfect, that usually meant something was off.

"This case has too many loose ends. Nothing makes sense," I said, shaking my head.

"Walk me through it again," Samantha requested.

For the next hour, we moved through the room, backtracking over every detail. We explored both angles—suicide and homicide—but nothing jumped out as the missing piece. No "Aha!" moment. By the end of it, I was just as frustrated as before.

Standing by the door, I took one last look at the room. "What are you thinking?" Samantha asked, watching me closely.

Without answering, I walked back to the side of the bed where Mrs. Ledmen's body had been. I bent down, pulling back the covers and the mattress pad. Beneath it, the smell of disinfectant hit me like a punch to the nose, but there it was—a dark outline, a water stain marking where her body had been.

"They didn't change the mattress," I said, disgust curling in my stomach. "When someone dies in a motel room and wets the bed, they don't bother replacing the mattress."

Samantha grimaced, her face pale. "I'm never staying in a hotel again."

My voice was high-pitched with disbelief. "Maybe hotels are better than motels."

"You know you'll be checking every mattress before lying down in any bed that's not your own," she said with a dark chuckle.

I nodded, feeling sick. We stepped outside and gulped the fresh air. "I think I like your first idea better," I said. "No more hotels or motels. Ever."

When I returned the key to Sveta, I didn't say a word. I doubted any city health department had rules about replacing mattresses after a death. I could only shake my head as I walked out of the office.

Ick.

Chapter Nineteen

T UESDAY MORNING, MY PHONE rang early. It was Mr. Ledmen, and I'd been expecting this call for a while. I hadn't reached out to him with updates, purposely withholding information. If it were my spouse, I'd be hounding the police daily for answers. But Mr. Ledmen? He'd been surprisingly quiet.

"Detective Jolett, I haven't heard from you," he said, a hint of frustration creeping into his voice.

"Hi, Mr. Ledmen," I replied, keeping my tone neutral. "Unfortunately, I don't have any new information to report."

He didn't press me for details, which was a little odd. "When will I be able to get my wife's body? I'm having her taken back to Texas."

"I believe the body was released. I'm sorry the mortuary hasn't contacted you yet." In truth, I wasn't sure if they'd reached out or not, but it seemed odd that he hadn't followed up himself sooner.

"Do you know what killed her yet?"

"I'm still waiting on the toxicology report. That could take another week." I didn't mention that Samantha, the county attorney, had refused my request for an arrest warrant. I understood her reasoning, but it didn't make it any easier to accept.

There was a pause before his next question. "Can I leave town?"

It was another one of those Hollywood myths that a police officer or detective could keep someone from leaving the city. Only a judge could make that order, not me.

"You're free to go, Mr. Ledmen. I'm sure your family needs you right now."

"I want to see my son. He's been having a hard time with this." His voice held a note of something that felt less like concern and more like dread. I wondered if his recent conversations with Gary were as strained as I imagined. Maybe Gary hadn't outright accused his stepfather of murder, but it was probably hard for him to hide his suspicions.

"I should be done with the investigation as soon as the toxicology report comes in," I assured him. What I didn't say was that I was also waiting on Mrs. Ledmen's medical records, which I had subpoenaed. Once I had all the pieces, I'd be knocking on Samantha's door again. The call ended shortly after that.

Bell was at my side almost immediately, sensing my frustration. Scratching her head, I ran through the case details again, out loud, hoping something new would pop up. "You have all the answers in that big head of yours, but you never like to share," I muttered, half-joking. Bell gave me a gentle lick on the hand before pressing her body against me. I leaned down and kissed the top of her head, grateful for her presence.

****

Six days later, I finally had the toxicology report and Mrs. Ledmen's medical records. The medical records revealed a previous suicide attempt and prescriptions for anti-depressants and anti-anxiety meds. The toxicology report showed alcohol in her system, along with the prescription drugs I had found on the motel dresser.

I called Dr. Thomas, the medical examiner, to discuss the findings.

"This is Detective Jolett. I wanted to talk to you about the toxicology report you sent over," I said.

"Good afternoon, Detective," Dr. Thomas replied, his voice heavy. "I was planning to call you before I left the office today. Do you have any new information?"

There was something in his tone that made my stomach drop. I recounted the call with Gary, telling him how the son believed his stepfather might have been involved in his mother's death. But even after hearing that, Dr. Thomas didn't sound any more optimistic.

"Nothing I have will definitively say Mrs. Ledmen was electrocuted," he said, his voice flat. "Her case will be listed as an accidental overdose."

I pressed him further. "Were there enough drugs in her system to support that conclusion?"

"Unfortunately, yes. The combination of prescription meds and alcohol could easily have caused her death. I wish I had more definitive answers for you."

I wasn't ready to let this go. "Nothing from the tissue samples? No signs of electrical trauma?"

"Nothing out of the ordinary. I spoke with the lab myself."

There was a heavy silence between us before I spoke again. "I think he killed her."

Dr. Thomas was quiet for a moment. "I think he did too."

This wasn't the outcome I wanted. I needed more. I needed something concrete to make my case. I wrote up my cause for arrest and decided it was time to confront Samantha again. Maybe now I'd have enough to push her toward a warrant.

I didn't bother calling ahead, hoping to catch her in the office. Thankfully, I did. I handed her the case file, and she flipped through it in silence, scanning the details carefully. When she finally looked up, her expression was thoughtful.

"You know this could be a suicide," she said.

"If that's the case, Mr. Ledmen covered it up," I countered. "He can explain everything once he's in custody."

"Or he lawyers up," she replied, her tone tight. "I'll get you the arrest warrant, but I want him interviewed before we take him in. You'll be flying to Texas tomorrow, if my secretary can book the flight. Call local law enforcement and let them know you're coming. You won't have the warrant in hand, so they'll make the arrest after you get home, assuming the interview goes the way we expect."

I leaned back in my chair, considering her plan. "He's not going to admit he did it."

Her lips curled into a small grin. "Of course not, but chances are good that if his story is bogus, he'll change it. A change in story would make this look better. Your case is circumstantial, and if he slips up, we can add that to the pile."

Now it was my turn to smile. "He'll change his story. They always do."

An hour later, I was booked on a flight to Texas, set to leave at three the next afternoon. I'd stay in a hotel and interview Mr. Ledmen the following day. After speaking with a local detective, he assured me Mr. Ledmen was home. They had sent a police cruiser by to check, and now it was just a matter of time.

I was ready for answers.

Chapter Twenty

B ELL WASN'T TRAVELING WITH me on this trip, and I needed to make sure she was in good hands while I was gone. I called Jack, her original trainer, the one person I trusted to take care of her overnight. Jack lived in the city, about four hours away, and had watched Bell before when I had to leave town. He knew her as well as I did, if not better. There was something reassuring about leaving Bell with him; it was like she was back with family.

Jack and I were more than just K9 handler and trainer—we were friends. Sometimes I wondered if there could be more between us, but life had its way of getting in the way. He was deeply committed to his role as the head of the state K9 program for law enforcement, and I couldn't see myself walking away from my job anytime soon either. We lived in two different worlds, even if they overlapped now and then.

"Sure, Bell can hang out here for as long as you need," Jack said when I called. His voice was easygoing, a reminder of the connection we shared. "How's she doing?"

I sighed, leaning against the kitchen counter as I watched Bell stretch out on her blanket. "Working homicide doesn't give her enough to do," I admitted. "I feel like she's wasted."

Jack's laughter came through the phone, warm and understanding. "You're too hard on yourself," he said. "Dogs are pack animals—they just want to be with you. It's not about what she does, it's about being by your side."

"She's a very expensive pack animal with very expensive training," I replied, still stubborn about it. Bell was one of the best-trained K9s I'd ever seen, and I couldn't shake the feeling that she needed more action, more work.

"She'll be there when you need her," Jack countered, his tone firm but kind. "You know that better than anyone."

I smiled despite myself. He was right. Bell had never let me down, and when the time came, she would rise to the occasion. "I'll see you tomorrow around one," I said, checking my watch. "That should give me enough time to get her settled and still make my flight."

"Sounds good," Jack replied, and I could hear the smile in his voice. In another life, maybe things could have been different. But for now, this was our reality.

****

By ten o'clock that night, I was already in bed, knowing the next few days would be long and grueling. Traveling never agreed with me, and I needed as much rest as I could get. But an hour after drifting off, my phone rang, pulling me out of a deep sleep.

"Hello," I answered groggily, not bothering to check the caller ID.

"Dispatch here," a calm voice came through the line. "We've got a barricade situation involving children. The chief requested you and David 16 on-scene."

My entire body tensed, the grogginess evaporating in an instant. "What's the location?" I asked, already reaching for my clothes.

She gave me the address, and something about it tugged at the back of my mind. I knew that place. "Do you have a name on the suspect?"

"Daryl Lewis."

The name hit me like a punch to the gut. Daryl Lewis. I knew him, and I knew his ex-wife, Melody. I'd handled a domestic violence call at their house three years before. It had been a messy, violent situation. Melody had finally left him after that incident, filing for a restraining order to keep him away from the kids. Daryl hadn't taken it well. We'd been called out several times for restraining order violations. Now, it sounded like things had taken a turn for the worse.

"How bad is it?" I asked, already moving through the house, pulling on my gear.

"We believe he shot his wife," dispatch said, her voice lowering. "She managed to call 9-1-1, but we haven't heard anything since officers arrived. Lewis came to the door with a gun."

"I'll be there in ten minutes," I replied, my heart racing as I hung up.

Bell whined softly from the bottom of the bed, sensing the tension in the air. Suii had been with me on that first call to the Lewis house. Now, as I geared up, all I could think about was how Bell would face a situation like that. K9s were trained to protect their handlers at all costs, even if it meant sacrificing themselves. The thought of Bell putting her life on the line like Suii had... it was almost too much to bear.

Twelve minutes later, I arrived on the scene, my hands shaking as I pulled the SUV to a stop. The area was flooded with police lights, and a familiar knot of dread twisted in my stomach. As soon as I stepped out, Sergeant Spence approached, his expression grim.

"Suit up and have Bell on standby," he said without preamble. "Lewis has his wife and kids at gunpoint. The wife's been shot, but as far as we know, she's still conscious." He glanced toward the house, then back at me. "County's hostage negotiator isn't available. You've got the cert, right?"

"I do," I confirmed, though it had been a while since I'd used my negotiation skills. "But I'm not sure how much good it'll do here."

"We don't have another option," Spence said. "We need you to talk him out. If you can get him away from the wife and kids, we've got a team ready to breach from the back. Bell may need to take him down on the porch."

The knot in my stomach tightened. Melody and her kids were in immediate danger, but all I could think about was Bell. If she went in and Daryl raised his gun, the officers wouldn't hesitate. They'd shoot. And Bell... Bell might not survive.

Sgt. Spence must have sensed my hesitation. "This is her job, Jolett. We need her."

I took a deep breath, pushing down the fear. "Get me a microphone," I said, my voice steady despite the turmoil inside. "Where do you want me and Bell?"

"Car on the far right," Spence said, pointing to one of the police cruisers. "When you're ready, I'll alert the team."

I opened the back hatch of my SUV and leaned down to Bell, placing my hands on her muzzle. "Stay," I told her when she tried to jump down. Bringing my face close to hers, I whispered, "I love you, Bell. Stay safe and come home with me tonight, okay?"

Her large brown eyes met mine, and she licked my face, her tongue catching a few stray tears. I gave her a firm pat on the head and let her jump down.

After suiting up in my additional tactical gear, I clipped Bell's leash to her collar and made my way to the police cruiser on the far right. Leo was there, crouched behind the car, rifle at the ready.

"I'll have your back," he said, giving me a thumbs-up as I grabbed the microphone.

I lifted the mic, trying to keep my voice calm and steady. "This is Detective Laci Jolett. I need to speak with you, Mr. Lewis."

There was no response, so I tried again. "Can you hear me, Mr. Lewis? No one needs to get hurt. I know you love your children. Come onto the porch and talk to me."

For about a minute, nothing happened. Then, suddenly, a chair crashed through the front window, sending glass flying across the lawn. Bell growled low in her throat, and I placed a hand on her head to calm her.

"Jolett!" Daryl's voice rang out from inside the house.

"I'm here," I called back. "Come out onto the porch, and we'll talk."

"I'm not coming out to be eaten by your crazy dog!" he shouted.

He was probably thinking of Suii. During that first call, Suii had taken him down. "Did you read the newspaper?" I asked, trying to keep my tone even. "My dog was shot and killed."

His laughter was cold, sending a chill down my spine. "Yeah, I heard about that. Poor doggy. Did you cry?"

I gritted my teeth, refusing to let him get under my skin. "Are your kids okay, Mr. Lewis?" I asked, steering the conversation back to what mattered. "I know you don't want to hurt them."

A long pause followed before Daryl's voice rang out again. "You want the kids? Come get 'em!"

"That's not how this works," I said calmly. "Bring the children onto the porch, and we'll talk."

Sergeant Spence slipped into the car beside me. "He doesn't seem too fond of you," he muttered. "But you've got him talking."

I nodded, my eyes focused on the house. "If we can get him to step outside, Bell can take him down. It's risky, but it's our best shot."

Spence glanced at Bell, then back at me. "If you're sure, get into position. We'll be ready."

Taking a deep breath, I unclipped Bell's leash and gave her a reassuring pat. "Stay low," I whispered to her, then turned toward the side of the house. Bell's body tensed beside me, muscles coiled, ready for action. Together, we moved quickly and quietly to the side of the house, keeping low behind the cars. I could feel the weight of the situation pressing down on me, every nerve on edge, my senses heightened. It was as if the world had narrowed to this one moment—Bell, me, and the unpredictable man with a gun inside the house.

As we neared our destination, Denise was stationed near the garage, her eyes wide, betraying the nerves of someone still green in these high-stakes scenarios. There was little time to comfort her or offer words of reassurance, but I would take a few seconds. Her breath was shallow and rapid, her gun gripped tightly in both hands.

"You okay?" I asked, my voice a little quieter than it should have been, trying to bring her back to focus.

Denise gave me a quick nod, though her expression remained strained. "Yeah. I'm good."

I didn't have to say it, but I reminded her anyway. "Remember to watch your tunnel vision."

Tunnel vision was the silent killer in high-stress situations. I'd seen seasoned officers fall prey to it—everything narrowing down to that one focal point, that one target, while the rest of the scene became a blur. I could see the adrenaline coursing through her, her eyes wide and her hands trembling ever so slightly. But she nodded again, her breaths steadying as she adjusted her grip.

I tapped my mic, "In position."

From the vehicle behind us, Sergeant Spence's voice crackled over the radio, calm but commanding. "Mr. Lewis, this is Lou Spence with the police department. We have medical assistance ready for your wife and children. We don't want anyone else to get hurt. Step outside so we can talk."

I felt Bell tense beside me, her body rigid as she waited for the command she knew might come. Every moment of her training, every instinct inside her, was tuned to this one task—subdue the threat, protect her handler. I could feel my heart hammering in my chest as I waited for Daryl's response.

The silence stretched for a few seconds, then his voice cut through the night air like a knife. "My wife isn't leaving here alive. If I go down, she goes down!"

My stomach twisted into knots. I tapped the mic again, signaling to Spence. "Focus on the kids."

"Mr. Lewis," Spence said, his voice unyielding but still calm, "You don't want to hurt your children. Send them outside, and we can talk this through."

For a moment, nothing happened. I held my breath, watching the front door with every fiber of my being straining toward what might come next. Then, slowly, the door creaked open. Daryl stepped out, his arm wrapped tightly around his daughter, using her as a human shield. Her small frame was nearly swallowed by his larger body, and she was sobbing uncontrollably, her face streaked with tears.

My heart broke a little at the sight. She was just a kid—no more than twelve now, maybe a bit older. And Daryl? He didn't seem to care one bit about the terror he was putting her through.

"Have her step off the porch," Spence's voice came again, softer this time, coaxing. "Or I can have an unarmed officer come up and get her. Whatever works best for you, Mr. Lewis."

"Stay back!" Daryl snarled, raising the gun that had been hanging loosely at his side. His daughter's scream cut through the night, sharp and filled with terror.

I unhooked Bell's leash, feeling the tension in my muscles as I whispered to her, "Hold. Wait for my command."

Her dark eyes stayed locked on the porch, watching every move Daryl made with laser focus.

"We don't want any more violence, Mr. Lewis," Spence continued, his voice unwavering. "Let the kids go. We'll work this out."

Daryl hesitated, then shoved his daughter toward the edge of the porch. She stumbled, crying as she fell onto the grass below. He kicked her hard, sending her sprawling a few feet away. That was the final straw.

"Take the lead. Attack," I whispered urgently to Bell.

She shot forward like a missile, her powerful body moving almost silently across the lawn. Daryl didn't see her until she was only a few feet away. His eyes widened, his gun lifting as if in slow motion. But Bell was faster—much faster.

She launched herself into the air, her jaws clamping down on Daryl's wrist with a sickening crunch. The gun flew out of his hand, skidding across the porch as Bell's momentum took them both down. He screamed in pain as her teeth sank deeper, shaking her head viciously as she tore into him. The sound was guttural, terrifying, the sheer force of her attack leaving no doubt she was in full protection mode.

I was already moving, running toward the porch as fast as my legs would carry me. The scene blurred around me—officers moving in, the little girl crying out as Denise scooped her up and pulled her to safety. But my eyes stayed on Bell and Daryl, every nerve in my body screaming for her safety.

I reached the porch just as Bell had Daryl pinned, her jaws locked on his shoulder now, dangerously close to his neck. His screams had turned into groans of pain, his body limp beneath her as she held him down.

"Bell, release!" I shouted, my voice sharp with authority.

She didn't let go, her grip tightening as she shook him one more time. Blood was dripping from his shoulder where her teeth had torn into him.

"Bell, release!" I commanded again, my voice louder, more forceful.

Finally, she obeyed, pulling back and releasing Daryl from her deadly grip. I grabbed her by the collar, pulling her away and praising her softly. "Good girl, Bell. You did good."

Officers swarmed the porch, cuffing Daryl and dragging him to his feet. His face was pale, and he was barely conscious, but he was alive. Bell had done her job, and she had done it perfectly.

In the chaos, Melody was carried out on a stretcher, her son walking beside her, his small hand gripping hers. She had been shot in the hand, but it wasn't life-threatening. She would survive. Thanks to Bell, they all would.

Once the situation was under control, Sergeant Spence walked over to me, a rare smile on his face. "Good job, Detective Jolett. That was a perfect takedown."

I looked at Bell, still panting at my side, her eyes bright and alert. "She did a good job. She saved those kids."

Spence nodded, his gaze shifting between me and Bell. "Yes, she did. But you let her do it. That takes guts. I'm proud of you."

I met his gaze, the flashing police lights still casting eerie shadows across the scene. "I didn't think I could do it," I admitted, my voice quiet.

Spence's smile widened. "I knew you would."

And for the first time in a long while, I believed him.

Chapter Twenty-One

OUR EVENTFUL NIGHT DIDN'T keep me from flying to Texas the next day, though it felt like I was moving through a fog. The drive to the K9 training center seemed longer than usual, but that was likely because I was operating on only two hours of sleep. Bell, always the lively one, had nudged me awake at the crack of dawn, desperate for playtime. She wasn't one to let me wallow, and maybe I needed that distraction, though my heart still felt heavy. The events of the previous night weighed on me, the close call with Bell leaving me shaken in a way I hadn't expected. I came so close to losing her, and my chest tightened just thinking about it.

When I finally pulled into the familiar parking lot of the K9 center, Bell was already pacing in the back, her tail wagging furiously. This place was like a second home for her, though it hadn't always been a place she liked. I grabbed her travel kit and opened the hatch, letting her out. She bounded toward me, excitement radiating off her as she darted forward, sniffing the air. She recognized this place immediately, and her happiness brought a small smile to my face.

Bell might have had a rocky start here, but she had grown, evolved into the dog she was today—my partner. The first time I brought her back after our initial training period, she refused to get out of the car. I had to promise her I'd come back for her. The next time wasn't much better, but at least she didn't dig her claws into the seat. Now, though, she seemed comfortable, eager even.

I scanned the training field for Jack, her original trainer, but he wasn't in sight. Instead, I headed to the inside kennels, knowing I'd find him there if he wasn't outside. Sure enough, Jack was cleaning out one of the kennels, which didn't surprise me in the least.

"I thought you had rookies for that job," I called out, smirking as I approached.

He looked up and grinned. "Hi, Bell. Nice of you to bring your human for a visit."

Jack was like Brett in many ways, preferring the company of animals over people. It had always made me wonder if he felt the same way about me as he did about the dogs, but I pushed that thought aside. No point in letting it linger.

"Save your insults for after I'm gone," I said, offering him a genuine smile despite my exhaustion. "I've got a long drive ahead."

Jack turned off the water hose and walked over, holding his hand out for Bell to sniff first. She licked him, her tail wagging happily, and with the same hand now covered in dog slobber, he shook mine. I didn't flinch or mention the slime. In the grand scheme of things, a little dog drool didn't matter. It was almost comforting, a small dose of normalcy after everything that had happened.

"You'll be taking care of a hero," I told him, my tone light but sincere. "Bell saved two kids and their mom last night. So please treat her like royalty. I really hate leaving her right now."

Jack's hand paused on Bell's head, his expression shifting to something more serious. He glanced up at me, his eyes locking onto mine. "Are you okay?"

He knew. Of course, he did. Jack had trained hundreds of dogs and worked with just as many handlers. He could probably sense my anxiety a mile away.

"I sent her in," I said, the words catching in my throat. I lifted my hand to brush my hair aside and noticed it trembling slightly. Jack noticed too.

"You both did your job," he said firmly, his pragmatism cutting through my emotions like a knife. "And that's what matters."

I nodded, though the weight on my chest didn't ease. He stepped back, giving me space, and I knelt down beside Bell, stroking her fur. "Tell him you deserve extra cookies before bed tonight," I whispered to her.

"I promise," Jack said with a small smile, overhearing me.

I stood, shaking his hand again, more firmly this time. "Thanks, Jack. I don't worry about her when she's with you."

"I've got her back," he reassured me. "You just make sure to stay safe out there."

The next leg of my journey was a long, uneventful hour's drive to the airport. I managed to board the plane without much trouble and settled in with my case file. I'd reviewed it so many times already, but I couldn't afford to let anything slip. Every detail mattered. Still, as I tried to focus on the pages in front of me, the words blurred together. My mind kept drifting back to Bell. I missed her already. It was like a part of me was lost without her by my side. With a sigh, I forced myself to concentrate, scribbling notes in the margins as I outlined the questions I had for Mr. Ledmen.

There was a slim chance I might be there for his arrest, and I hoped I would be. There was nothing like the satisfaction of closing a case with the suspect in custody. But even if I didn't get that moment, I'd at least have the peace of mind knowing that Mr. Ledmen wouldn't be hurting anyone else. That thought brought me a small sense of relief.

By the time the plane touched down at Dallas Fort Worth Airport, I was exhausted, but the adrenaline kept me going. I hailed a cab and made my way to the hotel booked by the county attorney's office. The room was standard—clean, but sterile, like most hotel rooms. Still, I couldn't shake the image of the Ledmens' motel room from my mind. Before I even put my bag down, I pulled back the bedding to inspect the mattress. No marks, no stains. It seemed safe enough, but that didn't stop the uneasy feeling crawling up my spine.

In one of my evidence collection classes, an instructor had told us she never slept between the sheets at hotels. Instead, she carried a sleeping bag with her on every trip, refusing to get under hotel bedding. It seemed extreme at the time, but now, I understood. A sleeping bag sounded pretty good right about now. I shuddered and pushed the thought away, reminding myself I was here to do a job.

Room service came shortly after, and I ate my hamburger in silence, reviewing my notes once more. The shower was hot and soothing, and by the time I crawled into bed, the sheets didn't feel quite so awful. Still, sleep didn't come easy. My mind was too busy with thoughts of body gunk and guns, and the image of Bell leaping to take down Daryl replayed over and over in my head.

Morning came too quickly. I grabbed a quick breakfast and called Detective Maltos, the local officer I'd spoken with the day before. He confirmed that Mr. Ledmen was still at his house, with two patrol officers keeping an eye on him. Perfect. I needed him to drive himself to the station. That way, he'd come in voluntarily, and I wouldn't need to Mirandize him. If he chose to talk, it would all be usable.

When I arrived at the station, I gave my name to the clerk at the front desk, and within minutes, Detective Maltos appeared. He was younger than I'd expected—probably in his thirties, which, in most departments, was still relatively young for a detective. He was tall, about six inches taller than me, with dark hair cut in that sharp, military style I'd seen so often in law enforcement. His white dress shirt was crisp, and his demeanor was professional but approachable. He had a vibe that put people at ease, and I immediately felt comfortable working with him.

After pleasantries, he led me to his office where I shared more details about the case. As I laid everything out for him, his eyebrows raised in disbelief.

"This is one for the record books," Maltos said, leaning back in his chair.

I nodded, feeling the weight of exhaustion settling in. "It is. I'm ready for this one to be over."

Truth be told, I just wanted to close the case, take some time off, and go home to Bell. A few days of rest with her at my feet sounded like heaven.

Detective Maltos escorted me to the interview room and left me alone to wait for Mr. Ledmen. Twenty minutes later, he was shown inside. His eyes met mine, and I could tell from the way his lips thinned into a line that he wasn't happy to see me.

"Hi, Mr. Ledmen," I said, extending my hand. "I've finished the investigation into your wife's death, and I'd like to review my findings with you."

He eyed me suspiciously, his gaze flicking around the room. "You came all the way to Texas just to tell me your findings?" he asked, his tone thick with skepticism.

I was ready for this. "We're a small department," I said smoothly, laying it on thick. "We always have money left in the budget at the end of the year. I like to give my cases a personal touch."

He looked unconvinced, but I didn't give him time to think about it. "Did your son mention I spoke with him a few days ago?"

His eyes narrowed slightly, but he nodded. "He said you called."

"I did. I wanted to know a few things about your wife from his point of view. It was enlightening. Why don't we sit down and go over what I've found?"

Once Detective Maltos excused himself, I wasted no time pulling out my file. I started with the photos of Mrs. Ledmen's hand and foot, pushing the pictures toward Mr. Ledmen one by one. His hands shook as he picked them up, and I watched closely, waiting for his reaction.

"She burned her hand on a hot plate," he said, his voice unsteady.

Original.

"And her foot?" I asked, placing the next picture in front of him.

"She bought some new sandals. The strap rubbed against her skin and caused that...rug burn."

The lies rolled off his tongue so easily, rehearsed even. He'd had time to plan his story. I kept pressing, asking if she had sought treatment for the burn. He fumbled through an explanation about visiting the local pharmacy, describing the pharmacist in vague terms.

I nodded along, though every instinct in me was screaming that he was lying.

"Excuse me, Mr. Ledmen," I said suddenly, standing up. "I need to use the ladies' room. I'll be right back."

Outside the interview room, Detective Maltos was waiting. "You buying any of that?" he asked.

"Not a word," I replied. "I need to call the pharmacy and check out his story."

Miles Atkinson, the pharmacist, remembered them immediately. A pleasant couple, he said. The burn had been nasty, but nothing had seemed out of the ordinary.

When I hung up the phone, I turned to Detective Maltos, the weight of disappointment heavy in my chest. "Remember that case for the record books?" I asked dryly. "It just fell to pieces."

Chapter Twenty-Two

I TOOK MY BEATING when I returned to the department, and by that, I mean the ribbing that followed the conclusion of the Ledmen case. At least Detective Maltos had been kind enough not to tease me too much, for which I was grateful. Still, the weight of the case lingered on my shoulders, the way unresolved cases tend to do. The feeling of missing something gnawed at me, and no amount of paperwork could shake it off.

Lou Macky, my fellow detective, entered my office an hour after I got to work, carrying two large coffees. He had a grin on his face that was both irritating and familiar.

"I figured you could use this," he said, placing one of the cups on my desk.

I sighed, already anticipating the teasing to come. "Go on, get it over with. My day can't get any worse."

Lou leaned against my desk, his grin widening. "Death by toaster. Only you could mess up a case that bad."

"Har, har," I muttered, rolling my eyes as I took a sip of the coffee.

"No, seriously," he continued, clearly enjoying himself. "The toaster wasn't even plugged in, and somehow you managed a full confession."

I crumpled a piece of paper from my desk and threw it at him. "Kill," I told Bell, pointing at Lou.

Bell, lying at my feet, didn't so much as budge. She didn't even open her eyes. Lou laughed all the way out of my office, leaving me to my paperwork and the lingering frustration of the case.

Just as I settled back into my chair, my phone rang. "Detective Jolett," I answered, hoping it wasn't another case waiting to land in my lap.

"I have Gary Ledmen on the phone for you," the receptionist said. "He says it's concerning his mother's case."

I rubbed my temples, feeling the headache forming. "Put him through."

The line clicked, and Gary's voice came through, soft and strained. "This is Gary Ledmen."

"Hi, Gary," I replied, keeping my tone neutral. "What can I do for you?"

There was a brief pause on the other end. "You don't think my father killed my mother, do you?"

I let out a slow breath, already knowing where this conversation was headed. "I'm sorry, Gary, but I don't have evidence that a crime was committed."

"He killed her. I know he did. He wanted the money, and he already has a new girlfriend."

That gave me pause. "A new girlfriend?"

"Yeah," Gary's voice cracked. "He's moving on like nothing happened. It hasn't even been that long."

I felt a pang of sympathy for him, but without concrete evidence, there was nothing I could do. "Gary, if you have any new information—anything at all—I will reopen the case and review it. But right now, I don't have enough proof to charge him with anything."

"He's going to get away with killing my mother." His voice was barely above a whisper, and then, before I could respond, the line went dead.

I sat there, staring at the phone for a moment, the weight of Gary's words pressing down on me. I knew how he felt. I had the same gut feeling, but gut feelings don't hold up in court.

An hour before I was ready to head home, the last person I wanted to see walked into my office—Officer Stanley Conners. His smug expression grated on my nerves, and even Bell, who was usually indifferent to people, lifted her head, bared her teeth, and growled softly at him. I had to admit, I was a little proud of her in that moment.

"How may I help you, Officer Conners?" I asked, barely keeping the irritation out of my voice.

"I heard how you screwed up your murder case," he said, his tone dripping with satisfaction.

I silently counted to ten. "Enlighten me. How exactly did I screw up my murder case?"

He faltered for a second, clearly not expecting me to call him out. "Well, I've heard the rumors."

Ah, he was fishing. Typical Stanley. I leaned back in my chair, giving him a measured look. "The case is concluded, and it's public record now. If you'd like to review my procedures, feel free. You can write up your findings and turn them in to Sergeant Spence. I'm sure he'll be thrilled to read your critique."

Stanley's smirk faltered. "I'll be sure to share my findings with my father too."

I resisted the urge to roll my eyes. "You do that. I'm sure it will give him something to do outside of his city council seat. Maybe suggest he attend the police academy if he thinks he can do better. We're always looking for good officers who can climb the ranks without needing their daddy to pave the way."

Stanley's face flushed red, his jaw tightening, but I wasn't done. "Just let him know that his city council position pays more. And while he's at it, he might want to push for a pay raise for us. You know, in case he decides to switch careers."

Bell let out another low growl, and Stanley's eyes darted toward her. "Bell's hungry," I said casually. "And she's looking at you like a nice piece of steak. So I suggest you leave my office. I'll inform records to pull a copy of the case for you. Review it on your own time, Officer Conners."

Stanley's mouth opened, but whatever retort he had died on his tongue. Without another word, he turned on his heel and left my office, leaving me with the satisfaction of knowing I'd rattled him.

Bell wandered back to her spot by my desk, settling down with a contented huff. I gave her a soft pat on the head. "Good girl," I murmured, grateful for her presence.

****

The following week, I finally took some time off. The weather was decent, and Bell and I spent our days hiking through our favorite trails. It was just the two of us, out in the fresh air, away from the stress of the department and the never-ending cases that weighed on my mind.

As we walked, I found myself talking to Bell, as I often did when we were alone. "Mr. Ledmen killed his wife," I said, my voice low. "I don't know how he did it, and there's nothing I can do about it. I've reviewed every detail a hundred times, and it all just... doesn't add up."

Bell trotted ahead, her ears perked, but she didn't offer any answers. She never did. Still, her silent companionship was comforting.

"I keep thinking about the life insurance policy," I continued, more to myself than to Bell. "That's the key. I sent a copy of the report to the insurance company, and they're paying out. He's getting the money, and there's nothing I can do to stop it. He's out of our jurisdiction now, and I'll probably never see him again."

Bell's ears twitched, and she pulled slightly at her lead, clearly spotting something ahead. I unsnapped her leash, letting her run free. She bounded off, her tail wagging as she disappeared into the trees. I sighed, watching her go, feeling the weight of the case settle back onto my shoulders.

"I missed something," I muttered, my voice lost in the wind. "I know I did."

Gary's voice haunted me at night. His certainty that his stepfather had murdered his mother echoed in my mind, and I couldn't shake the feeling that he was right. But without proof, my hands were tied. The only thing I could do was check in on Mr. Ledmen from time to time. Maybe if he did it once, he'd do it again. And if he did, I'd be there, waiting.

Bell came galloping back, a stick clutched between her teeth. She dropped it at my feet, her tail wagging furiously. I chuckled and tossed the stick, watching as she took off after it with boundless energy. She was happy, at least, and for the moment, that was enough for me.

We found a quiet spot to sit and eat lunch, and I pulled out a few treats for Bell. She munched them down eagerly, her big brown eyes turning sad when she realized I didn't have any more.

"Be careful," I teased, rubbing her head. "Or you'll grow fat and lazy."

She let out a short whine, then crawled closer, licking my hand with a wet, sloppy kiss. I smiled, grateful for her, even if she couldn't help me solve the case.

It's detective work—sometimes, we don't get our man. But if you have a K9, a little slobber is a close runner-up.

Chapter Twenty-Three

Part III

T HE COLD NOSE, LOW whine, and warm dog breath in my face let me know something was wrong. Groggily, I blinked into the darkness, trying to shake off the fog of sleep. Bell had a dog door leading out to my small back patio, and I always left it open during the warm season. It was mid-summer, and there was no reason for Bell to be waking me up at—I squinted over at the glowing numbers on my bedside clock—three a.m.

A groan escaped my lips as my eyelids reluctantly peeled halfway open, my brain struggling to make sense of Bell's sudden need for attention. Usually, she slept soundly at the foot of my bed, her rhythmic breathing a comforting reminder that everything was as it should be. But now, her cold nose pressed firmly against my cheek, nudging me with urgency.

As soon as Bell was sure I was awake, she gave a quick, high-pitched yap and padded over to the bedroom door. She stood there, her tail swishing in slow, deliberate motions as she turned to face me. Her behavior was strange. She wasn't barking in her typical protective mode, and yet there was something off about the way she paced near the door.

Bell had her specific skill set for protection and sniffing out explosives. Not exactly the usual partner for a homicide detective, but we made it work. If something was worrying Bell, I knew better than to ignore it. During our time together, her instincts had proven to be sharper than mine on more than one occasion.

I sighed deeply, pushing myself into a sitting position and rubbing my eyes. I was mentally exhausted from the ongoing murder trial at the courthouse, which had kept me tethered to a defense chair for what felt like an eternity. Too many hours spent under harsh fluorescent lights, listening to lawyers argue, taking notes, and occasionally passing them like some sort of delinquent school kid. It was a grind, and I was reaching my limit.

Most people didn't realize the psychological toll a murder trial could take on a detective. Even though the arrest was in the past, reliving the case in court felt like reopening old wounds. The case in question had been one of my first murder arrests after being promoted to homicide, and it was heavy. It had also taken almost two years to go to trial. Yesterday, I got the call that the jury was back. The verdict would be read at ten a.m. sharp, and I had planned to sleep until at least eight to prepare myself for whatever emotional aftermath the day would bring.

That was clearly not going to happen.

My legs slid to the edge of the bed, my feet hitting the cool floor as I tried to force my vision to clear. I glanced at Bell again, who was now standing rigid, her muscular frame silhouetted against the faint light creeping in from the hallway.

"Woof," she barked, a low, insistent sound. Her body quivered with impatience.

"I hear you, Bell," I muttered, grabbing a pair of shorts from the top of the dresser. I slipped them on with the same sluggish movements, my body still protesting the early hour. Next, I reached for my flip-flops and slid them on. Bell darted ahead, a few paces in front of me, heading straight for the front door.

Her behavior had my hackles rising. She wasn't acting aggressive, but there was definitely something off. I couldn't tell if she was alerting me to a danger outside, or if it was something else entirely. I watched her pause at the door, glancing back at me with an urgent whine.

"Hold on a second," I murmured, rubbing the sleep from my eyes as I turned back to grab my gun. I forced the holster's belt clip over the waistband of my shorts, though the weight of the weapon made them sag uncomfortably. It wasn't ideal, but better safe than sorry. I slipped my cell phone into my back pocket as an added precaution.

Once I was armed and ready, I cracked open the door cautiously. But before I had a chance to react, Bell's massive body barreled past me, slamming the door wide open with her momentum. I stumbled back, startled by the sudden force of her movement. I should have clipped her leash on, but this wasn't normal behavior for her.

"Bell!" I hissed, but she was already halfway across the yard, her powerful legs propelling her straight toward my neighbor Ed's condo.

My pulse quickened as I followed her. That's when I heard the faint, desperate scratching sound coming from inside Ed's front door, followed by a soft, pitiful whine. Sugarplum.

Ed's dog—a mop of a Shih Tzu—was on the other side of the door, and something was clearly wrong. My heart sank as I sprinted back to my condo, grabbing the spare key to Ed's place off the hook.

Fumbling with the lock, my fingers trembling, I pushed the door open, and Bell darted inside, her nose immediately meeting Sugarplum's as they sniffed each other, clearly aware of the situation.

"Ed!" I called out, my voice echoing through the quiet condo. "It's Laci and Bell."

No response.

I moved cautiously down the hallway, the layout of Ed's place a mirror image of mine. My pulse pounded in my ears as I reached his bedroom. My breath caught in my throat when I saw him lying on the floor, collapsed halfway between the door and his bed.

"Ed!" I rushed over, my hands already moving to check for a pulse.

Nothing.

Grabbing my phone, I dialed 9-1-1. "This is Detective Jolett. My neighbor is unresponsive, and I need an ambulance here now." I rattled off the address, though I knew they had it on file.

"I'm hanging up to start CPR," I added, tossing the phone to the floor as I began chest compressions. My hands pressed firmly against his chest, each push sending a jolt of desperation through me. His skin was warm, but his body was frighteningly still.

As I worked, I couldn't help but reflect on our rocky start as neighbors. Ed and I had clashed when I first moved in, mostly because I was angry at the world back then. I hadn't yet come to terms with Tony's death, and Suii hadn't yet entered my life to soften the rough edges. But over time, our dogs—now Bell and Ed's ridiculous little Sugarplum—had created a bond between us. Ed's patience and kindness eventually wore down my defenses, and while I wouldn't call us best friends, we had become something more than neighbors.

I could feel the seconds ticking by, each one an eternity as I continued CPR. Bell growled softly as the door opened, and I glanced up to see the EMTs charging in.

"Bell, down!" I barked the command, and she immediately dropped to her haunches, though her eyes stayed locked on me, ready to move if I gave the signal.

"She's good," I told the EMTs, who eyed her cautiously as they moved past me. "I'll get her and Sugarplum out of here so you can work."

I swiped Sugarplum off the floor, the little dog trembling in my arms as I backed away to give the EMTs space. Bell followed close behind, her steps matching mine as we exited the condo.

Ed had a daughter in California. Once they took him to the hospital, I'd find her information and make the call. But right now, I needed to focus on getting Sugarplum settled and finding out if Ed had any chance of pulling through.

I carried Sugarplum back to my place, setting her down gently on the kitchen floor. Her head barely reached the top of Bell's water bowl, and I realized one drink from Bell would leave the little dog high and dry. I grabbed a smaller bowl from the cabinet and filled it, placing it beside Bell's.

Sugarplum lapped at the water eagerly, her tiny pink tongue flicking out rapidly as she drank. When she finally stopped, she turned those big, sorrowful eyes up at me, her fuzzy white hair and ridiculous pink bow making her look even more pitiful than usual.

I sighed. "You're a mess, you know that?"

Bell gave her a gentle nudge with her nose, licking her face for good measure. Sugarplum's tail wagged furiously, her small body practically vibrating with joy at the attention.

I checked the clock. It was still too early to call Jack, the K9 trainer who had brought Bell into my life after Suii's death. Jack was the reason I had given a police dog another chance, despite the heartache of losing my previous partner. But I'd wait until a more reasonable hour to fill him in on this situation.

"Woof," Bell barked, as if reminding me there was still work to be done.

I smiled. "Alright, let's check on Ed."

We returned to Ed's condo just as the EMTs wheeled him out on a stretcher, CPR still in progress. My stomach twisted at the sight, but I forced myself to stay calm.

Roger, one of the EMTs I knew well, stopped beside me. "Do you have family information for him?" he asked.

"I'll grab it and bring it to the hospital," I replied, my voice steady despite the turmoil churning inside me.

"They're taking him to Mountain General," he added before they loaded Ed into the ambulance.

Once they were gone, I headed back inside and found Ed's wallet sitting next to his keys on a small table by the door. I rifled through it quickly, finding the emergency contact card with his daughter's name and phone number.

I dialed, hoping she'd pick up, but it went straight to voice-mail. I left her a message, explaining the situation and giving her the details for the hospital. My heart ached as I looked down at Sugarplum, who seemed to understand that something was very wrong. I assured Ed's daughter I would take care of the dog until she could make arrangements.

Returning to my condo, I set Sugarplum down again. Bell licked her face gently, and the little dog seemed to relax a bit. It was comforting to see them getting along, even if the situation was far from ideal.

Still, there was something about the quiet, about knowing Ed's life was hanging in the balance, that weighed heavily on me. I needed coffee, so I started a pot and busied myself by putting dishes away from the dishwasher, trying to keep my hands occupied while my mind raced.

As I turned to check on the dogs, I noticed Bell's ears were pinned back, her expression one of unmistakable discontent. Her tail swished in agitation, and I followed her gaze to Sugarplum, who was trotting happily behind her, tail wagging like she'd just won the lottery.

My eyes narrowed suspiciously as I watched the tiny dog. Bell, usually so composed, was not happy. And then, I saw it.

The nice, brown pile of evidence sitting squarely in the middle of my living room floor.

I pinched the bridge of my nose, trying not to lose my temper. "Oh, Sugarplum..."

Bell let out a triumphant yap, as if to say, *I told you so*.

"Oh, don't worry. I know this one's not on you," I said, grabbing some tissues to deal with the mess.

Bell wagged her tail in satisfaction, trotting off in search of her new little friend. I bent down to clean up Sugarplum's unfortunate mistake, shaking my head as I did.

It was going to be a long day.

Chapter Twenty-Four

I HAD DECISIONS TO make. Big ones. The sentencing for the trial I'd been involved in was starting in just under an hour, and I felt the pressure of time squeezing in on me. I paced back and forth, my thoughts bouncing between court and Ed's dog, Sugarplum. Ed had always been one to sneak her into places, grocery stores, even restaurants, claiming her undeniable cuteness won people over. I could almost hear him defending her, calling her "a cutie" as if that made up for her lack of manners. He wasn't wrong—most people let it slide—but this wasn't a situation where I could afford to be lenient.

I looked down at Sugarplum, her tiny body almost lost against the floor, and sighed. Leaving her alone would likely result in a mess. I had seen firsthand what happened when she was left to her own devices. Unlike Bell—or Suii before her—who both had impeccable training, Sugarplum didn't understand boundaries, and Ed had never bothered to instill them.

Bell lay nearby, her large brown eyes watching me intently, as if she could sense my inner turmoil. Bell was no stranger to staying home alone while I went to court. I never took her inside; it wasn't allowed, and besides, her presence could sway a jury. People either loved dogs or were uncomfortable around them, and I couldn't risk the trial being tainted by either extreme. Today, however, was different. The jury had already made their decision, and the judge had finalized everything. Bell could come with me—but Sugarplum? That was another story.

The phone rang, startling me from my thoughts. Jack's name flashed across the screen, and I answered with a heavy sigh, unable to hide the frustration in my voice.

"Ed, my neighbor, had a heart attack," I said quickly. "I'm stuck with his dog." I glanced at the little ball of fluff by my feet. "Or rat-like creature, depending on how you look at it."

Jack's laughter echoed through the line, breaking the tension that had settled in my shoulders. "Good morning, Detective Jolett," he teased.

I shook my head, refusing to be sidetracked. "Listen, Jack, I've been told that a K9 requires a one-dog household. Is that true?" I kept my tone as neutral as possible, but inside, irritation bubbled up. Jack was a dog lover through and through, and I knew he'd find Sugarplum charming, despite her lack of usefulness.

"It's true," Jack confirmed. "Another dog isn't permitted unless your K9 stays in a kennel at the department. That's the rule."

"Perfect," I muttered. "Just what I needed to hear."

Jack's tone lightened, amusement creeping back in. "How does Bell feel about her new houseguest?"

I glanced at Bell, who hadn't moved from her spot on the floor. Her head rested on her paws, but I knew she was paying attention to everything. "She hasn't eaten her yet, so I guess that's a good sign," I replied dryly.

Jack chuckled, but then grew serious again. "If Bell isn't showing any signs of aggression, it's probably fine for now. But play it by ear. If things change, give me a call, and we'll figure out another plan."

"Play it by ear?" I repeated incredulously. "That's your professional advice?"

"Hey, it's not an exact science," Jack said, the grin evident in his voice. "Besides, it'll be good for you to handle another dog for a change. And who knows, maybe Sugarplum will surprise you."

I highly doubted that. "Sure. Thanks for the help, Jack."

I hung up, shaking my head as I looked down at the two dogs. Bell's steady gaze met mine, while Sugarplum blinked up at me, completely unaware of the dilemma she was causing. I made my decision. Bell would come to court with me, and Sugarplum would stay at Ed's house. It wasn't ideal, but it was the best option I had.

After grabbing my blazer and slipping it on, I prepared to head out. Bell stood up immediately, her body language confident and alert, ready to work. I gave Sugarplum one last chance to relieve herself, taking her out front and watching as she sniffed around the lawn. Of course, she chose my lawn as her preferred spot, marking it like it was her personal playground. I had given up trying to fight the small brown spots her frequent visits left behind. It was just another reminder of the odd friendship Ed and I had formed over time.

Once we were back inside Ed's house, I made sure Sugarplum had water and gave the place a quick once-over. No obvious hazards, nothing she could destroy—at least, nothing I could see. Ed had never bothered to kennel train her, which would have made things much easier. But that wasn't Sugarplum's style, apparently. Bell padded after me as I walked to the front door, Sugarplum trailing between Bell's legs in a way that seemed almost natural. I opened the door and let Bell out first. Sugarplum, ever the escape artist, tried to dart after her, but I blocked her with my boot, gently closing the door behind me.

Bell gave me a long, soulful look, as if to say, *You're really leaving her behind?* I rolled my eyes and patted her on the head. "We've got work to do, Bell. Sugarplum will be fine."

But even as I said the words, I wasn't sure I believed them.

Bell trotted alongside me to the SUV, her ears perked up and ready for action, but the moment we reached the vehicle, she stopped. Her eyes flicked back toward Ed's house, and she sat firmly on her haunches, refusing to move. I tugged lightly on her leash, but she didn't budge.

"Bell. Up," I commanded firmly, but she continued to sit there, her gaze locked on the house as if she could see through the walls to where Sugarplum was no doubt whining on the other side of the door.

I gritted my teeth, frustration mounting. I didn't have time for this. Court was in less than an hour, and here I was negotiating with my dog. "Bell, get in the car," I repeated, my tone sterner this time.

Nothing. She didn't even glance at me.

With an exasperated sigh, I pulled out my phone and called Jack again. "Bell's refusing to get in the car without Sugarplum," I said the moment he picked up. "What do I do?"

Jack laughed, the sound almost infuriating in its ease. "Sounds like Bell's more attached than you thought," he said. "She's distressed because Sugarplum is upset. Dogs pick up on that kind of thing."

I pinched the bridge of my nose, feeling the tension build behind my eyes. "Jack, I need to be in court in fifty minutes. I don't have time for Bell's emotional breakdown."

"Well, you're not going to win this one," Jack said, his tone still light. "If Bell's upset, she can't focus on her job. You're going to have to bring Sugarplum with you."

I groaned. "That's not happening."

"Looks like it's already happening," Jack quipped. "Just put her in the car, and everyone will be happy."

I hung up without another word, knowing he was right but hating it all the same. I stomped back to Ed's house, the irritation in my steps probably visible from a mile away. I opened the door, scooped up Sugarplum—who immediately began licking my face—and carried her back to the SUV.

As soon as I had Sugarplum in my arms, Bell perked up, her tail wagging slightly as if to say, *Finally, you figured it out.* She hopped into the back of the SUV without hesitation, her previous defiance completely gone now that her tiny companion was with us.

"Unbelievable," I muttered under my breath as I climbed into the driver's seat, securing Sugarplum on the passenger side. She sat up straight, her tiny nose twitching as she took in the new surroundings, while Bell settled comfortably in the back, her crisis apparently averted.

The courthouse was only a short drive away, but the entire time, I kept glancing over at Sugarplum, wondering how I had gotten myself into this mess. I'd signed up for a career working with a strong, disciplined K9 like Bell, not a miniature mop with no training whatsoever. But here I was, chauffeuring both dogs to court as if this was just another day on the job.

When I pulled into the courthouse parking lot, I hesitated for a moment. I couldn't leave the dogs in the car—especially not in this summer heat—but I also wasn't thrilled about parading into the courthouse with Sugarplum in tow. It was one thing to bring Bell; she had a presence, an authority about her. Sugarplum was just... a distraction.

With a sigh of resignation, I attached Sugarplum's leash to her tiny harness and tucked her under my arm. Bell, ever the professional, hopped out of the SUV and fell into step beside me as we made our way to the courthouse entrance.

Dan, the courthouse guard, raised an eyebrow when he saw us approaching. "What's this?" he asked, nodding toward Sugarplum.

I gave him a half-smile, feeling the weight of the situation pressing down on me. "This is Sugarplum," I said dryly. "She's in training to be a drug sniffer."

Dan chuckled, bending down to ruffle Sugarplum's ears. "Well, good luck with that," he said, his tone amused. "She's got a lot of work ahead of her."

Bell stood stoically beside me, her posture calm and alert as usual, but I could sense her contentment now that Sugarplum was nearby. There was something comforting about the way Bell interacted with her, a protective instinct that I hadn't anticipated. I glanced down at Bell, feeling a mix of pride and frustration. This was not how I'd envisioned my morning going.

Inside the courthouse, we made our way to the courtroom. The room was already packed, and I could feel the curious stares from the moment I walked in. Bell was no stranger to the building—when I faced the judge for pretrial, I took her with me, or if I needed a warrant signed, I brought her along. But Sugarplum? She was a novelty.

A few of the local reporters were seated in the back, their eyes following me as I moved to the front of the room. I could already imagine the questions they would ask later, the playful comments about my "new partner." I wasn't in the mood to answer any of them.

I took my seat at the county attorney's table, positioning myself so that Sugarplum was partially hidden from view. She squirmed in my lap for a moment before settling down, her tiny body warm against me. Bell lay at my feet, her head resting on her paws as she waited patiently for the proceedings to begin.

Samantha Anderson, the assistant county attorney, glanced over at me, her eyes landing on Sugarplum with a look of mild confusion. "Should I ask what that is?" she said, raising an eyebrow.

I shot her a wry smile. "I've decided to start carrying a purse on duty," I replied. "This one just happens to match my blazer."

Samantha chuckled softly, shaking her head. "I'm not sure if I like the new fashion trend," she said, her tone playful.

Before I could respond, the bailiff called the room to order, and the judge entered, signaling the start of the sentencing. For the next forty-five minutes, I sat quietly, keeping one hand on Sugarplum to prevent her from squirming too much. Bell remained motionless at my feet, her body relaxed but her eyes sharp, watching everything around us.

When the judge finally announced the sentence—twenty-two years—I felt a sense of closure wash over me. The case had been a long, grueling process, but it was over now. Justice had been served even if the guilty didn't agree.

As soon as court was adjourned, I gathered my things, balancing Sugarplum in one arm while I picked up Bell's leash. We made our way out of the courtroom, and I felt the weight of the morning lift slightly. A well-deserved coffee was definitely in my future.

I pulled into the drive-thru of my favorite coffee shop, ordering the most sugar-filled concoction they had on the menu. It was a small victory, but one I intended to savor. Bell, ever the well-behaved partner, sat patiently in the back, her eyes on me as if waiting for her usual post-trial treat. I usually ordered her a cake pop, but today, with Sugarplum in the mix, I hesitated. One bite of that sugary ball, and the little dog might go into a diabetic coma.

Instead, I promised Bell a special treat once Sugarplum was back with Ed—assuming, of course, Ed recovered. As I sipped my drink and drove back toward the station, my thoughts wandered to Ed's condition. He was stable for now, but there was no telling how long his recovery would take. Until then, Sugarplum was my responsibility, whether I liked it or not.

When I arrived at the police department, the first thing I noticed was the unusually large number of squad cars in the lot. Something big was going on. I parked and grabbed Sugarplum, who was now fast asleep in my lap, and made my way inside.

Janice, one of the records clerks, met me at the door, her eyes widening slightly when she saw the dog in my arms. "The chief needs to see you," she said, her tone all business. "And... cute dog, by the way."

"Thanks," I muttered, following her down the hall. "What's going on?"

"Two high school students were hospitalized this morning," Janice explained. "Drug overdoses. One of them's in critical condition."

I nodded, feeling a familiar tension settle in my gut. Drug cases were always complicated, and when teenagers were involved, it only made things messier. "Is the drug task force on it?"

Janice shook her head. "The principal doesn't want them involved. Too much bad blood between them and the school. The chief wants you to handle it."

Of course, he did. I sighed, glancing down at Sugarplum. As if I didn't have enough on my plate. "Well, meet our new drug dog in training," I said dryly, holding Sugarplum up for Janice to see.

She chuckled, stepping aside to let me into the chief's office.

Inside, the mood was somber. The principal sat across from the chief and Sergeant Spence, along with two other men I didn't recognize. The conversation quickly turned to the overdose cases, and I listened quietly, my mind already working through possible leads.

The chief handed me an envelope containing one of the pills found on one of the students. I'd need to run some tests to confirm, but based on the early reports, it was likely fentanyl mixed with codeine—a deadly combination. I glanced at Bell, who sat quietly by my side, her keen eyes watching my every move. Sugarplum, oblivious to the gravity of the situation, yawned and snuggled deeper into my arms.

Yes, I'd been promoted to homicide detective, but I knew I was low man on the totem pole and if I objected to this case, no matter how badly I wanted to, it would be me who looked like a jerk. If a child died with another round of the drug, it would quickly turn into a homicide. I was here to stop that and had to do a mental reminder every few minutes because the very last place on earth I wanted to visit was the high school.

After the meeting, I made my way back to my office, my mind still racing with the details of the case. Bell and Sugarplum followed me in, and I could feel Bell's presence beside me, a comforting constant amidst the chaos.

I set Sugarplum down on Bell's bed in the corner of the office. The tiny dog curled up immediately, her small body relaxing into the plush fabric. Bell lay down beside her, her protective instincts kicking in once more.

I sat at my desk, making a few notes about the case and preparing for what I knew would be a long day ahead. As I worked, my phone buzzed with a call from Ed's daughter.

"We just got back from vacation," she said, her voice thick with worry. "I'm booking a flight to come see Dad."

I reassured her that Ed was stable for now and that Sugarplum was in good hands. "She's been... interesting," I added, glancing over at the two dogs now curled up together in the corner.

She laughed softly, clearly relieved that Sugarplum was being taken care of. "Thank you so much. I don't know what my dad would do if something happened to her."

"Don't worry," I replied. "Sugarplum's safe with me."

As I hung up the phone, I couldn't help but wonder how long this strange arrangement would last. But for now, Bell and Sugarplum seemed content, and I had a job to do.

Chapter Twenty-Five

O UR MID-SIZED RURAL TOWN had five schools—two elementary, two middle, and one large high school with around a thousand students. Sports were the town's pulse, and almost everyone, except me, rallied behind the football team as if it were a religion. It was more than just a game to them; it was a deep-rooted tradition. No matter if the team lost more games than they won, the town's spirit never wavered. Even other sports—basketball, baseball, or soccer—only garnered fleeting interest, and only if they made it to the playoffs. Then, in true small-town fashion, everyone suddenly acted like lifelong fans. But no matter what, football ruled supreme, as constant and immovable as the mountains that bordered us.

I couldn't relate. Sports and I were like oil and water. It wasn't that I lacked coordination—far from it. I'd always been capable but had never felt the urge to join in. While other kids were out running drills or rehearsing cheers, I preferred puzzles of a different nature. Books, mysteries, problem-solving—those were my fields. Long before I ever knew I'd end up in law enforcement, I devoured every detective novel I could get my hands on. There was something about peeling back the layers of a mystery, uncovering hidden clues, and putting together the pieces that fueled me in a way that no team sport ever could. It was like my brain had been wired from the beginning to investigate and analyze, and I stopped trying to figure out why a long time ago.

As I drove towards Mountain High School, memories of my own time in school gnawed at me. I gripped the steering wheel a little tighter, my knuckles whitening as I pulled into the parking lot. The sprawling campus, with its mixture of manicured lawns and artfully placed rock gardens, felt suffocating despite its design to feel open and airy. The towering building with its dull brick façade loomed ahead, triggering an old, familiar anxiety in my chest. I hadn't been one of the popular kids in school, and stepping back onto school grounds brought back that awkwardness and discomfort I thought I had buried. The same feelings I had spent years outrunning resurfaced as if I had never left.

Sugarplum shifted slightly in my left arm. Her small weight was becoming more noticeable, and my arm ached, but I kept her close. My right hand needed to be free at all times—police academy training ingrained that into me. Even in a supposedly safe place like a high school, that instinct to be ready, to be prepared, never left me. Bell, on the other hand, was in her element, her tail wagging enthusiastically as a couple of teenagers strolled by, their attention quickly turning to her.

"Is that the new department police dog?" one of them asked, his tone brimming with curiosity and just a touch of cockiness as he looked at the mop in my arms. His hair was too long, sticking out in uneven waves as if he hadn't bothered to comb it in days, and his baggy pants looked like they belonged to someone much larger. He had that carefree, slightly rebellious look typical of high school boys who spent more time goofing off than attending to their studies.

I gave him a cool smile, careful to keep my voice professional. "She is," I replied. "Sugar is our newest drug-sniffing dog." I didn't see the need to give him her full name—*Sugarplum* didn't exactly scream authority. Plus, I was trying to give her some credibility, even if she was undercover in the fluffiest way possible. Without waiting for a response, I continued walking toward the principal's office, feeling the boy's eyes on us as we passed.

The office, nestled at the heart of the school like most high schools, felt sterile, with its neutral-toned walls and the faint scent of cleaning products lingering in the air. The secretary greeted me warmly, recognizing the uniform, and ushered me in without delay. Principal Leland was already standing by his desk, hand outstretched. His grip was firm, the kind of handshake designed to put people at ease. I appreciated that.

I introduced Sugarplum more formally this time, aware that Leland wasn't the type to care about whether her name sounded "cool" or not. "She's new to my K9 team," I explained as he gestured for me to take a seat. "She'll be with me for a few days before she heads off to her permanent assignment."

Leland nodded, clearly satisfied with the explanation, and got right down to business. "I've contacted the parents of the students who were closest to the two boys in the hospital," he said, his voice steady but tinged with concern. "They've all agreed to allow their children to be interviewed, though only one of them has opted not to be present."

I nodded. Parents being present at this stage wasn't a concern for me. If any of the students raised enough suspicion, I'd handle the parents later. Right now, I just needed to gather information.

"We can start the interviews this afternoon if that works for you," he said.

"That's fine by me," I replied, mentally calculating the time I had left. "I'll be back at one. I need to walk the dogs and grab some lunch."

As I left the school, the knot of anxiety that had settled in my stomach loosened slightly. The park was a welcome escape. The heat of the day had driven most of the children indoors, leaving the playground deserted, and I welcomed the peace and quiet. Tall, mature trees cast long, cool shadows across the grass, providing shelter from the relentless sun. I let Bell and Sugarplum off their shorter leashes, watching as they trotted across the grass with a sense of freedom they hadn't had in the school halls.

There was something calming about watching them. Bell, usually so disciplined and alert, was in her element, sniffing the ground and wagging her tail as she explored. Sugarplum, for all her fluff and sweetness, had a spark of curiosity that kept her darting from place to place, her little nose twitching as she investigated every blade of grass. For a moment, I let myself relax, sinking into the comfort of the shade as I unwrapped my turkey sub. The faint smell of fresh-cut grass mingled with the earthy scent of dirt, and the rhythmic rustling of leaves overhead filled the silence.

The dogs continued to roam on their extended leads, and I couldn't help but smile at their antics. They sniffed the ground, then each other, tails wagging as they communicated in that unspoken canine language that always fascinated me. Bell's normally composed demeanor seemed to melt away in Sugarplum's presence, reminding me that despite all her training, she was still just a dog at heart.

Eventually, it was time to pack up and head back. I loaded Bell into the back of the car, and Sugarplum, ever the pro, hopped right into the passenger seat without needing my help. As I drove back to the school, the reality of the afternoon ahead settled over me. Interviews with football players and cheerleaders—the very kids I'd avoided during my own high school years. I couldn't shake the sense of dread that came with it. It felt less like I was heading into an investigation and more like I was bracing myself for a reunion with ghosts from my past.

The first student I interviewed was a bubbly girl with blonde hair tied back in a ponytail. She had the same wide-eyed, open expression that I'd seen on countless high school students—eager to help, but more interested in whatever shiny distraction caught their attention. And for her, that shiny distraction was Sugar. The girl was practically vibrating with excitement, her eyes fixed on the dog instead of me.

"She's a drug dog but has no problem sitting on laps," I told her with a small smile, finally giving in to her obvious desire to hold Sugar. As the dog settled in her lap, the girl's face lit up, and her parents, sitting quietly beside her, smiled in relief. It wasn't the most productive interview in terms of gathering useful information, but Sugarplum had clearly worked her magic, breaking the ice and easing the tension in the room.

The second interview followed a similar pattern, though the boy in question was less enthusiastic about cuddling the dog. Still, Bell and Sugarplum's presence seemed to put both the student and his parents at ease, and the conversation flowed smoothly.

It was the third interview that took a turn. Delaney, a pretty girl with long brown hair and an air of aloofness, entered the room alone. Her mother had given permission for the interview, but something about the way Delaney glanced nervously at Sugarplum set off alarm bells in my mind. When I mentioned that Sugar was a drug dog, the girl's posture stiffened, and she shifted in her chair, scooting as far away from the dog as possible. *She's hiding something*, I thought, mentally noting her behavior. I'd need to follow up with a visit to her home, away from the safety net of the school environment.

The last boy was Dayton, and his presence filled the room in a way that had nothing to do with his size. He was tall, muscular, and had an air of arrogance about him that made my skin crawl. The way he looked at me—no, at Sugarplum—was unnerving. "You have nothing on me," he said, voice dripping with contempt, "and I don't have anything to say to you."

His mother, sitting beside him, quickly apologized, her expression tense and uncomfortable. His father, on the other hand, remained silent, his eyes hard and unreadable. He wore a Mountain High football shirt and shorts that pegged him as a coach, and I didn't need to ask coach of what. His son's behavior said it all.

When they stood to leave, Sugarplum, normally sweet and docile, let out a low growl. I felt a surge of surprise—I had never heard her growl before. Even Bell, usually calm and collected, had her ears pinned back, her eyes fixed on Dayton with a quiet intensity. I couldn't shake the feeling that the dogs knew something I didn't.

After the family left, I met with Principal Leland again, who confirmed what I already suspected. Dayton was the school's star football player, practically worshipped on campus, and his father had been his coach since he was a child. A full-ride scholarship to a top-tier college was practically guaranteed, and Leland seemed to think that made him untouchable.

It didn't matter to me. Dayton's arrogance, combined with his behavior around the dogs, had already put him at the top of my suspect list. And while I wasn't about to jump to conclusions, I wouldn't ignore the gut feeling that had settled deep in my chest.

This case was more than just about drugs now. Something darker was lurking beneath the surface, and I had a feeling it was about to come to light. As I left the school and headed back to my office, the weight of what lay ahead pressed heavily on my shoulders. There was still so much to do—so many more interviews, so many more pieces to fit together.

But I couldn't shake the feeling that Dayton was at the center of it all. And if the dogs were onto something, then I had every reason to trust their instincts.

Chapter Twenty-Six

S UGARPLUM WAS CRAMPING MY style with her over-the-top cuteness. Every time she looked at me with those big, soulful eyes, it stirred something warm inside, the kind of fuzzy feeling I wasn't used to dealing with. I had to remind myself that her only job was to act cute and be an undercover pawn in my investigation. Nothing more. I wasn't here to bond with a dog who could fit in my purse. *Stay detached*, I thought, trying to fight the effect she had on me. The image of the stoic detective, cool and in control, with her champion K9 protector, was what I needed. That's who I was, who I wanted to be. But now I had Bell, my loyal and formidable partner, teamed up with Sugarplum—a pint-sized puffball who was slowly worming her way into my heart, and I hated it.

I sighed as I struck out contacting the parents of the two hospitalized kids. They hadn't answered their house phones, but I knew better than to rely on those in this day and age. I knew the parents would be at the hospital, so it made sense that my next stop would be there.

The only problem? Sugarplum. I wouldn't normally bring Bell to a place like a hospital unless I needed her, but there was no way I was dragging both of them into that environment. My dilemma was clear: *Could I trust Bell to take care of Sugarplum while I handled this alone?*

I wasn't so sure.

The drive home was filled with internal debates. Bell had proven herself a thousand times over in the field, but leaving her alone with Sugarplum in the backyard felt like leaving an older sibling to babysit the little one for the first time. It felt like a risk, but it was one I needed to take.

Once home, I let the dogs out into the yard to brown-spot the lawn. Sugarplum trotted across the patchy grass with an energetic bounce, while Bell, ever the guardian, followed closely behind. I stood by the back door, arms crossed, watching the pair. My backyard was little more than a slab of cement with a small patch of grass bordered by shrubs. It wasn't much, but the patio cover provided shade, and I figured Bell could handle herself if any trouble came their way.

She'll protect her, I reassured myself, feeling the knot of anxiety begin to loosen just a bit.

I set out two bowls of water—one for each of them—and locked Bell's dog door before I left. The look the dogs gave me as I stepped toward the front door was enough to make anyone feel guilty. Bell's typical stoic demeanor had morphed into something resembling sadness. Her usual unwavering confidence faltered just a little, as if she wasn't sure about being left alone with Sugarplum. Sugarplum, on the other hand, was giving me those wide, pleading eyes, her little head cocked to one side, lips quivering slightly. She was pulling all the stops.

I steeled myself, taking a deep breath. "You'll be fine," I muttered, more to myself than to them. I couldn't afford to picture them as twin prisoners behind the glass. Instead, I hardened my resolve and shut the door, reminding myself I was the tough detective who had dealt with far more difficult situations than leaving two dogs behind.

As I drove to the hospital, I forced my mind away from my four-legged partners and back onto the case. *Focus on the job*, I commanded myself. *Leave the guilt at home.* My human detective hat needed to be firmly in place, and I couldn't afford to be distracted by guilty feelings of a dog handler right now.

Mountain Hospital sat nestled between two pointed hills covered in thick trees and towering rocks. The three-story building, white and boxy, contrasted sharply with the rugged natural beauty of the surrounding area. The tall mountain pines swayed gently in the breeze, casting long shadows over the hospital grounds. I had always found the place to be oddly calming despite its sterile, clinical purpose.

Inside, the familiar smell of antiseptic and the low hum of hospital machinery filled the air. I knew most of the emergency room staff by name; they were often my go-to when I needed information. Today, however, I bypassed the ER and headed straight to the ICU. I approached a nurse, who nodded knowingly and disappeared to inform the parents that I had arrived.

Moments later, a woman in her late thirties emerged from the ICU doors, her eyes red and puffy from crying. Her hair, slightly frizzed from humidity, framed her round face, and despite the obvious grief and exhaustion in her expression, she managed a shaky smile. Her soft brown eyes held a weariness that only someone who had been to hell and back in a matter of days could carry.

"I'm Joshua's mother, Mandy," she said softly, extending her hand. Her voice wavered, but she held her composure. I admired her strength.

"Thank you for speaking with me," I replied, shaking her hand gently. "I'm Detective Jolett, and I've been assigned to your son's case. Do you have a moment to sit down and talk?"

Mandy nodded and followed me to a set of chairs in the waiting room. We sat, and I gave her a moment to settle herself before I asked, "How is Joshua doing?"

She dabbed at her eyes with a tissue and managed a faint smile. "The doctor thinks he'll be okay. He's responding to the treatment and starting to talk again."

That was good news. "I'm glad to hear that. Has there been any update on Nick?" I asked carefully, not wanting to press too hard.

Her expression darkened. "Nick's not doing as well," she admitted, her voice breaking slightly. She sniffed and wiped at another tear. "It's so awful for his family. I just can't imagine... I don't know what I'd do if I lost Joshua."

The weight of her words hung in the air between us, and I felt a familiar pang in my chest—the kind you get when you've seen too much loss and yet still feel the rawness of each new case. I had never had children of my own, but I had lost close friends. The kind of grief that Mandy was feeling was something I understood, even if I couldn't fully relate.

I shifted gears, gently moving the conversation forward. "Mandy, were you aware that Joshua had been experimenting with drugs?"

Her gaze faltered, and she looked away briefly before nodding. "I caught him coming home drunk from a party six months ago," she admitted, her voice barely above a whisper. "He promised me it wouldn't happen again. I believed him. This... this isn't like him at all." She sighed deeply. "I know most parents probably say that, but he really is a good kid. He's always gotten good grades. I just never thought...."

"I understand," I said, offering a small nod of sympathy. It was the same story I'd heard countless times—parents caught off guard by the choices their kids made, trying to reconcile the child they raised with the teenager before them.

"Did you have any suspicions about his friends?" I pressed gently.

She hesitated before answering. "There are a couple of football players I'm not too fond of. They don't seem like great influences, but most of his friends are good boys." She gave a half-hearted shrug.

"Could you give me the names of the boys you're not so sure about?" I asked, keeping my tone neutral. "This won't go into my report, but it might help me figure out who's involved. If other students are using or know something, it could help prevent another tragedy."

She bit her lip, clearly torn between protecting the kids and her need to help her son. After a long pause, she finally sighed and relented, giving me the names. I wasn't surprised when she mentioned Dayton. That kid had rubbed me the wrong way from the start, and hearing it confirmed my instincts about him.

"Dayton is the ringleader," she said with more conviction now. "I've never liked the way he treated Joshua, but my son seemed determined to be his friend. I guess it's the football thing." Her fingers drummed anxiously on the table, betraying her unease. I could tell she didn't like speaking ill of Joshua's friends, but she knew it needed to be said. I could almost understand, I thought. After all, wasn't I having a hard time admitting I was starting to like Sugarplum? The little rat dog had worked her way into my heart, even though I hadn't wanted her to.

I shifted the conversation back to Joshua. "Do you think Joshua would be able to speak with me today?"

Her eyes softened with worry. "I don't know. I can ask the doctor, but I really think he needs another day. He's improving, but I don't want to push him too soon. Maybe when he's feeling stronger, you can get him to talk about things he hasn't told me." Her face crumpled under the weight of her emotions, and she started to cry. "He's always been such a good boy. This... this isn't who he is. He's all I have."

I felt the gravity of her words. *All I have*—the raw vulnerability in that statement wasn't lost on me. She was clinging to her son in a way only a mother who feared losing him could.

"I appreciate your help, Mandy," I said sincerely, standing up. "I'll let you get back to him. I'm going to speak with Nick's parents now."

She stood up and offered me a grateful smile before walking back to her son's room.

Chapter
Twenty-Seven

TWO EXCITED DOGS GREETED me the moment I opened the back door. Sugarplum, in all her tiny exuberance, practically danced on the spot, her little paws tapping like a rapid drumbeat, and with her usual over-excitement, there might have been a tiny accident. I ignored the small wet drops on the cement, brushing it off without a second thought. At this point, she was too endearing for her own good, and the little droplets felt like a minor consequence of her enthusiasm. Bell was more composed, though her eyes sparkled with quiet joy, her wagging tail sending little waves through the air like she hadn't seen me in days.

I knelt down, giving both dogs all the attention they demanded—scratching behind Bell's ears, ruffling Sugarplum's fur as she pranced around me like I was the most exciting thing she'd ever encountered. The warmth of their unconditional affection soothed some of the day's tension, but before long, my growling stomach pulled me toward the kitchen.

Their bowls were prepped first, of course. Even though my hunger gnawed at me, I always took care of Bell before myself. I placed Bell's bowl on one side of the room and Sugarplum's on the opposite side, figuring that space might curb any potential disputes. Not that Bell was one to start anything, but Sugarplum, with her relentless appetite, could bulldoze through any sense of boundaries.

As I turned away to gather what I needed for my own meal, my attention snagged on Bell, who was sitting stoically next to her uneaten bowl. She wasn't looking at her food; instead, her gaze was fixed on Sugarplum, who was tearing through her meal like it was her last.

"What is it, girl?" I asked, feeling a slight unease creep in. Bell rarely hesitated when it came to food, and the sight of her sitting so still next to her bowl was unusual. She whined softly and nudged her dish, as though trying to communicate something.

I blinked, realization dawning. She cannot be serious.

Bell, my trained, disciplined K9, was waiting for permission—waiting, of all things, for her bowl to be moved closer to Sugarplum's. I stared at her, incredulous. We locked eyes, and she held my gaze, unwavering. It was a silent standoff between dog and handler, and as ridiculous as it was, I could see in her eyes that she wasn't budging. With a long, drawn-out sigh, I gave in, using my foot to slide her bowl across the floor until it was next to Sugarplum's.

Sugarplum didn't even pause, too busy devouring her food, oblivious to the world. Bell, acting as if this was completely normal, calmly walked over and began eating next to her like this had been the arrangement all along. It was such a bizarre scene—the big, powerful Bell, perfectly at ease beside Sugarplum, a literal puffball of energy.

"This is not a good scenario," I muttered, my voice catching in the quiet kitchen as I sat down on the nearest barstool. "You need to understand our part in this story, Bell."

She glanced up at me mid-bite, those deep brown eyes showing a flash of understanding. I could tell she knew what I was getting at. This arrangement was temporary. Sugarplum wasn't meant to be part of our permanent world, and Bell had to know that. I leaned in slightly, using my "dog discussion voice"—low, soft, but serious.

"We can't do this," I said quietly, shaking my head as if the gravity of the situation required us both to be on the same page. I moved closer, glancing over at Sugarplum, who was still happily chowing down, clearly not understanding the weight of what I was about to say. I lowered my voice even further. "She doesn't belong to us, Bell."

Bell paused, just for a moment, as if considering my words. She looked up at me with those baleful eyes that spoke volumes, eyes that seemed to say, *You don't believe that, and neither do I.* I sighed again, feeling a twinge of guilt. The truth was, I was starting to wonder whether Bell was right. Ed needs to get better, I reminded myself, trying to hold onto my resolve. This attachment can't happen.

After the dogs finished eating, and I had my dinner and cleaned the kitchen, the exhaustion of the day hit me hard. I could feel the weight of it pressing down, pulling me toward bed. I didn't bother fighting it. The dogs were still full of energy, but they followed me outside for one last bathroom break. I stood on the lawn, watching as they sniffed around, doing their business under the fading light of early evening. The cool breeze rustled through the trees, and for a brief moment, everything felt peaceful.

Afterward, I picked up Sugarplum, carrying her upstairs to the extra pillow on my bed. Bell, as always, claimed her spot at the foot of the bed, the same place Suii had once curled up. My heart gave a little squeeze at the memory, but I shook it off. Tonight was about rest. I climbed into bed, pulling the sheet up to my chin as I settled between the two dogs. Their soft, rhythmic breathing soon filled the room, and with it, I drifted off to sleep.

****

Morning came too early, heralded by small, warm licks on my nose. I groaned, blinking against the soft light filtering through the curtains. Bell's tail thumped against the mattress with quiet enthusiasm, and as I looked over, there was Sugarplum, staring at me expectantly. At least the sun's position told me it was a reasonable time to wake up.

I scooped up Sugarplum—no way was I trusting that tiny bladder to make it outside in time—and carried her to the back porch, where Bell followed. They sniffed and explored, establishing a routine together. I made myself a cup of coffee, the rich aroma filling the cool morning air as I sat on the patio, watching them with amusement. The backyard, with its limited space and the occasional ground squirrel droppings, was still a paradise for their curious noses. It didn't matter that they'd already sniffed every inch of it the day before—there was always something new for them to discover.

By the time I finished my coffee and had taken a quick shower, the dogs were loaded into the vehicle, and we were headed to the police department. My first call of the day was to Caldwell.

"What's up, Jolett?" he answered, his usual jovial tone kicking off the conversation.

"Good morning," I replied. "I still don't have the drug analysis back, but I wanted to ask if you could keep your ears to the ground in the surrounding counties. This stuff might pop up somewhere else soon."

He laughed, a deep, hearty chuckle that made me smile despite myself. "You know, you sound more and more like a dog person with your 'nose to the ground' comment. I remember when you weren't too fond of smelly mutts."

I glanced over at Bell and Sugarplum, curled up together in the office without a care in the world. You're funny, Caldwell, I thought wryly, but I wasn't about to admit anything. "Ha ha," I deadpanned.

After a few more jokes, Caldwell shifted into work mode. "We haven't seen any signs yet, which is weird. Usually, when something heavy like this hits, we get some early alerts from the usual suspects—people start overdosing, dealers go quiet. But right now? Nothing. How'd the interviews go?"

It was one of the reasons I respected Caldwell. Sure, he could poke fun, but when he needed to get serious, he didn't waste any time. "I've got some leads," I said, leaning back in my chair. "I'm hoping to talk to one of the hospitalized kids today. The other one was still critical when I left the hospital yesterday."

"I'll keep my ears open," he promised. "Let me know if you hit anything solid or need to brainstorm."

"You're my go-to wall for bouncing ideas off, huh?" I teased.

"Solid rock, baby," he replied with mock seriousness.

I couldn't help but groan. "You're going too far now. Get to work and stop wasting taxpayer dollars feeding your ego."

His laughter echoed through the phone, and when we finally hung up, I shook my head, smiling despite myself. Caldwell was one of the good ones, and in a line of work where allies weren't always easy to come by, I knew how lucky I was to have him in my corner.

Next, I checked on my three patients at the hospital. Joshua was going home in a few hours, which was good news. Nick, however, remained unresponsive. But the highlight of the call was hearing that Ed was awake and already complaining. I grinned at the thought—typical Ed.

When I asked if I could be patched through to his room, the nurse told me he was still in ICU and would be moved to a regular room once the doctor made his rounds. That was fine by me. The fact that he was awake at all meant things were looking up.

With Ed's daughter arriving later that day, she'd texted to ask how Sugarplum was doing. I assured her that I'd keep Sugarplum until Ed was back home. She didn't need to know I was growing soft. When Jack found out, he was going to laugh himself into a fit.

As I glanced at the clock, I decided it was time for Sugarplum's thirty minutes of training. Who knew? Maybe I could turn her into a real drug-sniffing dog—at least enough to keep up appearances. It couldn't hurt to try.

I opened the bottom drawer of my desk, pulling out the lockbox I hadn't touched in months. Inside were the items I'd used to train Suii—things that carried scents from past cases, imbued with the smells of marijuana, ash residue, and even a small child's stuffed dinosaur that had been left at the police department and repurposed for scent training. Each item told a story, a history embedded in every thread and fiber.

Bell had been trained for explosives detection, so her items were different—scraps of materials from dismantled pipe bombs, bullet casings, and the like. But this was different. With Sugarplum, I didn't need to train her to be an expert. I just needed her to *look* the part.

Bell's expression was downright pitiful when I left her behind in the office and took Sugarplum for training. I shot her an apologetic glance, mentally promising to make it up to her later. Hopefully, this experiment won't be a complete disaster.

Leo Franks, one of the other officers, looked up as I passed by his desk. "What's up, Laci?" he asked with a grin. "Heard you got stuck with the high school case. We're taking bets on when you'll sic Bell on one of the teenagers."

"Please, my Taser finger is just as good," I shot back, unable to resist the banter.

He laughed, the sound filling the room. "I can see the headlines now: 'Detective tases student while ferocious K9 watches.'"

"Not the headline I'm aiming for," I muttered, though it was a good reminder to always keep the "headline test" in mind. If it didn't sound good on paper, don't do it—that was a rule I lived by.

Before I could reply, a howl echoed through the station. I winced, recognizing it immediately. Bell. She was not taking kindly to being left behind.

"Is that what I think it is?" Leo asked, clearly amused.

I sighed. "Would you mind holding her lead while I work with Sugarplum?"

His brow furrowed in confusion. "Sugarwho?"

Between his bursts of laughter, I explained the whole situation. By the end of it, he agreed to help, though he still found the whole thing hilarious.

Once I had everything set up, I started working with Sugarplum, using crinkling treat bags and scent markers to guide her along. Bell watched from her spot with Leo, her big eyes tracking every move. It took a good forty-five minutes, but by the end of it, Sugarplum had picked up on the basics. She knew that following my hand and sniffing the scent meant a treat. Her phony drug alert might just fool a high schooler—if I was lucky.

Afterward, I took both dogs outside for a quick break. They sniffed around the fenced-in vehicle lot, noses to the ground as they took in the day's new smells. The sun had risen higher, and the heat of the day was starting to creep in, but the dogs didn't seem to mind.

When we returned to my office, Bell and Sugarplum curled up together on the dog bed. The sight of them, nestled together so perfectly, tugged at something in my chest. I couldn't resist snapping a picture to send to Ed. Who was I kidding? I was becoming a softie.

I wasn't sure what had happened to the mean, surly detective I'd been, but one thing was clear: things were changing, and maybe—just maybe—that wasn't such a bad thing after all.

Chapter Twenty-Eight

I CALLED MANDY AND lined up an interview with Joshua for the afternoon. She said he was feeling much better, physically at least, though she didn't have high hopes that he'd tell me anything useful. I wasn't surprised. Kids, especially teens, often clammed up in situations like this. They didn't want to rat out their friends or be the cause of more trouble. But it wasn't just about getting information from Joshua; it was about making him feel safe enough to share what he knew. Mandy had no problem with me interviewing him alone, so long as I did it at her home. I would have preferred the department's interview room, with video recording for documentation, but I understood that Joshua had just come home from the hospital. It was important to make this as easy as possible for both him and his mother. All of that would change if Nick didn't pull through. Unfortunately, he was still unresponsive, and the doctors were running further tests.

Leaving Bell and Sugarplum on the back patio, I felt a pang of guilt. Bell's eyes followed me as I locked the door, and Sugarplum, ever oblivious, bounced around her. But I couldn't bring them along. I didn't need distractions for me or Joshua during this interview. I had to stay sharp, and the last thing

I needed was the dogs demanding attention while I tried to crack through a teenager's guarded conscience.

As I drove to Mandy's home, I mentally prepared myself for what I was about to face. Joshua wasn't going to be happy to see me, and I couldn't blame him. He'd been through hell recently, and now here I was, showing up to dig through the remains of his mess. When I pulled up to the modest two-story house, the familiar tightness of anticipation settled in my chest. This was never easy, I reminded myself as I knocked on the door. But necessary.

Mandy answered quickly, her face pinched with worry and fatigue, though she gave me a polite smile. "He's in the living room," she said softly. "I told him you'd be here, but... well, he's not thrilled."

"I'll do my best to make this quick," I assured her, though we both knew that might not be possible. I stepped into the house, following her through a narrow hallway that opened into a cozy living room. The soft scent of lavender lingered in the air, probably from a nearby diffuser, and the muted tones of the furniture and walls gave the space a calming effect. But the tension was still thick.

Joshua sat on the couch, his posture stiff, head bowed, fingers interlocked and thrumming rhythmically against his knuckles. His shoulders were hunched, his body language practically screaming discomfort. He looked younger than I had expected, his features still caught in that awkward stage between boyhood and manhood. He wasn't as physically imposing as Dayton, and his smaller build and softer demeanor gave me hope that I might be able to reach him.

"Joshua, this is Detective Jolett," Mandy said, her voice gentle as she introduced me. Joshua barely glanced up, his eyes darting to his mom as if hoping she would stay. But when she quietly left the room, his anxiety visibly spiked.

I took the closest chair, making sure not to crowd him. We shook hands briefly—his grip weak, his palm clammy—and his eyes followed his mother out the door. It was clear he didn't want to be alone with me, and I could see the nervousness building in the way he fidgeted, tapping his foot lightly against the floor.

"How are you feeling?" I started with something simple, keeping my tone light.

He shrugged, not looking up.

"Did the doctor schedule a follow-up for you?"

He gave a brief nod but remained silent. It was going to be a challenge getting him to talk, but I wasn't in a rush. I needed to break the ice. Find something that would make him more comfortable.

"I should've brought Sugarplum with me," I muttered, almost to myself, but loud enough for him to hear.

"Huh?" His head tilted slightly, a flicker of interest crossing his face.

"My new dog, Sugarplum," I explained. "She's still in K9 training, but she's more of a cutie than anything else. People tend to relax around her. I could go get her if you think that would help."

Joshua's lips twitched, and for the first time, I saw a small, reluctant smile. "No, that's okay," he said. "I do like dogs, though."

I seized the opportunity, glad to have found something to build on. "Do you have a dog?"

"We did," he replied, his voice softening. "But he died a few years ago. My mom said we were too busy to get another one."

"I didn't grow up with dogs either. I'm pretty new to it myself. What kind of dog was he?"

A small chuckle escaped him, and his expression softened a little more. "Spaz was a mutt," he said. "He was kind of crazy. Always acted like a puppy, even when he got old. He was a good dog, though."

"I like the name," I said with a grin. "It fits. My first K9, Suii, he was strong and protective. He saved my life." I paused, feeling a pang in my chest as I spoke. The memory of Suii's loss still stung, and I didn't have to fake the emotion on my face. Joshua saw it, and I think it helped him understand that I wasn't just some hard-nosed detective. I'd lost something too.

"I'm sorry he died," Joshua said quietly, and the sincerity in his voice was clear.

I nodded, grateful for the connection we were forming. "Thanks. He was a great partner. But now I have Bell and, of course, Sugarplum, the newest addition."

For a brief moment, the room felt less tense. Joshua seemed a little more at ease, and I took the opportunity to steer the conversation back to the case. "I know you don't want your friends to get into trouble, Joshua. That's not why I'm here. But you need to think about Nick. If he doesn't make it, someone will be responsible for his death. And I know you don't want that on your conscience."

His eyes dropped to the floor, and I saw the first tear hit the carpet. His hands clenched, but he remained silent, his shoulders hunched even further. The weight of everything was crashing down on him, and I knew I had to be careful not to push too hard too fast.

"I'm not here to make your life harder," I said, keeping my voice soft. "But if there are more of those pills out there, Joshua, then someone else could get hurt. Maybe worse."

Joshua's lip quivered as he finally looked up at me, and then his tears flowed freely. His body shook with quiet sobs, and I knew I had hit the core of his guilt. Silence stretched between us as I waited, giving him the space he needed to gather his thoughts. People hate silence, I reminded myself. It forces them to fill it.

Finally, he spoke, his voice barely above a whisper. "I bought the pills. This is all my fault."

It was a breakthrough, but it also presented a new problem. He had admitted to buying the drugs, which put him in a precarious legal position. Legally, I wasn't obligated to read him his rights—he wasn't in custody, and this wasn't an official interrogation. But ethically, it was a tightrope walk. I couldn't just go on the attack, not with him like this.

I leaned forward slightly, keeping my tone neutral. "You bought the drugs?"

He nodded, still crying.

The weight of his admission settled in the room like a heavy blanket. I had to tread carefully here. I wasn't about to arrest him right then and there, but I needed to get as much information as I could. "Joshua, I think it's time we bring your mom back in. She deserves to hear this from you."

His head shot up, panic flashing in his eyes. "No, please. She won't understand."

"She's your mother, Joshua. She'll understand more than you think. And I've already spoken to her. She knows something's wrong. I'm not going to arrest you. I don't think the county attorney will want to press charges either, but that depends on what happens next. What you need to do is cooperate. The hospital stay was punishment enough, but if Nick dies, this will get worse. Telling the truth now will help."

His body tensed, and for a moment, I thought he would shut down completely. But then he broke, his face crumpling as fresh tears flowed. "I didn't bring the drugs into town. I swear I didn't. But I can't tell you who sold them to me. I just can't."

I stood and sent a quick text to Mandy, asking her to return to the living room. She came in with a worried expression, but I gave her a reassuring smile, signaling that everything was under control. The moment Joshua saw her, he completely broke down, throwing himself into her arms. She held him tightly, whispering soft reassurances while he sobbed.

I envied him for a second, seeing the way his mother held him, her love unwavering despite the situation. It reminded me of the rare moments in foster care when I found someone who cared enough to wrap me in their arms. It didn't happen often, and watching it now made me ache for something I hadn't realized I missed.

"I'm so sorry, Mom," Joshua cried. "If Nick dies, it's my fault."

Mandy's eyes widened in panic, but I shook my head subtly, silently urging her to stay calm. She caught on quickly and kept her voice gentle. "It's okay, Joshua. Just tell us what happened. I'll love you no matter what."

Those were the magic words. Joshua's sobs quieted, and he took a deep, shaky breath. "I bought four pills," he confessed.

Mandy's hand flew to her mouth in shock, and I saw her struggle to hold back a reaction. This was why parents shouldn't be present during interviews, I thought. But she did her best, giving me a helpless look. I gave her a small shake of my head, silently asking her to stay calm.

"I'm sorry," she whispered. "I'll stay quiet. You just need to talk, Joshua. Get it all out. I'm here for you."

Joshua wiped his face with the back of his hand, the raw emotion still etched on his face. "I've never done anything like this before, I promise. I took one and gave two to Nick. I also gave one to Delaney."

His sobs started again, and my stomach twisted at the mention of Delaney. She had lied during her interview, and now I knew why. This was getting more complicated by the minute.

"Does Nick know who sold you the pills?" I asked gently.

Joshua didn't answer, just shook his head and kept his gaze fixed on the floor. I knew I wasn't going to get any more out of him today. He had already given me more than I expected. I explained to Mandy about the possibility of charges and how cooperation would help Joshua's case if it came to that.

"I can't tell you," Joshua whispered again, his voice filled with guilt and fear.

I stood to leave, placing a hand on Mandy's shoulder. "I think it's important to get him into counseling immediately.

It'll help if this goes to court, but more importantly, it'll help him deal with everything he's feeling."

She nodded, her eyes brimming with tears as she looked at her son. "Thank you," she whispered, her voice thick with emotion.

As I drove away from their house, I couldn't stop thinking about Joshua. He was just a kid—a kid who had made a stupid decision that might cost him his future. I hoped for his sake—and for Nick's—that this wouldn't be a tragedy they couldn't come back from.

Chapter Twenty-Nine

LUNCH AT HOME CONSISTED of leftover lasagna I had made the night before Ed's heart attack. It wasn't gourmet by any stretch, but it did the job. Cooking for one was never exciting, and I'd gotten used to throwing together meals that just barely satisfied hunger. Adding a bunch of herbs helped mask any culinary mistakes, but I wasn't delusional—I wasn't a chef, just someone who learned enough to avoid starvation. If all else failed, I had Bell, who, with her iron stomach, could usually handle whatever went wrong in the kitchen. Just one more reason she made such a great partner—she never complained about what I gave her, even if it didn't exactly taste like it came from a five-star restaurant.

The lasagna was serviceable, though the thought of how close Ed had come to never having another meal weighed on me. He was a staple in my life, and that near-miss made me appreciate the small things more. I gave the dogs the last of their kibble and loaded them into the car for another trip to the station. The way Bell and Sugarplum followed me everywhere made me feel less alone, even when the weight of the case pressed hard on my chest.

When we arrived at the department, I put off the inevitable paperwork as long as I could. I should have written my initial report last night, but exhaustion had won. Sitting at my desk, I caught myself procrastinating by checking on Nick. The hospital reported that he had finally shown signs of awareness. That bit of good news lifted some of the darkness hovering over the case. I even spoke briefly to Ed, who was, true to form, cranky about being stuck in the hospital.

"I've got Sugarplum here with me," I told him, a small smile creeping onto my face. "She and Bell are fast friends now. Your job is to get better so you can take the fluff mop off my hands."

"You're a good woman, Detective Jolett," he said, his voice raspy with exhaustion, but there was a warm sincerity there that settled my nerves.

I ended the call quickly, not wanting to tire him out. His daughter would be in town shortly, and she'd texted that she'd go straight to the hospital and find her own way to his house. That was a relief—one less thing for me to worry about.

After hanging up with Ed, I called Delaney's mother. There was no easy way to tell her that her daughter had one of the pills, especially without implicating Joshua. "I don't want Delaney in trouble," I reassured her, keeping my tone calm. "But I do need to speak with her. If she still has the pill, or if she passed it to someone else, it's crucial that we get that sorted. Otherwise, if I have to talk to her at school, we're looking at an automatic felony for bringing drugs on campus."

Her mother, understandably horrified, didn't want to wait until after school. "It'll be easier if you bring her here, to my office," I said. "I don't intend to charge her, but I need to know if she still has the pill or if it's been passed on. And I think she knows more than she's letting on about who's distributing these pills at school."

With reluctance, Delaney's mother agreed, and I told her I'd be ready when they arrived. That left me with about forty-five minutes to work on my report—precious time, considering how much paper the case had generated so far.

When Delaney and her mother, Rene, arrived, I left Sugarplum behind. Her newly honed treat-induced skills would be saved for the right moment. If I needed her, it would likely be a one-shot deal, and I couldn't risk wasting it here. I started the interview with Rene, a woman who immediately struck me as someone who took care of herself—dyed blonde hair, green eyes, plump lips that had likely seen a bit of Botox. She looked tired, though, like life had thrown too much at her in a short time.

"Thank you for bringing Delaney in," I said as we sat in the interview room. "I want to make sure she's safe, and I appreciate your cooperation."

Rene nodded, her eyes sharp as she listened carefully. "I should have been there yesterday," she admitted, her voice tinged with regret. "My husband's traveling, and my younger son had his tonsils out. I had my hands full. I asked my mother to babysit, but she had a prior engagement."

I liked Rene immediately. There was a genuine concern in her voice that I didn't always hear from parents. She wasn't making excuses; she was explaining, and that made all the difference. "I know Delaney lied to me during her interview," I said gently. Rene's lips pressed together in frustration. "It's natural—she's scared. But we need to make sure she understands the stakes here. This could have ended a lot worse."

Rene sighed, shaking her head. "I know when Delaney's lying. I would have stopped her. We could have three dead kids right now, and one of them could've been my daughter." Her voice cracked, and the pain in her eyes mirrored the horror of what could have been. "Nick's poor family. We go to the same church. This has destroyed them."

Her honesty, her ability to acknowledge the situation, made me like her even more. It was rare to meet parents who could see the truth about their kids, and I knew I had her on my side. "If Delaney doesn't speak honestly with me, I'll bring you back in as backup," I told her.

Rene nodded, clearly willing to do whatever it took to get Delaney to talk. I decided to give Delaney the chance to come clean on her own, without her mother present. As I led Rene out, I could see the worry lines etched deeper into her face. She was as scared as Delaney was, and I didn't blame her.

Delaney entered the room looking like she was walking into a tomb. Her shoulders slumped, her eyes darted around the room, and her hands trembled as she sat down. She wore jeans and a flowered shirt, her hair pulled back from her face, but no amount of grooming could hide the fear that radiated from her.

I waited for her to settle, studying the way her hands fidgeted in her lap, her eyes brimming with unshed tears. It was clear she was scared out of her mind, and I had a good feeling I wouldn't need to read her Miranda rights today.

"I spoke with Joshua," I started, but I barely got the words out before Delaney spilled what she knew. There was no hesitation, but she stopped short of giving me the name I needed.

"I threw the pill away after I found out the boys got sick," she said, her voice shaky. "When you talked to me at school, I was scared your dog would smell it on me. I should have told you then."

I leaned forward, keeping my tone even. "Delaney, I need a name. Even if you didn't see the sale, I need to know who you think it was."

But the wall went up again. Despite my efforts to nudge her with guilt, the fear of naming the dealer was stronger than anything I could say. After a while, I called Rene back in, hoping she could help push her daughter to talk. But even with her mother's pleading, anger, and threats, Delaney wouldn't budge. Her fear outweighed the consequences, and I could see that whatever or whoever was scaring her had a grip stronger than her family's influence.

Delaney left in tears, her mother fuming with disappointment. It was frustrating, knowing how close I was to the answer but unable to cross that final hurdle. Though Nick was doing better, there was always the chance that changed.

The rest of the afternoon was spent writing my report. The steady rhythm of typing didn't do much to ease the frustration, but at least I was making progress. I got a text from Ed's daughter, Maggie, confirming that she would meet me at his place at six to pick up the key. I finished up at the department around five, threw together a quick microwave meal at home, and took the dogs for a walk. The routine helped ease my mind a little, giving me a much-needed break from the chaos of the case.

Maggie arrived a few minutes after we returned home. She looked weary, the kind of bone-deep exhaustion that comes from worrying about someone you love. Ed had told me she was in her late thirties and worked as a medical transcriptionist, and I could see the resemblance to her father—dark eyes, easy smile, though tonight, her smile was strained.

"Thank you for taking care of Sugarplum," she said sincerely as I handed her the key.

"I've actually enjoyed it," I replied, meaning it. I'd never admit that to Jack, though. If he found out, I'd never hear the end of it. Jack had always teased me about secretly being a dog lover, and I'd pretended to hold onto my tough exterior for as long as I could. But lately, I was starting to think Jack had seen right through me from the start.

After getting Maggie settled and hearing more good news about Ed—he'd be getting a stent in the morning and should be home in a few days if all went well—I finally crashed for the night. Bell curled up at my feet, as always, and Sugarplum nestled into the extra pillow beside me. When I woke up the next morning, I was greeted by a familiar warm tongue on my face. Nope, I thought as I rubbed their bellies, I am not getting used to this. But I couldn't deny that I lingered a little longer before getting out of bed.

The next few days passed in a frustrating blur. Dead ends piled up, and none of the kids would talk. After Joshua's mother called Nick's family to apologize, Nick's parents lawyered up, which was no surprise. They were just protecting their son, but it made everything more difficult. I knew Nick wasn't responsible for what his parents did, and as much as I wanted to hold him accountable for withholding information, I wasn't about to charge him unless he was deeper in this mess than I suspected. My real target was whoever was bringing the drugs into town.

The kids wouldn't talk. No matter what angle I tried, no one was giving me the name I needed. But I had one option left—someone I'd been holding in reserve. Caleb. He owed me a favor, and now was the time to call it in.

It took me half the day to track him down. If I could've put out word on the street, it would've been easier, but I didn't want Caleb's name tied to this. He was my quiet informant, the type who lived in the shadows, and I needed him to stay there. Eventually, after circling through his usual spots, I found him outside his mom's apartment building.

"Hey, Jolett," he greeted me, all smiles, as he approached the passenger side of my SUV. Sugarplum stuck her head out the window, and Caleb reached out to scratch her head. "Nice puppy," he said, grinning.

If I had to describe Caleb, it would be "skinny and all teeth." He wasn't the brightest when it came to the world around him, and lying came easier to him than the truth. But if you had patience, Caleb could come through. He had a rough past, but deep down, there was a gentle soul in there. He wasn't a bad kid, just misguided.

"Take a ride with me," I said, keeping my tone light. "We'll head to the airport. I want to keep this between us."

"Oh, is this dark detective stuff?" he asked, his grin widening as his teeth flashed in the sunlight.

"Very dark," I warned, motioning for him to get in.

As we cruised toward the airport, Sugarplum happily settled on Caleb's lap. I reminded him of the favor he owed me, then got to the point. "Who's supplying the fentanyl-laced codeine and putting our high schoolers at risk?"

Caleb shifted uncomfortably, his usual cocky demeanor faltering for a moment. "Rumors everywhere," he said evasively. "You got a bum case, Jolett."

I wasn't in the mood for his games. "I'm not interested in rumors, Caleb. I need a name."

He hesitated, his eyes darting to the window as if he might make a run for it. "This is a bad deal," he muttered, clearly on edge. "I don't want any part of it."

"You owe me," I reminded him, keeping my voice steady. "You know what I let go last time. Don't forget that."

Caleb sighed, leaning back in his seat. "Come on, Jolett. Everyone knows the players. It's no secret." He paused, glancing at me out of the corner of his eye. "But there's only one person controlling the drugs and thugs at the high school."

"Who?" I asked, the impatience creeping into my voice.

He shifted again, finally expelling a long breath. "The fentanyl is probably a one-off," he began. "There are two drugs at the high school—marijuana and steroids—and they're both supplied by the same person. The scandal's going to be huge."

He drew out the word "huge," and I could tell he was enjoying the drama. But he still hadn't given me a name.

"Who, Caleb?" I pressed.

He gave me a side-eye before finally spitting it out. "Lanigan. All three of them."

My stomach tightened. Dayton Lanigan. "Who are the three?" I asked, keeping my tone calm despite the storm brewing inside me.

"Coach and his two sons," Caleb answered with a shrug. "Everyone knows it. Dayton's the supplier at school. His older brother Bo brings in marijuana and steroids from college. Broke his leg senior year and lost his scholarship, so now he's dealing."

"And the coach?"

Caleb rolled his eyes dramatically. "Coach wants a winning team. He tells the players to do whatever it takes to get those wins. Dayton handles the business at school, but everyone knows it's all coming from the top."

The implications hit me hard. The coach, involved in this mess? I shouldn't have been surprised, but it was still a punch to the gut.

"I owe you for this," I said quietly, grateful for the lead but already dreading where it might take me.

Caleb grinned, his teeth flashing again. "I thought I owed *you*."

I smiled back. "You've gone above and beyond. I can't get you out of every scrape, but if you need help next time, I'll see what I can do."

"You got it, Jolett."

I dropped him off at his mom's place, then immediately called Caldwell to set up an in-person meeting. It had taken years to build up the kind of connections I had with people like Caleb, and I knew other officers didn't always understand my methods. But my end game was different—I wanted the big players, the felons, not a group of misguided teenagers.

I needed ten more Calebs.

Chapter Thirty

ALDWELL WAS THE ONE who whistled, long and low, as the weight of the information I shared with him sank in.

"This is going to be a firestorm," he said, leaning back in his chair, his eyes narrowing as he processed the implications. I didn't offer the name of my source—Caleb—and Mike, as always, respected that. He understood the delicate dance of informants and knew better than to press for details I wasn't ready to give. But we both knew what was coming, and neither of us liked it.

I nodded in agreement, though I felt a pit form in my stomach. This wasn't going to be the kind of case that stayed quiet, and the fallout would ripple far beyond just the kids involved. "What about the steroids?" I asked. "Have you heard any inkling that they've been going around the school?"

For a second, Caldwell's blank look made me wonder if I'd said something absurd, but then he let out a short laugh that quickly morphed into a cough at the sight of my unamused expression. "Laci," he said, shaking his head, "I don't think you get high school football. It's all about the win."

I stared at him, incredulous. "What are you saying?" I asked, already bristling.

He held up a hand, cutting me off before I could launch into a tirade about law enforcement ethics. "I'm on your side, Laci. Trust me. But you have to realize that, around here, football isn't just a sport. It's a way of life. Of course, we've heard the rumors at the task force about steroids. But whenever there's an investigation? It goes nowhere. It's like trying to punch through water. People don't want to talk. And when they do, it's all hushed whispers. Nobody wants to be the one who takes down their Friday night religion."

I crossed my arms, unable to hide my irritation. "You're telling me that this town is just going to look the other way while high school kids are pumped full of drugs?" My voice was tight with disbelief.

He met my gaze, unflinching. "I'm telling you it's been going on for years, and nothing's changed. This town has two Gods: the one they worship on Sundays, and the football team they cheer for on Fridays. They'll protect that with everything they've got, even if it means turning a blind eye to what happens off the field. Steroids in sports? It's like an open secret no one wants to acknowledge. It's probably the same in most high schools. People see it, but they don't talk about it."

The frustration bubbled up inside me. "That's wrong, Mike. You start making kids think they can take drugs—steroids, pills, whatever—and it leads to where we are now. Kids taking God knows what, without knowing what's inside. It escalates. And now we've got overdoses and kids in the hospital."

He sighed, nodding. "I know. And I agree with you. Marijuana, alcohol, cigarettes—they're all gateways. I drank my first beer at sixteen, not because I liked it, but because it pissed off my parents. Rebellion. That's how it starts. I was lucky, didn't get pulled into the drug scene, but a lot of my buddies from back in high school? They weren't so fortunate."

I leaned back in my chair, listening. His words hit close to home. I hadn't been much of a rebel, aside from sneaking out to parties or driving my foster parents' car a little too fast. But I'd always had an aversion to drugs, something deep in me that kept me away from that spiral. The one time I'd tried beer, it made me so sick I hadn't touched it since. Even now, just thinking about the taste of it made me queasy.

"You need to keep this close to the vest, Jolett," Caldwell warned, snapping me back to the present. "I'll help where I can, but this isn't going to be easy. You start poking around a football coach, especially one who's pushing steroids? You're going to find yourself on the wrong side of a lot of people."

I felt a wave of anger surge through me, but I kept my face neutral. "So you're telling me I won't get any support from the school if I take down their precious coach?"

"Not a chance," he said bluntly. "Not with football involved."

I left the meeting with Caldwell feeling like I was walking on hot coals. The more I thought about what he'd said, the angrier I got. I had more faith in people than Caldwell did—or at least I wanted to believe I did—but maybe he was right about the football culture here. Still, I couldn't let this go. I might have to play the long game and leave the steroids and marijuana for now, but the truth was going in my report. When I handed this case over to the county attorney's office, they'd be the ones dealing with the fallout. Not me.

My next stop was Sergeant Spence's office. I trusted the guys I worked with—well, most of them—but I knew better than to let the rumor mill get started. With the football coach involved, things could spiral fast, and I didn't want this blowing up in my face before I had solid evidence.

"What do you have for me, Laci?" Spence asked, motioning for me to take a seat as I entered.

I laid out everything I'd uncovered, from Caleb's intel to Caldwell's warnings. Spence listened carefully, his face unreadable as I spoke.

When I finished, he didn't hesitate. "Go for it," he said, his voice firm. "I don't like hearing that we have a drug problem at the school, especially not with steroids involved. Illegal drugs are illegal, no matter who's behind them."

Relief flooded through me. At least Spence wasn't part of the football fan club that would blindly protect their own. He also agreed that I needed to keep the investigation quiet until

I had more concrete proof. There was no point in stirring up trouble without something solid to back it up.

"I see you still have Bell's new friend," Spence added, glancing at Sugarplum as she poked her head out from her spot between Bell's legs. "I'm surprised she's still with you."

He wasn't the only one. The two dogs had become inseparable, acting like they'd been partners from day one. I didn't know whether to be amused or jealous. "Ed's getting out of the hospital soon, so I won't have to deal with the fluff mop for much longer," I said, though there was no denying that Sugarplum had grown on me. "She's been good for Bell. Or at least, Bell seems to think so."

Spence chuckled, patting Bell's head. "Bell's a good dog."

"The best," I agreed, feeling a swell of pride. Spence had been the one to order me to get a K9 partner in the first place. He probably had no idea how much it would change my life, but Bell had done more than just become my partner—she'd given me a reason to love my job again.

Back in my office, I cleared off my desk and started laying out the case with sticky notes. Each note held a name or a fact, and I began moving them around, connecting dots in a way that helped me visualize the bigger picture. I had a lot of people who knew something, but none of them were talking. The puzzle in front of me was still incomplete, but I was determined to make it work.

After a few minutes of studying the mess of notes, I picked up the phone and dialed Joshua's mother. She answered on the second ring, her voice sounding cautious but polite. "Hi, this is Detective Jolett. I wanted to follow up with you."

"Hello, Detective. How can I help?" Her tone was cooperative, and that was a good sign.

"As my investigation continues, a few things have come to light. I didn't ask before, but I need this kept quiet," I said, cringing a little as I heard the words leave my mouth. Asking for secrecy felt wrong, but necessary.

Her voice shifted, concern lacing her words. "Is my son in more trouble?"

"No, not legally," I assured her. "But I think it would be wise to have Joshua tested for steroids and marijuana."

There was a long pause on the other end of the line, and I imagined the gears turning in her head. When she finally spoke, her voice was heavy with resignation. "I'll call you as soon as I have the results. This is bad, isn't it?"

I felt a weight lift. "Yes, it's bad," I admitted. "And because of some of the people involved, it's important that Joshua keeps quiet about this. No talking to his friends."

"If my son tests positive for any of that, he won't have friends to talk to," she said firmly. "But I'll make sure he stays quiet regardless."

"Thank you," I said, relieved. "Is he back in school yet?"

"No, he returns on Monday."

After we hung up, I turned to see Bell stretched out with Sugarplum nestled comfortably against her belly. The sight made me smile, and I couldn't resist snapping another picture, texting it to Ed's phone. "I feel better now, girls," I said, watching as Bell thumped her tail and Sugarplum trotted over for her hourly dose of attention. "Let's let this case rest for a couple of days while I tie up some loose ends. Sound good?"

Bell's tail thumped harder, and Sugarplum, always eager for affection, happily rolled over for a belly rub. For the next two hours, I did exactly what I promised, tackling the various loose ends that had piled up. I had a homicide trial coming up in two months, though it was likely to be postponed again. Homicide cases always took forever to go to trial, and this one was no different.

Just as I was getting into the groove of reviewing audio testimony, my office phone rang. "Detective Jolett," I answered absentmindedly.

"You have a Ms. Camp on the line," the receptionist said. "She wants to speak with you about her son."

Mandy. I felt a jolt of anticipation. "Put her through," I said quickly.

There was a pause, followed by two clicks, and then Mandy's voice came through, trembling with barely contained emotion. "Hi, Detective Jolett."

I could hear the tears in her voice, and my gut tightened. "Hi, Mandy. What's going on?"

"Can you come to my house? Joshua needs to speak with you." Her voice broke on the last few words, and I knew this wasn't going to be an easy conversation.

"I'll be there in fifteen minutes," I said, already standing and grabbing my keys.

"Thank you," she whispered before hanging up.

I turned to Bell and Sugarplum, who both perked up at the change in my tone. "Looks like we might have a break in the case," I said, my voice laced with excitement. Bell yapped, catching my energy, and Sugarplum wagged her tail furiously, bouncing on her little legs. "Sorry, girls, you're staying here for this one," I added. Both dogs immediately deflated, but I softened the blow with the promise of a quick potty break before I left.

Chapter Thirty-One

JOSHUA'S LOOK OF DREAD greeted me the moment I stepped into their home. His eyes flickered to mine briefly before dropping to the floor, his shoulders hunched in a familiar posture of guilt and shame. I could tell this wasn't going to be easy for him.

"Hi, Joshua," I said evenly, trying to keep my tone neutral and non-threatening. The last thing I wanted was to make him clam up again.

"Detective Jolett," he muttered, barely audible, his voice tinged with a mixture of fear and regret. His head remained down, avoiding eye contact.

"We can all sit down, and Joshua will tell you what he knows," Mandy said, her voice calm but firm. She sat next to her son, placing a reassuring hand on his leg. "He came clean with me, and we didn't need a test. He's ready to talk."

I took the same chair as last time, settling into the familiar rhythm of the interview, though today felt different—heavier, more charged with the weight of what Joshua was about to admit. I could feel the tension in the room as Joshua gathered the courage to speak. Mandy gave him an encouraging squeeze, and I waited, letting the silence fill the space between us.

"I've been taking steroids for football," he finally confessed, his voice barely above a whisper. "But I haven't touched the marijuana." He lifted his head slightly, his face red with shame. "Most of the starting lineup is using steroids."

I took a deep breath, careful to keep my expression steady. His admission wasn't exactly a surprise, but it still hit hard knowing how deep the problem ran. "I know the last thing you need right now is another lecture, but I have to tell you a few things from my perspective as a police officer," I said, my tone soft but serious. "I've dealt with far too many domestic violence cases, and a lot of them start the same way—with steroids."

Joshua's eyes flickered with surprise, and I took that as a cue to continue. "Young guys start using them in high school for football, and it doesn't stop there. After graduation, it turns into a habit for some of them. The problem is, steroids don't just mess with your body—they mess with your mind. You start getting angry, aggressive, and that violence? It spills over into your family, your relationships. I've seen it turn into assault charges or worse." I paused, letting my words sink in. "My lecture's over now. I just wanted you to understand what you're playing with."

Joshua remained silent, his face crumpling as the tears began to fall. I glanced at Mandy, who gently wrapped her arms around her son. They shared a quick hug before she released him, and Joshua wiped at his face, finally looking up at me.

"Dayton Lanigan gets the steroids from his brother. He gets the marijuana from him too," Joshua said, his voice raw with emotion.

I nodded, taking it all in. Dayton Lanigan. That name was going to cause waves, but I wasn't surprised. I'd suspected as much. "Does Coach Lanigan know what's happening?"

Joshua shrugged, his body slumping further. "Everyone knows," he said, his voice low.

I leaned forward. "Everyone as in the school staff?"

"No," he shook his head quickly. "The guys on the team, the other coaches... They don't want to see it. As long as we keep it out of sight, we get a green light. Coach tells us to juice up over the summer for bulk, and we do."

The words hit hard. It was worse than I thought. "What about random drug testing? Doesn't the school require that?"

Joshua shook his head again, more firmly this time. "We don't have that here. Coach says we'll keep it that way as long as we keep our use under wraps."

My gut tightened. No random testing? That was news to me. I'd assumed all high school athletes were tested, at least randomly, to discourage this exact kind of thing. "How does Dayton get the drugs from his brother?"

Now that the truth was pouring out, it seemed easier for Joshua to talk. He glanced at his mom, then back at me, his voice gaining some strength. "Bo brings them up on the first Thursday of every month. He meets Dayton right after practice to do the handoff. But this month, he had to come up early, in the middle of the month, and that's when he brought the speed. He said it would give us a boost at practice." His voice shook with barely-contained anger. "I bought four pills, but I didn't want them anymore. That's when I gave three away. I never thought anyone would get hurt."

His tears came again, and I softened my tone, trying to reassure him. "The good news is Nick is doing better," I said gently. "I'll talk to the county attorney's office, and, I can't make promises, but you'll likely be off the hook, as long as you keep your nose clean. Make amends with your mother, and make sure your name doesn't come up in any more police reports."

Joshua nodded, his tears slowing, and I could see the relief in his eyes. He had been carrying this weight for a while, and letting it out was a first step toward healing. I also knew the county attorneys I worked with well enough to believe they'd go easy on him, especially given his cooperation. I'd make sure they knew about his hospital stay and emphasize that he came forward on his own. I could replace this interview with the first one in the report to give the impression Joshua was forthcoming from the start. It wasn't the first time I'd done something like this.

If the case went to trial, the defense would likely question why I didn't go after Joshua harder. But that kind of questioning usually backfired. Once I explained my reasoning—that I was after the bigger fish—the jury usually sympathized with my decisions. And Joshua wasn't the big fish here. Dayton and his brother Bo were.

"He starts counseling next week," Mandy said, breaking through my thoughts. "Our insurance will cover twenty sessions a year, and he's going to use every one of them."

I nodded approvingly. "That's going to look really good with the county attorney's office, Joshua. It shows that you're taking this seriously."

He nodded again, more resolutely this time.

"I need you to tell me everything about those Thursday nights when Bo brings the drugs into town," I said, pulling out my notepad. "Leave nothing out. Every detail matters."

Joshua went into more detail than before, outlining how the handoff took place and who was usually around. The more he talked, the clearer my plan became. Tomorrow was the last Thursday of the month, and Bo was due to bring another batch of drugs into town. I had about a week to prepare, and I wasn't going to waste a single second.

As I wrapped up my notes, a plan formed fully in my mind. I thanked Joshua for his honesty and Mandy for her support, then left their house, feeling the weight of responsibility settle firmly on my shoulders. This case was going to resolve itself soon, one way or another, and I was ready to see it through.

Back in the parking lot at the department, I barely had time to exit my car before my phone buzzed in my pocket. Caldwell's name flashed on the screen. I answered quickly.

"Jolett speaking."

"I think your pills have shown up in the county," Caldwell said, his voice serious. "We've got a dead druggie out here. I've been assigned to the case."

My heart sank. I'd hoped this wouldn't get worse. "Do you think the high schoolers were involved?"

"I don't know yet," he replied. "But this guy was bad news. It might be connected."

I took a deep breath, steadying myself. "Meet me at my office. I've got information you need, and I think I have a plan that could work."

"I'll be there in ten," Caldwell said, hanging up.

I quickly let Bell and Sugarplum out for a potty break, promising them a romp in the park once I'd finished with Caldwell. As soon as he arrived, we sat down to go over our respective cases. I laid out my plan, explaining how I intended to use the Thursday drug handoff to catch Bo and Dayton in the act. Caldwell was skeptical at first, but as I walked him through the details, I could see the gears turning in his mind.

"This could work," he finally said, though his tone was cautious. "It's risky, but it might just work."

With our plans set, Caldwell left to follow up on his lead, and I kept my promise to the dogs, taking them to the park for a well-earned break. I let Bell run on her long lead, tossing her favorite tug rope as far as it would go. Sugarplum, ever eager to be part of the action, chased after her with a pinecone in her mouth, perfectly happy with her little part of the game.

As I watched them play, my mind churned with ideas. A text notification buzzed on my phone, and when I read it, a smile tugged at my lips. My weekend plans had just been confirmed. For once, I had something to look forward to outside of work.

Chapter Thirty-Two

O N SATURDAY, I LOADED Bell and Sugarplum into the extended cab of my new truck. It was still a sore spot, trading in the old truck—but life changes, and I needed to adapt. Bell needed comfort, especially with how much we traveled, and the old truck without a backseat had been cramping her style. She'd made her feelings known by shedding enough dog hair to make a second dog in protest.

Now, Bell sprawled comfortably in the back seat, her head resting between the center console and the passenger seat, where Sugarplum perched, looking out the window like a queen surveying her kingdom. The little dog seemed to enjoy the ride, her nose twitching with every new scent that drifted in through the vents.

As we turned the last corner, Bell's excitement ramped up. She let out a soft whine, her tail thumping against the seat in anticipation. This was one of her favorite places, a home we visited every few months—Tina's house. Tina's husband had been my partner Suii's handler before me, and after he'd been killed in the line of duty, Suii had been removed from the family. It had broken their hearts, especially their two boys, Kyle and Daniel. I had reintroduced Suii into their lives, but that had been short-lived. Suii had died saving me, and though the wound still felt fresh, Bell had helped me carry on, and bringing her here seemed to lift the boys' spirits every time.

As we pulled up, Tina and the boys came out to greet us. Kyle, the oldest, was a spitting image of his father. His serious expression softened as soon as he saw Bell, and I could see the boy his mother described, the one who still grieved for Suii. Daniel, younger and shyer, had more of his mother in him, with a gentle demeanor and curious blue eyes. They both shared the same striking blue eyes as their dad—eyes that always hit me with a wave of bittersweet memories.

"Hey, you three!" Tina called as I opened the door. Bell bounded out, her tail wagging furiously. Sugarplum, ever the diva, hopped down gingerly, looking up at the boys with her big eyes. She didn't know it yet, but she was about to be doted on like royalty.

The boys immediately fell in love with her. "She's so small!" Daniel exclaimed, crouching down to pet her. "Can we play K9 with her?"

I smiled, knowing full well what they meant. Playing police K9 was their favorite pastime, a way to stay connected to their dad's legacy. Bell always played the hero, and I was sure Sugarplum, with her fluffy cuteness, would be cast as the villain. "Sure," I said. "She'll love it."

With that, the boys raced to the backyard, the dogs following close behind. Bell was already in her element, and Sugarplum, eager for attention, quickly adapted to her role in their game.

Tina and I sat on the porch, catching up while the boys entertained the dogs. "They're getting so big," I said, watching them play. "Seems like just yesterday they were little boys."

Tina smiled softly. "Yeah, time flies, doesn't it? I've been thinking... They're old enough now. Maybe it's time we got a dog of our own."

I raised an eyebrow, surprised. "Really?"

She nodded. "I wasn't sure when they were younger—it felt like too much responsibility. But now? I think they're ready. The problem is, I'm torn between getting a big dog, like Suii or Bell, or maybe going the small-dog route." She chuckled. "A small dog would eat less...and poop less."

I laughed with her. "That's a solid point. I can ask Jack to keep an eye out for a K9 that's not quite cut out for police work. They make great pets, and they're usually large dogs. If you want to go the smaller route, though, you're on your own."

Tina laughed again, shaking her head. "We'll see. Either way, it's time."

The afternoon passed easily, the warmth of the sun and the sound of the boys' laughter filling the yard. When it was time to leave, the boys were reluctant to let Sugarplum go.

"Will you bring her next time?" Kyle asked, his eyes pleading.

I smiled, knowing I couldn't promise that. "She'll be back with her owner by then. But you can come visit Bell anytime—and Sugarplum, too, if you're lucky." I glanced at Tina, and she gave me a nod. I knew Ed wouldn't mind them visiting once he was settled back home.

On the drive back, Bell sprawled out in the back seat, exhausted but content. Sugarplum, ever the princess, curled up in the passenger seat, her head resting on my arm as I drove. It had been a good day, the kind that reminded me of Suii and made me feel closer to him in a way I hadn't in a while.

Sunday was spent catching up on housework—laundry, cleaning, and trying to keep Bell from running off with my socks. With Ed still in the hospital due to a small complication, I figured Sugarplum would stay with me a little longer. I didn't mind. In fact, I had grown quite attached to the little fluff ball. But I knew Bell needed her K9 training soon, and the presence of Sugarplum made that difficult. I hadn't realized how much of a distraction she'd become for both of us. I couldn't afford to slack on Bell's training; if we ended up in a serious situation and she didn't perform, her K9 book would be scrutinized. I didn't want to be explaining to a defense attorney why we'd missed aggression trials or sniff tests.

By Monday, I was back at my desk, organizing the case and making phone calls. The warrants were in hand, and everything was lining up perfectly. I could feel the case building toward its conclusion, and I was ready to see it through.

Later in the week, I touched base with Caldwell after getting the warrants signed by the judge. "I've got the warrants," I told him. "We're set for Thursday."

"Great," he replied. "I'll be there in plain clothes. Got the overtime squared with my supervisor."

"You're lucky," I muttered. "I had to flex time. Our budget's running low again." We always hit the same problem at the end of the fiscal year, trying to stretch funds. I didn't mind too much—I had taken a half-day to rest up for the operation.

Thursday finally arrived, and as I waited near the high school field, I watched Bo Lanigan's vehicle pull into the lot. The timing was perfect. Practice was still going on, and I had Leo stationed nearby as backup. Caldwell was in position, and the stage was set. I texted Caldwell to let him know Bo had arrived, and I settled into my hiding spot, Sugarplum in tow.

Once practice ended, Bo made his move, meeting Dayton outside the locker room for the handoff. It was subtle, but I caught it. My heart raced, but I stayed calm, stepping out of the shadows with Sugarplum at my side.

"Hey, guys," I called out as I approached. Both brothers froze, their heads snapping toward me. "I came to talk to your dad. Is he around?"

I casually crinkled the treat bag in my pocket, and Sugarplum, ever the eager beaver, sat down obediently, waiting for her cue. Her whine was perfectly timed, and I allowed myself a small smirk. "That's odd," I said, furrowing my brow. "Looks like my drug dog has alerted."

The brothers stiffened, glancing at each other nervously. I could hear the coaches approaching from the field, and I knew I had to act fast. Using my finger, I drew an imaginary line up Dayton's leg, pretending Sugarplum was following the scent. When I reached the waistband of his pants, Sugarplum let out a frustrated bark.

"What's going on here?" Coach Lanigan's voice boomed from behind me.

I turned, feigning confusion. "Not sure," I said. "I came to talk about last week's overdoses, but my dog's alerted on your son. I find that...strange." I let the implication hang in the air.

Coach Lanigan's eyes darted left and right, clearly searching for an escape. He towered over me, his broad frame imposing, but I held my ground. "I think you should search your son," I said firmly. "My dog doesn't alert unless there's a reason."

He stepped closer, using his height to intimidate, but I wasn't fazed. Before he could respond, Principal Leland arrived, stepping between us.

"I'm making a formal request that you search the student," I said, addressing the principal directly. Kids didn't have privacy rights on campus, and school administrators could search them anytime. It was a loophole I intended to exploit.

"This is ridiculous," Coach Lanigan growled, but I could see the panic in his eyes.

Dayton, clearly distressed, looked to his father for help, but the coach's response sealed their fate. "Keep your mouth shut," he snapped. "I'll get a lawyer."

Thank you, Coach, I thought. You've just confirmed everything.

Bo turned and took off running. I didn't even give him a second look as he disappeared. Principal Leland, reluctant but knowing his duty, stepped forward to search Dayton. The boy, realizing he was cornered, pulled the package from his waistband and handed it over with a glare.

Inside the bag were vials—not pills like I expected, but injectable steroids. My stomach churned. They were shooting it.

"Dayton Lanigan, you're under arrest," I said, snapping the cuffs onto his wrists. As I read him his rights, I felt a strange sense of satisfaction. It wasn't about punishing a kid—it was about justice. Dayton would get off lightly as a juvenile, but at least there would be consequences.

As for Bo, his attempt to flee had been short-lived. Leo had taken him down around the corner, and now he was being led back, handcuffed and defeated.

"You can't do this," Coach Lanigan said, his red face going purple.

"Actually, I can," I told him and gave a nod to Calwell who had just arrived. "Mr. Lanigan, you are under arrest for distribution of narcotics to minors."

"That's bull—,"

I held up my hand, cutting him off. "Think about what you say next. Everything can be used against you in a court of law."

Caldwell took Coach Lanigan into custody and the reality of the situation finally seemed to hit him as his rights were read. His face went bloodless, and for a moment, I thought he might have a heart attack right there on the field.

It was a textbook bust. The look of disbelief on the coach's face as Caldwell walked him away was priceless. His arrogance, his belief that the rules didn't apply to him, had finally caught up with him.

After the dust settled, I took Dayton to juvenile detention, walking him through the cold, echoing halls. He kept his head down, his earlier bravado replaced by quiet tears.

"I know this is scary," I told him as we entered the booking area. "But the officers here will treat you fairly. It's up to you to give them the same respect."

He didn't respond, but his tears dried up by the time we arrived at the intake desk. I watched as the process unfolded, my mind already racing through the next steps of the case.

When I finally got back to my car, Sugarplum greeted me with an excited bark. For a moment, I let myself smile, grateful for the small reprieve she offered.

The case wasn't over yet, but we had taken a major step forward. As I drove back to the station, I sent quick texts to Franks and Caldwell, confirming that Bo and the coach had been processed smoothly. Then, as promised, I took the dogs for a celebration.

We hit the local fast-food joint, and I ordered three soft-serve cones. Sugarplum, lacking all manners, started licking the cones the second I set them down in the car. I shot her a mock glare. "No patience," I muttered, but I couldn't help laughing.

At the park, I let Bell and Sugarplum off their leashes, watching as they danced around excitedly. I placed Sugarplum's cone in the grass, knowing full well it would probably lead to some unfortunate consequences later, but I didn't care.

"Good girl," I told Bell as I handed her the cone. She devoured it in one gulp, barely chewing. I had no idea how she avoided brain freeze.

As I ate my own cone, savoring the small victory of the day, I realized how good it felt to celebrate, even in the little moments.

Bell and Sugarplum seemed to agree.

Chapter Thirty-Three

DAYTON WAS RELEASED INTO the custody of his mother the following day. Bo and Coach Lanigan posted bond and were also released, but the weight of the charges hung heavily over them all. They wouldn't be able to escape the consequences of their actions this time. The gears of justice had already started turning, and I intended to see this through.

I dropped my report at the county attorney's office and sat down to review the specifics with Samantha Anderson, the prosecuting attorney assigned to the case. Samantha was sharp, no-nonsense, and one of the few lawyers I trusted to handle delicate situations like this. As we went through my findings, I could tell she was satisfied. "You've got a solid case here," she said, flipping through the documents. "We'll keep you updated, but there's still more to be done."

I nodded. There were always loose ends to tie up, follow-ups to conduct. That's how cases worked—never truly over until they were airtight. Samantha thanked me again before I left her office, and I felt a sense of accomplishment. But the work wasn't over.

Officer Caldwell was deep into his own investigation, trying to make his case just as strong. He was chasing every lead, working every angle, trying to connect Bo and the coach to his dead druggie. I knew it would be a tough link to establish; with street drugs, even from the same supplier, chemical compositions could vary enough to muddy the waters. If the pills from the teen overdose matched those from the county victim, it could help strengthen both our cases.

My meeting with Principal Leland went about as expected. He'd had time to recover from the shock of the arrests, but his confusion had turned into questions—mostly about why I hadn't looped him in before making the bust.

"Principal Leland," I said, keeping my tone firm but respectful, "with all due respect, my investigation uncovered long-term drug use by members of your football team." I watched him cringe at the words but pressed on. "I didn't know how deep the corruption went, and I'm a detective. My job is to keep people safe. I don't care about last names, who sits on city council, or who's a football God. I protect this town, and I'll do it to the best of my ability."

He flinched but didn't argue after that. By the time I left his office, I was confident I wouldn't be receiving a complaint from the school. Still, I could feel the ripple effects of the arrests, especially as Friday night approached. The game went on, but not without changes. The team had lost its head coach and a starting player. Dayton faced mandatory suspension for possession of drugs on campus, and even if he managed to avoid further juvenile detention, his future at school was looking bleak.

I contacted Nick's parents, but they still weren't willing to let him talk to me. I let it go. His testimony shouldn't be necessary at this point, though the defense might try to muddy the waters by pointing out that Joshua gave Nick the pill. We'd cross that bridge if we came to it. Joshua had since revealed that Nick had been present when the money changed hands. Apparently, the only reason Nick didn't buy his own was because he'd lost his allowance that week. I relayed this to

Nick's parents, letting them know the full extent of their son's involvement, and left it at that.

All in all, I was satisfied with the case's progress so far.

On Saturday morning, Bell and I had one of our long talks. "I know you deserve to visit Ed too, girl, but you're just too big for me to sneak into the hospital," I explained, scratching behind her ears. Bell let out a soft bark of understanding, though I could tell she wasn't happy about it. "If you're good, I'll buy you a hamburger as a treat," I added, knowing full well that burgers gave Bell terrible gas. Still, sometimes a girl needed a little indulgence, and Bell had more than earned it.

She gave me a look, as if to say, *I'll hold you to that,* and then padded over to her bed with an air of forgiveness. Leaving Bell behind had never bothered me too much before, but now, the idea of taking Sugarplum and leaving Bell behind felt wrong. Maybe it was another reason K9s should live in single-dog homes.

I used a small backpack to sneak Sugarplum into Ed's hospital room. The little fluff ball wasn't exactly cooperative—she squirmed and whined the whole way there, making the whole covert operation a little more complicated than it should have been. But I walked with purpose down the hallways, ignoring the curious glances, and somehow, no one stopped me.

Ed's eyes fluttered open when I entered his room, a sleepy but welcoming smile spreading across his face. "Detective Jolett," he greeted me.

"You know it's Laci," I reminded him for what felt like the millionth time. I walked over and squeezed his hand. He looked older, more fragile than the last time I'd seen him. The heart attack had taken a toll, and I hoped he would pull through without lasting damage.

His eyebrows shot up in surprise when Sugarplum let out a tiny yip, announcing her presence. I pulled her from the backpack and placed her into Ed's arms. His face lit up, and for a moment, he looked like his old self again, all the years melting away as he hugged the excited little dog. I stood back, watching as Sugarplum wriggled happily in his arms, her tail wagging like crazy.

"You brought my girl," Ed said, his voice thick with emotion. He held Sugarplum tightly, tears forming in his eyes as he cuddled her close.

"I figured you could use the company," I said, smiling. "She's been a handful, but Bell and I have managed."

Ed laughed, his face crinkling with genuine joy. "I can't believe you taught her to be a drug dog in forty-five minutes."

I shook my head, grinning. "No, I taught her to whine for a treat in forty-five minutes. There's a difference." I winked. "But hey, you never know—she might need her own badge one day."

Ed laughed harder, hugging Sugarplum closer until she squirmed for freedom. He loosened his grip, letting her settle into the crook of his arm where she promptly closed her eyes, content to nap after her little adventure.

"They should let me out of here in a day or two," Ed said, his voice softer now. "Have you been in touch with Maggie?"

"We've texted a few times," I replied. "She's been a good daughter, staying by your side. I haven't been the best neighbor lately, with this case keeping me busy, but she's got everything under control."

Ed nodded, his eyes growing misty again as he looked down at Sugarplum. "She's a good kid. Always has been."

I couldn't help but smile. Maggie was in her late thirties—hardly a kid—but I understood the sentiment. "She got here quickly, which is what matters. You gave us all a scare, Ed."

He reached over and patted my hand, his grip weaker than I remembered. "I owe you, Laci," he said, his voice filled with warmth. "If it weren't for you, I might not be here."

I hadn't really thought about it that way, but I told him about the night of his heart attack and how Sugarplum had saved him. He held the little dog closer when I finished the story, shaking his head in disbelief.

"To think this little ball of fluff saved me," he murmured. "I was too old when I got her, but I needed the company."

"You weren't too old," I assured him, though I could hear the unspoken worry in his voice.

He sighed deeply. "She'll outlive me, Laci. That's the hardest part. I don't want her neglected when I'm gone."

I gave his hand a reassuring squeeze. "Don't worry, Ed. If it comes to that, Sugarplum will be part of my family. Bell's already attached to her, and separating them now wouldn't be easy."

Tears filled Ed's eyes again, but this time they were tears of gratitude. "Thank you," he whispered, his voice thick with emotion. "That means everything to me."

I understood. With Bell, I had peace of mind knowing she'd end up with Jack if something happened to me. It was a comfort knowing your best friend would be taken care of. And despite Sugarplum's yapping and fluffiness, I'd grown fond of her. She'd wormed her way into my heart just like Bell and Suii had. Maybe, one day, I'd even call myself a dog lover.

****

Later that night, I had a long conversation with Maggie, Ed's daughter. She sounded exhausted but grateful for my help. "We've been trying to get Dad to move in with us for years," she confessed. "But he won't give up Sugarplum, and our rescue dog doesn't tolerate other dogs. It's been a constant struggle."

I chuckled softly. "Stubborn man," I said. "But I understand. She means a lot to him."

Maggie sighed. "She does. I just hope one day he'll agree to move in with us. Thank you again for everything."

"You don't need to thank me," I replied. "Ed's a good man. I'm just glad I could help."

We said our goodbyes, and I hung up the phone, feeling a quiet sense of peace. All in all, it had been a nice and quiet weekend, and after the chaos of the case, I was grateful for it.

Chapter Thirty-Four

E D WAS RELEASED FROM the hospital on Tuesday, and by Friday, his daughter Maggie had headed back home. I made it a point to check on Ed throughout the week, making sure he was adjusting to life after his health scare. Our nightly sit-downs had become a comforting routine, with Bell and Sugarplum happily playing while we chatted. It felt like we were all in this together—two old friends and our dogs, sharing the weight of life's changes.

Bell seemed to handle Sugarplum's move back to Ed's place without any issues. It was as if she understood that her role as caretaker was over, and now they could just be friends, no responsibilities attached. I envied her ability to let go so easily.

One evening, as the sun set, casting a soft glow over Ed's small yard, he sighed heavily. "I miss my daughter," he said quietly, his gaze distant.

I nodded, knowing how much he cared for Maggie. "She misses you too, Ed. She told me they'd love for you to move in with them."

His eyes shifted to Sugarplum, who was curled up on his lap. "Did she tell you they already have a dog? And that Sugarplum wouldn't be able to come with me?"

I nodded again, feeling the weight of his words.

He scooped up Sugarplum, holding her close to his chest, as if trying to draw strength from her small, furry body. "I think the two of us are meant to spend my final years together," he whispered, his voice thick with emotion.

I left his place that night with a heavy heart. Ed's love for Sugarplum ran deep, but so did his love for his daughter and grandchildren. He was torn, stuck between two loves, and I couldn't help but feel the weight of that. Sugarplum wasn't just a dog; she was family. She gave Ed love, and in return, she received it tenfold. It was a bond that went beyond simple companionship—something I understood all too well with Bell by my side.

****

The high school drug case finally came to a close after another two weeks. The county attorney decided not to charge Joshua, which was a relief. Nick and Delaney's parents played a big part in that decision, not wanting to see Joshua punished for what had essentially been a foolish teenage mistake. Joshua was suspended from school for three days, a lenient sentence considering the circumstances. His time in the hospital had likely factored into the decision. Mandy was overjoyed, and I hoped this experience taught Joshua a valuable lesson—that the police could be trusted and that actions had consequences. More than that, I hoped it scared him straight enough to avoid making any more stupid decisions.

Coach Lanigan, on the other hand, wasn't as lucky. He was fired from the school, and both he and his sons took a plea deal before quietly leaving town. Caldwell and I had hoped to tie the pills to the drug death in the county, but that connection never materialized. It was a long shot from the start, but that's the nature of police work. Sometimes, you follow every lead, and it just doesn't pan out.

A friend in probation told me that the judge agreed to let the Lanigans serve their sentence and probation in another county. I felt a sense of relief knowing they wouldn't be lingering around the high school or town. It was the best outcome for everyone involved. With a criminal record, Coach Lanigan wouldn't be teaching again. I could only hope that this experience would serve as a powerful lesson for the entire family. Slim chance, but I still had to hope.

Over the next two months, my nightly visits with Ed continued. I could see him slowing down, his energy waning with each passing day. It was hard to watch, knowing that time was catching up with him. He said he felt fine, just a bit more tired than usual, but I knew there was more to it. The spark that once lit up his eyes had dimmed.

One evening, he finally admitted the truth. "I think it's time," he said softly, his voice barely above a whisper. "I want to be with my family before it's too late."

His words hit me like a ton of bricks. I had seen this coming, but hearing him say it out loud made it real. I wanted Ed to be happy, and I wanted Sugarplum to be happy too, but I wasn't sure how to make that work.

It took two weeks to finalize everything. Ed's condo sold quickly, within a week of being listed, and the day came when I had to drive him to the airport. Watching him say goodbye to Sugarplum was one of the hardest things I'd ever witnessed. His old hands trembled as he held her close, whispering words of love and reassurance. Sugarplum, in her innocent way, didn't understand what was happening. She whimpered softly, licking his face as if trying to comfort him.

I stood back, giving them their moment, but my own heart ached. I knew this was the right decision—Ed needed to be with his daughter and grandchildren—but it didn't make it any easier. I would miss Ed, and I knew he would miss Sugarplum terribly.

That night, after I brought Sugarplum home with me, she whimpered softly in her sleep, curled up on her pillow. Bell, sensing her sadness, scooted closer, pressing her warm body against Sugarplum's tiny form. They slept like that all night, side by side. It was a small comfort, but it eased the ache in my heart just a little.

The next morning, I loaded both dogs into my truck. I had already made arrangements with Tina and the boys, and I knew they were eager to welcome Sugarplum into their family. When I pulled up to their house, the boys came racing out, their faces lit up with excitement. Bell and Sugarplum jumped from the truck, and soon enough, chaos ensued. The boys had Sugarplum in their arms, Bell was running circles around them, and the whole scene brought a smile to my face.

Tina and I sat on the porch, watching the kids and dogs play. It felt good to see Sugarplum so happy, to know she was going to be loved and cared for. When the boys finally took a break, Kyle came running over, squeezing Sugarplum to his chest.

"We really get to keep her?" he asked, his eyes wide with hope.

I smiled, my heart full. "She's yours," I said, my voice steady. "She'll be your forever friend, and she'll always love you."

Daniel, not wanting to be left out, chimed in. "Me too?"

"Yes, you too," I assured him, ruffling his hair.

This was the solution Ed had needed to find peace with moving to his daughter's house. Though he'd never met Tina or the boys, he knew Suii's connection to them, and he knew Sugarplum would be in good hands. I promised him that if there were ever any issues, Sugarplum could always come back to me and Bell. It wasn't an easy decision for him, but it was the right one—for everyone involved.

Before I left, I took videos and pictures of Sugarplum playing with the boys, sending them to Ed so he could see how happy she was. I also gave Tina his number so she could continue sending him updates. It wasn't much, but I knew it would bring him some comfort.

As I drove away, I couldn't stop the tears that welled up in my eyes. Bell, ever the empath, whined softly from the back seat and rested her head on the console, her large brown eyes watching me.

"I know, girl," I said, reaching over to pat her head. "We'll visit. Sugarplum has a great life ahead of her, and we've still got cases to solve."

"Woof," she responded, her tail thumping against the seat.

I smiled, feeling a sense of closure. The gift of having Suii in my life had come full circle with Sugarplum. Each dog, in their own way, had left paw prints on my heart, and I realized, more than ever, that a K9's love was forever.

Chapter Thirty-Five

Part IV

I HEARD BELL GROWLING from the back patio again, and I decided that maybe losing my mind wasn't just an option—it was the *perfect* option. The past two weeks, following what had been a blissfully quiet vacation of doing, well, pretty much nothing, had turned into a whirlwind of chaos. Between work piling up and the persistent drama involving Bell and the back patio, it was enough to make anyone snap.

With a heavy sigh, I closed my eyes, rubbing my temples in a futile attempt to fend off the pounding headache that seemed to be lurking just out of reach. I inhaled deeply, willing calm into my frazzled nerves, but when I opened them again, the sharp growls and occasional high-pitched barks still pierced the air, setting my teeth on edge.

"God help me," I muttered under my breath as I walked toward the back door. This had to stop.

Pushing the door open, I was met with the exact sight I'd expected, though it didn't make the situation any less infuriating.

Bell's new personal demon was perched on top of the block wall we shared with our new neighbors, staring down at her with an air of superiority that only a cat could muster. His orange fur gleamed in the morning light, and his tail flicked lazily, as if taunting her, daring her to make a move.

"Bell, no," I called out, trying to inject some firmness into my voice. But my trusted K9 didn't even glance my way. She was laser-focused on the creature sitting smugly on top of the wall, her muscles tensed and ready to spring, her growls intensifying with every second that passed.

And there he was—Rat Cat, in all his arrogant, king-like glory. He licked his paws, completely unfazed by the menace that Bell promised him.

I'd dubbed him Rat Cat because it somehow made me feel better. It was a small, childish victory. But Bell? She hadn't bought into the nickname, not fully. I had the feeling she simply called him Dinner. Her patience with the smug feline was nonexistent, and I could hardly blame her.

Rat Cat had shown up in our lives with the new neighbors from Virginia, who had moved into Ed's old condo. And maybe—just *maybe*—it was the fact that the cat had a Southern twang in its strangled meow that rubbed me the wrong way. Not that I minded a Southern drawl. On the contrary, I actually found it charming—when it came from humans, at least. But from a cat? The incongruity made it unbearable.

The orange furball had no idea how close he was to becoming a delightful snack. Or maybe he did, and that was part of the fun for him. He knew full well that I'd hide the evidence of his demise in a heartbeat if Bell ever got her paws on him. Over the years, dogs had wormed their way into my heart, turning me into a K9-loving fool. But cats? Cats were just evil incarnate, walking around with their noses in the air, like they were better than the rest of us. On this, Bell and I were in total agreement.

"Come on, Bell. He won't leave until you do," I said, exasperated. This had become our daily ritual—our little morning and evening nightmare.

Bell glanced at me, just for a second, before snapping her gaze back to Rat Cat, as if she couldn't afford to look away for too long. It was a battle of wills, neither of them willing to back down.

For weeks now, the same scene had played out. Bell would run out through the dog door to do her business, only to find Rat Cat waiting for her like some kind of gatekeeper. The moment he spotted her, he'd arch his back, all puffed up and menacing, throwing out a hiss or two for good measure. Bell, like clockwork, would respond with a growl. And that's when the show really started—Rat Cat would sit down, nonchalantly lick his paws, and let Bell know, in no uncertain terms, that he wasn't scared of her.

It was almost painful to watch.

Each time, Bell fell for it, her growls growing louder, her body rigid with the promise of pending menace. And Rat Cat? He reveled in it. The more Bell barked, the more he basked in her frustration, savoring every second of the power he held over her. It was beyond pathetic.

"Bell, it's time to go to work," I said, this time using my *command* voice—the one that meant business. As with every other morning, it finally snapped her out of her trance. She gave one last, solid bark in Rat Cat's direction, but this time, it was half-hearted. She knew the game was over. For now.

Rat Cat, on the other hand, took his time. He stretched luxuriously, tail flicking in triumph, then strolled along the length of the wall before disappearing into his own yard.

"Rat Cat twenty-two, Bell zero," I muttered, shaking my head.

Bell, ever the professional, wagged her tail like none of it mattered. I couldn't help but smile as I strapped her into her K9 vest. With the last piece of Velcro in place, the change was immediate. Her playful stubbornness vanished, replaced by the focused, disciplined dog I trusted with my life. Her eyes told me she was ready—ready to protect, to serve, to do whatever the day demanded of her.

I knelt down, giving her chin a gentle scratch. "Rat Cat is beneath you," I said softly. "His tiny little skull can't hold a brain big enough to make him worth your time. If you keep barking and growling at him, you'll just keep getting the same outcome. And that's embarrassing, Bell. He *enjoys* watching you lose. The only way to beat him is to ignore him. Trust me."

It was wishful thinking, I knew that. The truth was, Rat Cat wasn't going anywhere. But I liked to fantasize about a world where maybe, just *maybe*, he'd run into traffic one day and solve the problem for us.

Bad detective, I chastised myself.

Bell, of course, had no interest in my musings. She ignored my attempt at wisdom and trotted toward the front door, eager to get the day started. I clipped my gun and badge to my belt, then followed her to the car.

It was a bright, sunny morning, the air carrying the faintest hint of fall. The kind of day where the light was still warm, but you could feel the promise of cooler weather lurking just beneath the surface. I preferred the heat of summer—always had. Bell, naturally, loved the cold. Her thick coat was made for it. But weather wasn't something we had a say in. We took what we got.

Bell jumped into the back of the SUV as I opened the hatch. With that, we were officially on duty. Detective Jolett, homicide division, and her faithful K9 partner, Bell.

Unfortunately, today's case wasn't a homicide. Far from it, actually.

I strapped into the driver's seat, glancing over at Bell in the rearview mirror. She was already in full work mode, eyes scanning the streets even as we pulled out of the driveway. My current assignment? Gathering town gossip to help solve what was essentially a glorified property crime. Hardly thrilling, but it paid the bills. At least I had the distraction from the usual tedium of petty crime.

The case wasn't mine, originally. One of our property crimes detectives had taken paternity leave for his first child, and in a department as small as ours, reassignments happened fast. I wasn't thrilled about it—homicide was my bread and butter—but the paycheck still came every week, so I couldn't exactly complain.

My last big case had been a high-profile drug crime involving high school students—an age group I wasn't particularly fond of. This current case couldn't have been further from that. Apprehending a window shooter wasn't the worst assignment, but it didn't exactly get my blood pumping. If I was lucky, it'd be wrapped up soon, and I'd be back to doing what I did best—solving murders. If all the killings expected over the next few months could happen at once, that would suit me just fine.

I smiled at the dark thought, even though I shouldn't.

My main objective today was to find someone to rat out a friend. Someone who knew about the incident, about the person who'd shot up the window at Lucky Gas and Wash. It was a long shot, but fresh ideas were running thin, so stirring the local gossip mill seemed like the next logical step. Preferably without any threats of bodily harm, though I wasn't making any promises.

I chuckled softly as I drove, my fingers tapping rhythmically on the steering wheel. My sense of humor, I often thought, was wasted on today's world. I would've made a great detective in the mob days of the '40s and '50s. "Someone messes with me, I'm gonna mess with them, right, Bell?" I said in my best Al Capone voice.

Bell let out a bark from the backseat, and I couldn't help but laugh. She'd seen *The Untouchables* as many times as I had, and I liked to think she knew all the one-liners too, though she was much more modest about it.

The number one place in town to get the juiciest gossip wasn't where most people would think. It wasn't the beauty salon or the local diner. Nope—if you wanted to know what was really happening, you had to find the old men. Middle-aged women had nothing on a group of retired men when it came to gossip. The mob movies got it right: old men knew everything.

So where did you find old men at this time of morning? That was easy. Lucky Gas and Wash—known to the locals as Lucky's—had the cheapest coffee in town, and every morning, like clockwork, the gray-haired crowd would gather outside, shooting the breeze and sharing whatever morsels of information they'd gathered. Lucky's was also ground zero for my current case.

A week ago, the owner had raised the price of coffee by a quarter. Even with the increase, Lucky's still undercut the other shops in town, but it had clearly ruffled some feathers. Twenty-four hours after the price hike, someone had shot the front window with a .22 caliber bullet, aiming dead center at the sign announcing the new price. It didn't take a detective to see that was a clue.

No one had been in the store at the time, but the shooter couldn't have been certain of that, which made the incident serious enough to warrant attention. But there were no leads—just a single bullet hole and a lot of questions.

I pulled into the gas station and found a parking spot in the dusty lot. The place wasn't much to look at—just a grayish storefront with a recently replaced window—but it had that small-town charm that felt like it belonged in a postcard. A large U.S. flag waved proudly from a fifty-foot pole, and the four gas pumps out front had seen better days. Still, it beat the other station in town, which was a soulless corporate chain.

Lucky also had a drive-through car wash, which, in the eyes of the department, was a godsend. The police chief had struck up a deal with the owner, and we could run our vehicles through the wash anytime, free of charge. Before that, we'd had to deal with city council complaints about how our cars weren't as clean as the fire department's. Because, clearly, we didn't have enough on our plates already.

I still remembered how the councilmen had squabbled over the issue, oblivious to the fact that if officers had time to polish their cars to a shine, we'd probably need fewer officers on the streets in the first place. But I'd kept my mouth shut, like a good public servant.

I should mention, we did have another gas station in town, a giant chain with twenty-four pumps, but no local in their right mind would be caught dead there. The place was a tourist trap—TT, as we liked to call it. It sold overpriced souvenirs and everything else you'd expect from an out-of-state corporation that didn't understand the town. The tourists were their main customers, and we were more than happy to leave them to it.

As I stepped out of the SUV, I noticed the group of old men standing on the pavement, huddled together in their usual fashion, talking in low voices. One of them, a man in a frayed denim jacket, spotted me first.

"Good morning, Detective," he called out, his raspy voice cutting through the murmur of conversation.

"Good morning, gentlemen," I replied, offering a smile. The group of them—wrinkled, gray-haired, most with clothing that hadn't seen an iron in decades—murmured greetings in return, their eyes flicking toward me warily. These were the kind of men who avoided their wives until a respectable hour in the morning. If they were lucky, they'd make it past lunchtime before going home.

I glanced around at the lot, taking in the scene before zeroing in on the real reason I was there.

"I was hoping to talk to one of the clerks inside about what happened a few nights ago," I said, making my voice as casual as possible. I watched their expressions closely—each man's eyes darting away, down at the ground, shuffling their feet like schoolboys caught sneaking a cigarette. Exactly the reaction I'd been hoping for.

"Shooting a gun into a building, even when it's closed, is a felony," I added, giving my words weight. "And I plan to prosecute to the fullest."

They didn't catch the fact that I didn't actually prosecute cases—that was the county attorney's job. But they weren't focused on my words so much as the uncomfortable reality of standing face-to-face with a cop who wanted answers. They all had the same look, the one that said they'd rather be anywhere but here.

Finally, one of them—Leroy, if I remembered correctly—spoke up. He was a regular complainer, known for calling in about loud music, unruly teenagers, and other minor irritations. He squinted up at me, revealing the gap where an eyetooth should've been. His hair was an unconvincing comb-over that had seen better days.

"I heard it was a high school rival," he volunteered. "You know, kids from the other football team. Seems like a juvenile thing to do."

I smirked. Leroy had just given himself away. His attempt to pawn the crime off on high schoolers only made me more suspicious of him. His name had already been on my list of suspects, and now it was creeping higher.

"That's a good observation," I said slowly, making sure to speak loudly enough for their selective hearing to catch every word. "But the bullet hit dead center in the sign announcing the coffee price increase. And don't forget the threatening letter the next day."

The note had been brief, just a few hastily written lines: *Your coffee doesn't taste good enough to be priced so high. Change it, or else.* On its own, it wasn't much of a threat. But when paired with the bullet hole, it was a little harder to ignore.

Jeb Garland, one of the scruffiest members of the group, spoke next. I knew Jeb too well—he was notorious for flirting with every woman in town, regardless of age or marital status. His gut hung over his belt, and his personal hygiene was always questionable at best.

"Probably a disgruntled customer," Jeb grumbled, giving me a slow, lecherous once-over before quickly averting his eyes.

I took a deep breath, trying to keep my composure. Don't lose it, Jolett, I reminded myself. Not yet, anyway.

"I'm glad you think so," I said, my voice calm but firm. "And I've got a lead. I'll be speaking with the clerk soon. Enjoy your coffee, gentlemen."

I turned on my heel and made my way back to the SUV, but just as my hand closed around the door handle, I heard it.

A loud whistle cut through the air—the unmistakable sound of a catcall.

I froze, heat rising up the back of my neck. Every. Damn. Time.

I knew better than to engage, knew I should just let it go, but I couldn't. Not today. I'd had enough.

Without a word, I walked around to the back of the vehicle, opened the hatch, and clipped Bell's leash onto her collar. She leapt out, her posture alert, ready for whatever came next.

"It's time to work," I said softly, my voice barely audible over the rush of blood in my ears.

Bell stayed by my side as we approached the group of men again. I stopped just a few feet away, and without turning my head, I spoke in a calm, measured tone.

"I think you all know Bell."

The effect was immediate. The men stiffened, their gazes locked on the K9 at my side. They knew full well what she was capable of, and none of them wanted to find out firsthand.

"Hold," I commanded. Bell sat obediently at my feet, her eyes trained on the group, ears twitching as she picked up on the subtle sounds of nervous shuffling.

I stepped closer to Jeb, the smell of stale sweat and cheap cologne assaulting my senses. I'd intended to get right up in his face, but his protruding gut made that impossible.

"Would you like to whistle again?" I asked, my voice low and dangerous.

Jeb's eyes dropped to the ground, his confidence evaporating. "Most women take it as a sign of respect," he mumbled. "All I was saying is, you're hot."

I didn't even have to think about my reply. "Hot is something that will burn you," I said, my tone icy. "And Bell's not holding position to protect me. She's here so your friends don't leave before I'm done with you. I'm standing in front of you because you think an obscene whistle is a compliment. Bell's a female, and she has better taste than I do. Why don't you try whistling at her and see how that goes for you?"

One of the other men snickered, and Jeb shot him a dirty look before turning back to me, his face flushed. "You made your point," he muttered.

I took a step back, allowing myself a small, satisfied smile. Oh, no. Not yet.

"Actually, I haven't," I continued. "If another woman files a complaint about you, I'll charge you with harassment. Maybe the charge won't stick, but it'll cost you time, and probably money for a lawyer. And here's the kicker—I'll be paid for every minute I spend in court." I leaned in slightly, just enough to make him uncomfortable. "So, unless you want to spend your golden years in a courtroom, I suggest you keep your mouth shut."

"Bell, release." I slapped my thigh, and she followed me as I walked away without saying another word.

As we drove away, my phone rang, and I glanced at the screen—Gabe Macky, the department's senior homicide detective.

"Jolett, your friendly detective to the rescue," I answered, putting the call on speaker.

"I thought *you* were the one who needed rescuing?" Gabe's voice crackled through the speaker, a hint of amusement in his tone.

"Only from catcalls and devil cats," I replied dryly. Gabe knew all about my ongoing battle with Rat Cat.

He laughed. "Well, lucky for you, I've got a case that might get you out of property crimes purgatory. Sergeant Spence cleared you to take it. He's impressed you haven't had a single complaint."

I snorted. That could change by lunchtime.

"I might have pushed my luck this morning," I admitted, smiling to myself as I thought of my run-in with Jeb. "I put Jeb Garland in his place, and I did it in front of his cronies."

Gabe groaned. "You're playing with fire. But hey, I've got your back. If you can get out of your current assignment, I'll even cook your favorite meal."

The tension I'd been carrying around for the past few days eased a little. "Sounds like a plan. What've you got for me?"

"I'll send you the details, but it's a fresh case, and you're the best legwork detective we've got."

"I'm flattered," I said, though my mind was already racing with the possibilities.

"Just call the hospital as soon as you can. Victim's name is in the file."

"Got it," I said, scribbling down the details.

As I pulled into the police department parking lot, I glanced in the rearview mirror at Bell.

"We're off the hook," I said, smiling. "No need to take a bite out of any old men today."

She barked once, her tail wagging in agreement.

Chapter Thirty-Six

After getting situated in my office, I called Mountain General Hospital and asked to speak with Doctor Timmons, someone I wasn't familiar with. As I was placed on hold, Bell, ever the professional, settled into her bed in the corner with a soft thud. Meanwhile, I absentmindedly played a game of solitaire on my computer, the endless cards flipping over as the minutes ticked by. My ear wasn't as lucky—it was assaulted by a nauseating barrage of tinny organ music, the kind that made you question if it was designed to irritate on purpose.

Just when I thought I couldn't take another second of the grating sound, a gruff voice finally cut through the torment. "Dr. Timmons," the voice announced, abrupt and straight to the point.

"This is Detective Jolett," I said, straightening in my chair. "I'm contacting you about Jennifer Chaplin, a patient admitted last night."

He sighed heavily, the kind of tired exhale that said he'd already been through the wringer. "Hello, Detective. I was expecting your call. Ms. Chaplin is in critical condition and unresponsive to vasopressors. I've been consulting with a specialist in New York. Her bloodwork has come back negative for known toxins, but Dr. Eagan and I believe we're dealing with a poison of some sort. I've reached out to toxicologists to see if they have any treatment ideas."

I quickly jotted down the word *vasopressors*, mentally bookmarking it for research later. It didn't take long to learn as a detective that doctors liked to speak in a foreign language and rarely realized they were doing it. If I let on that I wasn't medically fluent, Timmons would probably oversimplify things and risk leaving out something vital. "If Ms. Chaplin isn't able to answer my questions, I'll need her mother's information," I replied, keeping the conversation on track. There was no need to waste time with sympathy—the doctor and I both had jobs to do.

"She spoke with me earlier," he continued, his voice taking on a more clinical tone. "Ms. Chaplin's mother mentioned that her daughter's been staying in a safe house for several months, and she suspects the ex-husband might be involved. Apparently, he's threatened her daughter multiple times, and one of those threats included poison. That led me to my current line of treatment."

That's when the proverbial lightbulb flickered on in my mind. I'd heard this name before, and it wasn't from a casual case file. I scribbled faster. "The mother said anything else that might help?" I asked.

"She mentioned calling her daughter last night. Ms. Chaplin's speech was slurred, and she was having hallucinations. By the time the ambulance arrived, she was already unresponsive and has remained that way ever since. The critical issue now is determining the exact cause of her condition. I can't rule out other possibilities, but poisoning is my leading theory."

The conversation veered into territory I wasn't fully equipped to follow, with talk of serology and toxicology that made me wish I'd paid more attention in science class. But I kept scribbling notes, nodding in all the right places until Dr. Timmons provided the mother's contact information. That was the golden nugget I'd been waiting for.

After the call ended, I ran Jennifer's name through our police department database. It didn't take long to find the report I'd written years ago, back when I'd covered a shift for one of the patrol officers.

Victim: Jennifer Chaplin.Suspect: Beau Chaplin.

Beau's name rang a series of bells, all of them dark and unpleasant. More lightbulbs popped on as I reread the old report. Beau had been a regular user of his fists, and death threats had been par for the course in their toxic relationship. During my interview with Jennifer at the time, she'd told me how often he threatened to kill her. Though poison wasn't something she mentioned to me back then, she did recall some of his more psychotic behavior—locking her in closets without food or water for hours on end. Despite her bruises, I had left that case doubting she'd ever truly leave him. It was nice to be wrong.

I picked up the phone and dialed Jennifer's mother.

"Hello?" came the strained voice of an older woman, weary and worn down by the ordeal.

"Mrs. Rogers, this is Detective Jolett. I'm following up on your daughter's condition and hoping you might have some information."

There was a soft sniffle on the other end of the line. "Thank you, Detective. I've been waiting for someone to call. I know Beau did something to her—I just know it." Her voice trembled with a mix of certainty and helplessness.

Knowing something and proving it were two very different things. "I need to understand more about their relationship," I said gently. "I've read the report from a few years ago, but I could use your perspective. Could you walk me through it, from the beginning?"

"Please, call me Marge," she replied. Her voice steadied, but the pain was still there, just beneath the surface. "The abuse started soon after they were married, but Jennifer didn't tell me until much later. I knew something was wrong—she started pulling away, stopped coming to family events, and always had excuses that didn't add up. Then one day, I surprised her at home while Beau was at work, and I saw the bruises. Her poor face..." She trailed off, choking back more tears. "She still wouldn't say much, but I did some digging and found out about his arrests. The last time he beat her, she finally agreed to leave and went into a safe house. I was so proud of her."

Her voice dropped to a whisper, and I gave her a moment to collect herself. "Marge," I began carefully, "what happened when you spoke to her last night? You mentioned her words were slurred."

"She was saying strange things," Marge answered. "She told me the clothes she was wearing didn't fit—they should have, but they didn't. Then she started talking about the kitchen, saying it was all wrong, that things weren't where they were supposed to be. I honestly thought she was drunk or on drugs, but that's not my daughter." Her voice cracked again. "I called the ambulance right after. They told me it was the right thing to do, that I might've saved her life."

I jotted down every detail. The slurred speech, the hallucinations about the kitchen, the odd clothing comment—all could be symptoms of poisoning, or something else entirely. "The doctor mentioned that you're worried about poison. Why is that?"

"It's something Jennifer told me after she went into the safe house. She said Beau had threatened to poison her. I didn't believe it at the time—it seemed too far-fetched. But now..." Her voice trailed off, leaving the implication hanging heavy in the air.

Poison wasn't typically a weapon men used, but every now and then, you found an exception. "Did she mention a specific poison?" I asked, though I doubted it.

"No," Marge replied. "The doctor asked that too, but she never said."

"Do you know where Beau is right now? Does he have a job?" I asked, switching gears.

"He's working at the tomato plant," she answered. "Monday through Friday."

The local tomato plant was known for hiring ex-cons, including those fresh out of jail. The fact that Beau worked there told me he hadn't strayed far from trouble. "Do you know if her cell phone was brought to the hospital? Or where it might be?"

"I don't think so," Marge said. "I haven't been to her place since the hospital called."

"It's best to stay away from her house for now. I'll look into getting her phone records, which might help us piece together what's been happening. If you think of anything else, please call me." I gave her my direct line, and she thanked me softly before hanging up.

I ran Jennifer's number through the internet to find her cell provider, then faxed a hold order to the company. Her texts, voicemails, and call records would be preserved for 180 days. Unfortunately, the law now required a warrant for me to obtain them, rather than a simple subpoena, but I'd cross that bridge when I had enough evidence.

I glanced at the clock. There was still time before Beau's shift ended at four p.m., and I preferred to approach him after he left work. In the meantime, I decided to update Bell's K9 training book. She'd earned a bit of playtime before things got serious.

Just as I was about to grab her toys, Officer Leo Franks poked his head into my office. His five-o'clock shadow had darkened over the course of the day, only enhancing the Italian heritage written all over his face. He looked like the brother I never had, complete with that familiar smirk.

"I hear you're back on homicide," he said without preamble.

I nodded. "News travels fast."

"It does when I get stuck with your stray bullet case," he replied, sounding suitably grumpy as he pulled a pout that would make any three-year-old proud.

I stifled a laugh, biting my lip. "Hey, you've got five solid leads," I said, deadpan. "The only problem is any one of them could die of old age before you get around to interviewing them. I suggest calling the gang task force—these suspects all wear suspenders and ball caps and reek of Fixodent."

Leo's eyes narrowed in mock irritation, but I could see the glimmer of amusement beneath. "Are you done?" he asked, trying to sound serious.

"Not quite," I grinned. "But I'll hand over the case. If Jeb Garland whistles at you, let me know. I'd love to sic Bell on him. Made some promises earlier I'd be happy to keep."

Leo groaned. "Forward me what you've got, and I'll handle Jeb and his old man gang."

"If you gang-identify them, maybe you'll get a life sentence out of it," I said sweetly. "Even thirty days could be a death sentence at their age."

With an eye roll, Leo turned on his heel and walked out, leaving me laughing behind him.

I turned back to Bell, who had been watching our exchange with mild interest. "Well, partner, that could've been more fun if Conners had the case. Leo's too quick for me."

Bell's tail thumped lazily against her bed as she closed her eyes, ignoring me again. But the moment I reached for her toy box, she perked up, her eyes snapping open. Her tail started wagging furiously as she sprang to her feet, ready for work. Nothing got her more excited than a good K9 training session—and sniffing out explosives always got her blood pumping.

Chapter Thirty-Seven

I DON'T LIKE APPROACHING Beau Chaplin without Bell by my side. She's my backup, my muscle, and a very persuasive presence. But I also know that having her along for this interview could be counterproductive. Intimidation won't get me what I want. I need to lock Beau into a story, something solid enough to uncover the truth. People lie because they have something to hide, and I'm ready to find out exactly what he's hiding. Jennifer has a current restraining order against him, so legally, he shouldn't have had any contact with her. Whether he tells me the truth or not, I'll find out soon enough. But this first interview is critical.

Leaving a very sad-faced Bell behind in my office, I park down the street from Beau's house, blending in with the neighborhood. His place is a one-story, run-down blue house that hasn't seen any real maintenance in over a decade. The kind of place that makes you wonder if anyone still cares about it—or about themselves. The trees out front are dead, their branches bleached by the sun, frozen in place like they're trying to become petrified wood. And to top it all off, a broken toilet sits about five feet from the front door, adding to the overall ambiance of neglect. Every town seems to have at least one house with a broken toilet in the yard, but ours had more than its fair share. Personally, I would take a trip to the city dump any day to avoid that particular decoration.

I don't have to wait long before Beau is dropped off. It's a quiet, unmarked car, and neither man in the vehicle looks in my direction when they drive past. It's only when Beau steps out that I recognize him. I jot down the license plate of the car before it drives off, leaving Beau standing alone in the dusty yard.

Once he's inside the house, I give him a minute, then get out of my car and jog to his door. The moment I knock, the door opens—he hadn't even bothered to close it all the way. His initial, cheerful expression fades as soon as he sees me.

Beau Chaplin is short, wiry, with brown hair that sticks out from under his ballcap in messy tufts. He's not much to look at—certainly not the type of man you'd think could charm anyone—but at one point, Jennifer must have seen something in him. I remember his sour expression all too well. Men like Beau never forget a female officer arresting them, and they certainly don't forgive. Our last encounter was years ago, but I can still feel the lingering anger rolling off him. His grudge against me is probably as strong as the one he holds against Jennifer. The thought of it sends a small, perverse sense of joy through my veins.

"I need to speak with you about your ex-wife, Jennifer," I say before he can slam the door in my face. I have a recorder turned on in my pocket, already picking up our conversation. This is going to be one of those front porch interviews, and I want every word on record.

"I've got nothing to say to you," he snaps, his face hardening.

"That's your statement?" I let my voice drop, incredulous, as if I'm giving him one last chance to reconsider.

"What do you mean *statement?*" he demands, puffing up his chest and standing straighter. To me, he looks like one of those inflatable Christmas decorations, half-full and about to collapse.

"Your ex-wife is in the hospital," I say. "I need to ask you a few questions. If your only statement is 'I have nothing to say,' that's fine with me." I take a step back, acting like I'm ready to leave.

He freezes, panic flashing in his eyes. "Why would I have anything to do with her being in critical condition?" His voice rushes out, and the nervous edge tells me exactly what I need to know—he's worried, but not about her. He's worried about himself.

I don't smile, though it's tempting. He's just tipped his hand without realizing it. I never mentioned that Jennifer was in critical condition, and his lack of surprise is telling. It's possible he heard through the grapevine—small town news spreads fast—but this feels different. I can practically see the hatred he harbors for Jennifer radiating off him, fueling his every response. Beau's the kind of man who thinks he's smarter than women, and that's the downfall of most abusers. His ego blinds him to the fact that he's already given me more than he intended.

"My questions are quick and simple," I said sweetly. "You can answer them, or you can stay quiet. Either way works for me." I lean back slightly, letting him stew. There's no rush—I have all the time in the world.

Beau shuffles his feet, his jaw working as he debates what to do. "Ask, but I'm not saying I'll answer," he grumbles, sounding more like a petulant child than a grown man. I half expect him to kick the broken toilet in a fit of frustration.

"Do you know if your ex has any allergies the doctor should be aware of?" I ask, watching his face closely. The question throws him off-balance, as I intended.

His face scrunches in concentration as he tries to think. "Uh, she's allergic to some medication a doctor gave her years ago for an infection, but I don't remember what it was called."

"Thanks, that's helpful," I said. "Does she have any enemies that you're aware of?"

"No," he said immediately, too quickly.

I fire off the next question before he has time to think. "When was the last time you saw her?"

He shifts his weight, his gaze darting to the side. "It's been months, I don't know the exact date. Is that all?" He sounds like he's in a hurry to end this.

"Not at all," I reply, forcing a smile. "Were you aware she's in the hospital?"

His eyes narrow to slits, his voice turning cold. "You just told me."

"Thank you, that's all I have," I said, my smile widening as I turn and walk away. I can feel his eyes burning into the back of my head, but I don't look back. The door doesn't close, and I know he's watching me all the way to my car. I don't even glance over my shoulder as I drive away. Sometimes, it's better not to engage. I can't always watch my back, and my decision not to bring Bell hits home.

When I finally step back into my office, Bell lifts her head and thumps her tail against the bed. Her expression says it all—she's forgiven me for leaving her behind, but she expects a reward. She stretches lazily, first her front legs, then her back, with all the grace of a jungle cat.

"Come on, I'll take you outside for a break," I said, using my guilty mom voice. Bell wags her tail even more, licking my hand in forgiveness.

Unfortunately for me, it's my rotten luck that Officer Stanley Conners pulls into the parking lot just as Bell and I head outside. Conners and I have butted heads ever since I started at the department. His father sits on the city council, which gives Stanly an overinflated sense of importance. Thankfully, his dad hasn't managed to pull the strings necessary to get his son into a detective or supervisory position yet, but that hasn't stopped Conners from acting like he's already in charge.

As soon as he spots me, he makes a beeline in my direction. *Why me?* I groan inwardly. "If you accidentally bite him, I'll look the other way," I whisper to Bell. She stays at perfect attention, her loyalty unwavering. She's not fond of Stanly either.

"I hear you're back on homicide detail," he says as he approaches, stopping a few feet away. He's in uniform, which always grates on my nerves—not because of the uniform itself, but because of how he wears it, like it's a crown. He's in his thirties, been a cop for over ten years, and no matter the time of day or night, he wears those ridiculous dark sunglasses. Someone must have told him they were cool once, but that person lied. His grin is as fake as his dimples, and I know he's gearing up for some kind of power play.

He stays just out of reach, probably because of Bell. He used to have a habit of stepping into my personal space—something Bell, and my old partner Suii, quickly cured him of.

Leo gave me a hard time earlier today about the stray bullet case, but it was all in good fun. Stanly, on the other hand, never jokes unless there's a threat or insult wrapped in it. I decide not to answer him right away, letting the silence stretch just long enough to make him uncomfortable.

"Bell needs to do her business," I finally said, not even bothering to hide my disdain. "She's still upset I left her for the afternoon, so don't make any sudden moves."

I told Bell to "release," watching as she trots over to her favorite spot in the weed-infested patch we call grass here in Arizona. Meanwhile, I turned my full attention back to Stanly. "Homicide needs me, I guess," I said lightly, curious to see what he was up to.

Conners smirked, a calculated move that he thinks passes as charming. "There's a rumor that DJ's applying to another agency. There might be a detective spot opening up."

And there it is. He's buttering me up, hoping I'll put in a good word for him. Not in this lifetime.

"DJ's a good detective," I said flatly, shutting down his angle immediately. "I'd hate to lose him."

Stanly puffs up his chest, looking more like Beau with every passing second. It's sad, really. I've disliked him for as long as I can remember, but at least I can admit I had my own chip on my shoulder when I started. I was abrasive, and everyone knew it. I've changed since then. Stanly hasn't.

His smile turned saccharine, but the fire in his eyes betrayed his real feelings. "I just wanted to give you a heads-up. I'll be moving into the detective division soon. Macky will be retiring in the next few years, and I've got my sights set on homicide. I think we'd make a great team."

I had to swallow down the bile threatening to rise. "Best of luck if DJ leaves," I said, forcing a smile. I glance over at Bell, who's now sniffing the fence line. "Come on, girl. It's time to go home." Bell runs to the back of the car, eager to leave.

"I know I'll make a better partner than your dog," Stanly called out, his voice smug. "You can count on that."

His parting shot stops me in my tracks. I turned, smiling sweetly. "I wouldn't bet on that," I said, my voice dripping with fake sincerity. "Bell has four shoes to fill, and you only have two."

I laughed lightly, as if we're just having a friendly chat, but we both know this is anything but.

Once Bell is loaded into the car, I slid into the driver's seat and immediately dial Gabe. He barely had time to say hello before I launch into it.

"If you retire in the next few years, I will never buy you a Christmas present again," I growl.

Gabe laughed, the sound echoing through the speaker. "Since you've never bought me a Christmas present, I'll assume your favorite officer cornered you, like he did me."

"Did you tell him you planned to retire?" I ask, irritated.

"No, but he hinted that I should," Gabe says, still chuckling.

"Well, don't," I snapped, hanging up before he can say more. I twisted around in my seat and glared at Bell. "If I'm ever forced to work with that jerk, you'll have free rein to bite him every other day. When you're not on duty, I'll take over and punch him in the face. We'll take turns."

Bell didn't bother to respond. She was probably already plotting how to turn Stanly Conners into dog food.

Chapter Thirty-Eight

R AT CAT PACED AT his front door when we pulled up, his sleek black fur catching the late afternoon light as he moved with that irritating feline grace. His sharp yellow eyes followed my car like I was trespassing on his personal kingdom. He stopped briefly, flicking his tail with a deliberate, calculated swish that oozed disdain. Even from this distance, his arrogance was palpable. He knew exactly what he was doing—taunting Bell and, by extension, me.

Bell growled through the window, low and menacing, the sound rumbling deep in her chest. The sharpness of it sent a tremor through the car, her eyes locked onto Rat Cat with an intensity I hadn't seen in her for anything other than a suspect. Her whole body trembled with anticipation, her muscles tight and ready to spring. Despite all her training, she looked like she could barely control herself, as though she were on the edge of launching herself through the window to settle the score.

Rat Cat, ever indifferent, flicked his tail again—this time slower, more deliberate, as if to say, "You can't touch me." He sat down, his back to us, and began cleaning his paws with casual, slow licks. The audacity of him. I felt my own irritation rising, mirroring Bell's frustration.

I practically dragged Bell, who should have known better, through my front door. She fought me every step of the way, her body resisting my tug on the leash as if her sole purpose in life had shifted to ending this cat once and for all. "Come on, Bell," I muttered through clenched teeth, barely able to keep her from lunging back toward the door. Her growls continued, vibrating through her tense frame. She was acting like she'd forgotten every bit of K9 training we'd drilled into her over the years.

Inside, the house felt stiflingly quiet compared to the growling and tension of moments before. I could feel my pulse slowing as I shut the door behind us. But Bell wasn't calming down. She paced back and forth near the front window, glancing out every few seconds as if expecting Rat Cat to somehow reappear, still taunting her from his throne.

I needed to break this tension, for both of us. That familiar itch to call Jack at the K9 division kicked in. Any excuse would do, and a dog who was hell-bent on eating the neighbor's cat seemed like a solid one. Plus, if I was being honest with myself, I didn't need much of an excuse. My finger hovered over his number on the screen for a second before I hit call.

The phone barely rang once before Jack answered. "K9s are Us, at your service," he said, and I could hear the amusement in his voice. He knew it was me, and something in the casual warmth of his tone made my heart give a little flutter I wasn't prepared to acknowledge. Leo, with his movie-star looks, never made me feel this way. But Jack? He made me wonder what it would be like to have someone I could just talk to, without needing an excuse. That thought was foreign to me, unsettling even.

"We have a cat situation, and Bell isn't handling it well," I said, trying to keep my voice light, though the tension still coiled inside me.

"I'm with Bell on this one," Jack replied smoothly, his voice full of mock seriousness. "Cats have something called dander, and it makes everyone around them crazy."

"You just made that up," I said, shaking my head, though a smile tugged at my lips despite myself.

Jack laughed, a deep, easy sound that I found myself enjoying a little too much. "Nope. They do have dander, and I'm allergic. If Bell has the good sense to dislike cats, I wouldn't worry about it."

"I don't like cats either," I admitted, leaning back against the kitchen counter. The coolness of it seeped into my skin, grounding me a little. This conversation was a welcome distraction, a way to shake off the tension Rat Cat had stirred up.

"Does this mean we have something in common?" Jack asked, his voice teasing but with that edge of curiosity that made me wonder if he was testing the waters.

I hesitated just a fraction too long. "Do you have any suggestions other than misplacing the cat on my next trip to the dump?"

"Drastic times call for drastic measures," he replied, that mock-serious tone still in place. "I have a special ops friend who handles these types of situations for a fee. He could make the problem disappear, and there'd be no evidence left behind. Though, full disclosure, I think my friend is a sociopath."

"Now I'm unsure if you're joking or not," I replied, feeling the tightness in my chest ease as his laughter filled the line again. His laugh had this way of cutting through the stress, the heaviness of the day, and it made me feel lighter, like maybe things weren't as bad as they seemed.

"We're talking about cats," Jack said, his voice turning gruff with amusement. "Nothing's off the table, even potential serial killers."

"I'll remember to never make you sneeze," I said, but I could feel the conversation starting to slip away, that inevitable end approaching. It left a pit of disappointment in my stomach, like I was grasping at straws to keep him on the line. I gave myself a mental shake. Pathetic, thy name is Laci.

"You do that. They say an allergy can start at any time," Jack continued, and I felt a glimmer of hope that maybe he wasn't in a rush to end the call after all.

"I'm back on homicide," I said, trying to stretch the conversation just a little further. "I might be investigating a missing cat case soon. It could really mess up my eighty-five percent case clearance rate if I protect Bell and don't turn her in."

"Bell's tough," Jack replied, his tone shifting slightly, a bit more serious now. "She can take the heat. Congrats on the reassignment, by the way. I'm sure working the trenches of the lower echelon of detectives wasn't easy."

"An old man whistled at me," I deadpanned, leaning more comfortably against the counter as I settled into the banter again.

"The nerve," Jack said, matching my tone perfectly. "Did Bell attack?"

I chuckled softly. "He wasn't a cat, so the old man was safe."

"And we're back to cats," he said warmly.

"It's an ugly cat," I muttered, as Bell whined, perfectly timed to express her discontent over not having dinner in front of her. "See? Bell agrees."

"Even kittens are ugly," Jack replied, with a hint of seriousness that made me smirk.

I gasped, playing along. "Now you've gone too far. A man should be ashamed for not liking kittens." I wasn't even sure if we were flirting, but this was the rhythm we had, a strange mix of sarcasm and affection, and I wasn't complaining.

"I hate to cut this short, but I have a date," Jack said suddenly. My heart plummeted for a brief second before he added, "His Majesty is having some behavioral issues, and I brought him home for some extra training."

I let out a breath, my pulse steadying. "His Majesty?" I asked, grateful that I could breathe again.

"It's his name—capital H, capital M," Jack said, his tone returning to its usual lightness. "He's a Belgian Malinois and he's in explosives training like Bell was."

"I'm sure you'll find him the perfect partner," I said, feeling a strange mix of relief and curiosity.

"If I could afford him, he'd be mine," Jack admitted, his voice turning wistful for a moment.

I hadn't ever asked why Jack didn't have a dog of his own. "It must be rough, giving them up when it's time for them to go to a new owner," I said softly, picturing him with His Majesty, the way he must bond with these dogs, only to say goodbye.

"Some are harder than others," he said, his voice thick with emotion he rarely let show.

I placed Bell's dinner bowl on the floor and started searching the refrigerator for something for myself. "If you need a shoulder to cry on after he finds his forever home, give me a call," I offered, remembering how Jack had been there for me after Suii died. I wouldn't have made it through without him.

"It's a deal," he said, and there was something warm, something almost unspoken, in the way he agreed. "Call me if the cat situation gets worse, and I'll drive down and save the day with my rifle."

"You're all heart."

"We're talking about cats," he reminded me, laughing softly.

"I'm not disagreeing."

We ended the call with me smiling, a strange mix of emotions swirling inside me. Maybe, just maybe, when we were old and gray and both retired, things could work out between us. Until then, Jack was a good friend, and I was glad to have him in my corner.

I popped a frozen dinner into the microwave, telling myself that if the box said it was healthy, it had to be, right? I ate in front of the evening news, my mind drifting back to Jack's laugh more than the headlines flashing on the screen. After dinner, I threw a load of laundry in the washer while Bell went out back to inspect the yard, her usual routine.

It wasn't long before her barking started up again, and I sighed, walking out to see what the fuss was about. Of course, there he was—Rat Cat, sitting on his makeshift throne on the fence, casually grooming himself without a care in the world.

"Come inside, Bell," I called, exasperation creeping into my voice. "He's got your number, and you're letting him win."

Bell cast one last, longing look at her sworn enemy, but she trotted back toward the door, albeit reluctantly.

It's a hard life when a K9 has a feline nemesis. Kind of like Conners. But shooting him would be a terrible idea.

Chapter Thirty-Nine

MY FIRST BREAK CAME after I checked out the location of the safe house. It turned out that Lucky Gas was just around the corner. Like many safe houses in small, rural communities, everyone—including the abuser—was aware of the house's location. In extremely dangerous cases, the caseworker would pull the victim out of town, but that wasn't an option for everyone. Funds were scarce, and they had to pick and choose who needed an escape the most. Jennifer hadn't been lucky enough to make that list.

The safe house was a modest white stucco building with a red door, its simplicity belying the refuge it offered to those inside. I took pictures of it—front, sides, and the surrounding area—just in case I ended up needing a warrant. I'd need the precise details for the paperwork. The house itself didn't seem out of place in the neighborhood, though there was a quiet sadness to it, knowing the kind of desperation it shielded. After I was sure I had everything documented, I turned my attention toward Lucky Gas and Wash.

The scent of gasoline, faint but distinct, greeted me as I parked. The dingy sign above the gas station buzzed with life, though it had seen better days. Larry, the owner, was at the counter when I walked in. He was in his seventies but could have easily passed for sixty-nine, as he liked to joke. His broad frame still held strength, and his large, welcoming smile radiated a warmth that was hard to fake.

He'd run this place for years, known to everyone in town as someone who helped people in need. Even a month ago, he still hadn't raised the price of a cup of coffee in over a decade—a small act of defiance in the face of rising costs. The place had an air of nostalgia, the kind of worn but comfortable vibe that made it a local staple.

"I heard you put the dust on old Jeb," Larry said with a twinkle in his eye as I approached the counter. "Wish I could've seen it. You think he's the one who shot my window?"

"He fits the profile of an old lecher," I replied, smiling at the memory of Jeb, "but I'm not sure about the bullet hole. Officer Franks is handling that case and will stop by to speak with you soon."

Larry nodded, a frown crossing his face. "Franks already came by. I told him what I told you—the coffee gaggle here is full of mean old men. Any one of 'em could be responsible. Still, they keep buyin' my coffee, even at the higher price."

"If you raise it again, you might get rid of them for good."

He chuckled, a deep, hearty sound that seemed to warm the room. "And ruin all the gossip they share every morning? Not a chance." He shook his head. The thought of losing his regulars, no matter how grumpy, clearly didn't sit well with him.

I laughed along with him before getting to the point. "I'm actually here to spend some quality time with your video system. It might help with my latest case."

Larry leaned forward slightly, his curiosity piqued. "I haven't heard of any homicides recently," he said, posing it as a question. Larry was just as much a gossip hound as his regulars.

"Hopefully, you won't," I replied, sidestepping the topic. Anything I said to Larry would be spread across town in less than five minutes.

"Be my guest," he said with a wave toward the back, turning to greet another customer as they walked in.

I made my way to the rear of the store, where a built-in ladder led up to a small loft. The familiar hum of the surveillance equipment greeted me as I climbed up. The space was cramped but organized. Whoever had shot into the store knew what they were doing—they'd stayed just out of camera range. It was one of the reasons I had the coffee gaggle on my suspect list. Teens wouldn't know about the system or how far back they needed to stay to avoid detection.

I'd worked with Larry's equipment more than a few times and knew my way around the system. My first check was for last Tuesday, starting at four p.m., when Beau usually got off work. The footage sped by in a blur as I fast-forwarded through the hours. It only took a minute before I spotted Beau's friend's car, both of them inside, heading home after their shift. I slowed the footage and watched closely as they drove past Lucky's without turning down Jennifer's street.

I continued running through the next hour, eyes scanning the footage for any sign of Beau. Finally, at 6:25, the familiar faded-green Mazda appeared on the small screen. Even in the grainy footage, I could make out the spots where the paint had chipped away. Beau was driving, and he was alone. I watched as he turned down Jennifer's street, disappearing from the camera's view.

"Thank goodness," I muttered to myself. Finally, some confirmation.

Back in the car, Bell waited patiently in the backseat, her ears perked up as I got in. "It's time to hit the neighbors and ask about a green Mazda," I informed her, pulling out of the lot. Bell sighed, her body sinking down as if resigning herself to the fact that this was not her kind of job. "Where's a good bomb threat when you need one?" I teased her.

The first house I knocked on was empty, so I moved to the neighbor on the east side of the safe house. An older woman answered the door. Seventy maybe? She was about five feet tall, but what caught my attention was her gym attire—black leggings and a tight shirt that boldly proclaimed, *"If it jiggles, it's available."* I smiled. This lady had spirit.

After introducing myself, I asked, "Have you noticed an older model green Mazda with peeling paint parked near your neighbor's house?"

She squinted slightly, her sharp eyes glinting with the kind of keen observation that comes from years of watching everyone and everything. "He doesn't park in front of Jennifer's place," she corrected. "He parks about five houses down, across the street. I'm guessing he's the woman-beater sneaking into the safe house?"

"You might have assumed correctly," I said. I wasn't about to lie to her. It wouldn't get me anywhere, and she seemed like the kind of person who appreciated directness.

"Tuesday nights, sometimes on weekends. I keep an eye on that place," she added with a nod, crossing her arms.

"If I showed you a photo lineup, do you think you could identify him?"

She raised an eyebrow. "I could, but I can also give you his name. My nephew works with him at the tomato plant. Told me all about him." She paused, eyeing me carefully. "My nephew had some issues with drugs a few years back, but he's doing good now. You won't be lookin' for him anytime soon."

I nodded. "A name would be great."

"It's Beau something." She frowned slightly. "I can call my nephew and get his last name if you need it."

"Beau will do for now. Can you call me if you see him again?" I handed her my card, knowing full well she'd keep an eye out.

"If you could arrest him right here on this block, where I could watch, I'd appreciate it," she said with a mischievous smile. "I know it might not work out that way, but it doesn't hurt to plant the idea in your head."

I smiled back. "It's there, but no promises."

I felt lighter as I walked back to my car. She was more than willing to go on the record about seeing Beau at the safe house. He'd violated the restraining order, and now I had the foundation for my warrant. Time to sit down and write it.

Two hours later, I had my preliminary report written along with the warrant paperwork. With fingers crossed, hoping I could find a judge in a cooperative mood, I headed to the courthouse. I bypassed the justice of the peace and went straight upstairs to the superior court judge's chambers. The judge wasn't available, but John Eship, the Judge Pro Tempore, was in.

John was in his forties, with a thin face, large teeth, and an impeccably neat suit beneath his black robe. His brown hair was perfectly in place, and he greeted me with the kind of smile that felt genuine. He'd practiced law in town before accepting this appointment a few years ago. To my advantage, he was also a fan of Bell.

"How are you, Detective?" he asked, his eyes twinkling as Bell walked over for some well-earned attention. He scratched her neck, then under her chin, knowing just where to pet without making her uncomfortable. She liked him, which was a good sign. Not that Judge Eship would ever sign a warrant without cause, but having Bell on my side didn't hurt.

"She's having a great day," I replied with a smile. "I'm doing well, too."

"What can I help you with today?" he asked, straightening as I handed him the paperwork.

"I have a warrant that needs a signature," I said.

He flipped through the pages quickly at first, then slowed down as he reached the probable cause section. He paused to pull a pair of reading glasses from his desk, grunting quietly as he scanned the text. Finally, he looked up, his expression thoughtful. "I've had this gentleman in my courtroom before. I sincerely hope your case isn't what it looks like."

His head dipped back down as he reviewed the document from the beginning, this time carefully checking for any potential errors.

My relief was palpable. If he was this thorough, it meant he was preparing to sign it. It took him about ten minutes to finish reading through the entire warrant before handing it back, signed and ready. "Take it to the court clerk for filing. You're good to go."

"Thank you, Your Honor," I said sincerely. I knew he wouldn't badmouth Beau in front of me—if the case ended up in his courtroom, any bias could overturn a verdict. But his agreement to the search was enough for now.

I immediately dialed Investigator Wilson from the hazmat unit, setting up a time for them to meet me at the house the next morning. The investigator taught a training I attended, and he'd handed out his business card to offer his help if we ever needed it.

I headed back to the station to request an officer to keep watch overnight and maintain the integrity of the warrant. Sergeant Spence was in his office, surrounded by the never-ending stack of paperwork that came with the job. Bell perked up as we entered, and Spence ignored me entirely in favor of greeting her. "How you doing, Bell?" he asked, giving her a hearty scratch behind the ears. It was their little ritual. After a moment, he turned his attention to me. "You owe me for putting you back on homicide."

I blinked, genuinely surprised. "Was I being punished?"

He laughed. "Teaming you with a K9 was punishment. Taking you off homicide while Detective Marin was out was a necessity. Now I find it more necessary to have you back on homicide. I convinced the chief the other detectives could handle the extra workload."

I raised my hand in mock seriousness. "I owe you and will repay my debt with honor, sir." I clicked my heels together dramatically, like Dorothy from *The Wizard of Oz*.

Spence shot Bell a look. "How do you put up with her? No respect for authority."

I grinned. "I have a warrant for the safe house, and hazmat's meeting me there first thing in the morning. I need a rookie to keep watch overnight."

He nodded, already picking up the phone. "Consider it done."

It was time to head home and get some rest. Search warrants always made for long days.

Chapter Forty

I WAS DEAD TO the world when Bell's low growl pulled me from sleep. Before I could even register what was happening, she flew off the bed and bolted for the front of the house, her nails clicking against the hardwood floor. My mind was sluggish, but instinct kicked in, and I reached for my gun from the bedside nightstand. Groggily, I followed her, barefoot, with no phone or shoes—just a cold grip of metal in my hand.

Bell stood at her locked dog door, her entire body rigid, hackles raised, and a low, continuous growl rumbling from deep within her throat. Her intensity was contagious, setting my nerves on edge. I flipped on the backlight and peeked through the window, squinting into the night, my pulse quickening as I tried to make out the cause of her distress.

Of course. It was Rat Cat. He was on the patio, chewing on something. His silhouette hunched over in the dim light, and for a moment, I thought he'd caught a mouse and decided to make my porch his personal dining table. Or worse—a rat. I blinked, trying to clear the fog of sleep from my brain as I watched him gnaw at the mystery meal.

Something strange caught my eye, and without thinking, I commanded Bell to stay as I unlocked the door. The cool night air hit me as I stepped outside. Rat Cat, unfazed by my presence, let out a long, drawn-out meow but didn't budge. His green eyes flicked up to me, almost lazily, before he returned to whatever he was eating. That's when my groggy brain finally registered what I was seeing.

I moved forward quickly, heart pounding in my chest. The cat hissed at me but reluctantly backed off, jumping onto the brick wall that bordered my yard. From his new perch, he glared down at me, his tail flicking in annoyance, but I was no longer focused on him.

I crouched down, squinting at the partially eaten lump of meat on my patio. My hands trembled as I processed what I was looking at. This wasn't a mouse. It wasn't even a rat. It was a chunk of raw meat, too neatly placed to be anything but deliberate. My breath hitched in my throat as the realization settled over me like ice.

Someone had thrown poisoned meat into my yard. And it wasn't meant for Rat Cat—it was meant for Bell.

With shaking hands, I grabbed Bell's water bowl, dumping its contents on the ground. Scooping the meat into the bowl, I stood there for a moment, my legs weak beneath me. My mind raced as I quickly washed my hands, trying to steady my nerves.

I called dispatch, my voice more strained than I intended, and requested an officer to be sent to my house. I dressed in record time, barely able to focus as I slipped Bell onto her lead and kept her by my side. My flashlight cut through the darkness as I swept the backyard for anything else—another piece of meat, anything out of place. But the yard was still. Rat Cat had vanished, and despite my usual irritation with him, I found myself hoping he hadn't eaten any of the poisoned meat. As much as the tabby annoyed me, I didn't want him suffering.

Part of K9 training with Jack had always involved understanding that your dog was both your protection and a liability. If someone wanted to get to you, they could go after your dog. I'd never fully grasped just how real that threat could be until now. The thought of losing Bell twisted my insides with fear and anger.

Minutes passed, but my heart refused to slow down. The rage simmered beneath the surface, growing with every second that ticked by. How dare someone come after Bell? How dare they try to hurt her?

When the patrol car pulled up, I had a sinking feeling that my luck wasn't improving. Officer Conners got out of the vehicle, his dark sunglasses on even at this hour. My initial reaction was to bite back a sarcastic comment, but I managed to hold my tongue, focusing instead on keeping Bell calm beside me.

He walked over with his usual cocky swagger, but as soon as he examined the water dish and saw the meat, his expression shifted. He was all business now, and for once, I appreciated it.

"Someone tried to poison your dog," he said grimly, shaking his head in disbelief. He didn't need to state the obvious, but hearing it from him made the situation all the more real. It was clear he wasn't pleased, and I could tell that even with our differences, we were on the same side when it came to something like this. Bell wasn't just my dog—she was an officer, and that meant Conners took this personally too.

"The case I'm working might involve poisoning," I admitted, my voice tight. I hated giving him any details about my investigation, but he needed to know the potential connection. "I don't believe in coincidence."

Conners frowned, his lips pressing into a thin line as he thought it over. "Beau would do this," he said finally, the disgust clear in his tone. "I've handled too many domestic calls at his place. I know what he's capable of."

My stomach churned. The thought of Beau coming anywhere near my home, near Bell, made my blood boil. I lived nowhere near the safe house, but that didn't mean Beau wouldn't make the connection and come after me.

"The cameras between Beau's place and mine…" I started, but Conners beat me to it.

"I'll run his license and get a plate number," he said, already pulling out his notepad. "Then I'll check the cameras in town. If I can place his vehicle near your house, it gives us a stronger case."

"Thank you," I said, surprising myself with the sincerity in my voice. Normally, I'd keep everything I knew about Beau's vehicle to myself, but these were two separate cases, and Conners needed to follow his own leads.

The next words out of my mouth shocked even me. "I'll talk to Sergeant Spence about keeping you assigned to the case. Bell needs a hero right now, and I'm a mess."

It was the truth. The possibility of losing Bell had shaken me more than I wanted to admit. Conners nodded, seeming to understand the gravity of the situation. "I need to pay my neighbors a visit," I added, thinking of the cat. As much as Rat Cat drove me crazy, I didn't want him to suffer from whatever poison might have been in that meat.

"I'll bag the evidence and get it to the lab," Conners said. "We'll figure out what was used. And check your yard before you let Bell out. We'll have patrols cruise by more often until we get this settled."

I gave him a small nod, my worry subsiding just enough to appreciate his professionalism. "Thank you," I said again. The roof didn't cave in, and I meant it. If Conners dropped his usual attitude, he could be a great cop. He just needed to stop relying on his father's name and start pulling his own weight.

After he left, I headed next door and knocked. It was four in the morning, and the exhaustion was starting to catch up with me, but I had to check on Rat Cat. He hadn't returned, and I was worried.

Bill answered the door, his wife Molly standing behind him, both of them looking groggy but curious. I'd only spoken to them a handful of times since they moved in, but they'd always been friendly.

"I'm really sorry to bother you," I started, feeling the weight of the situation pressing down on me. "Someone tried to poison my dog tonight. I think they may have tossed some meat over the fence, and I'm worried your cat might have gotten into it."

Bill looked confused. "The tabby cat?"

"Yeah, I've been calling him Rat Cat," I admitted, feeling a little embarrassed now. "He's been hanging around on the fence between our yards since you moved in."

Bill exchanged a look with Molly, who had a strange expression on her face. "That's not our cat," he said slowly. "We thought he was yours."

I blinked, stunned. "What? He paces in front of your door all the time. I just assumed he was yours."

Molly shifted uncomfortably. "I feed him," she confessed, looking sheepish. "I thought he needed a little extra meat on his bones. I didn't think you fed him enough."

I almost laughed at the absurdity of it. "I've never fed him." If I had known Rat Cat didn't belong to them, I could've gotten rid of him weeks ago. "I'm really sorry to wake you both. I'm going to grab Bell and see if we can find him. I don't want him suffering."

Bill offered to help, but I could see the tiredness in his eyes. "It's okay, Bell and I have it covered. Again, I'm sorry for waking you."

I fetched Bell, and the next two hours were spent scouring the neighborhood for Rat Cat. With each passing minute, my concern grew. By the time dawn began to creep over the horizon, I had to admit defeat. I couldn't find him.

"Sorry, Bell," I murmured as I prepared for my shift. "I don't think the cat's coming back. We'll solve this case, and you'll have your dog door open again, I promise."

For now, I would have to check the yard before letting Bell out. I wasn't taking any chances.

As I finished getting ready, Bell started barking at the back door. I reached for my gun, instinct driving me, but when I glanced outside, I couldn't believe my eyes. There, perched on the wall like nothing had happened, was Rat Cat, looking every bit the arrogant king surveying his kingdom.

I felt a ridiculous sense of relief. "It's stupid," I muttered to myself, "but I'm actually glad you're okay."

Bell, however, wasn't in the mood for sentimentality. She barked furiously, her eyes locked on Rat Cat as if this morning's drama hadn't happened at all.

"Come on, Bell," I said, grabbing my keys. "We've got a criminal to catch. I think he's a serial poisoner, and we need to put him out of business before someone dies."

Bell gave one last bark at her furry nemesis before eagerly following me to the car, leaving behind her very-much-alive antagonist.

Chapter Forty-One

WE WERE OUT EARLY, and I had about an hour before I was scheduled to meet the hazmat unit at Jennifer's house. As we passed the police department on our way out of town, I mentally mapped out the day ahead. First stop: the tomato plant. I needed to find out what kind of employee Beau was and maybe, if I was lucky, slip in a few other questions that could shed more light on the case.

About five miles outside of town, I took the turn leading to the plant. The place was set back from the road by about a quarter of a mile, a sprawling facility spread across a hundred acres of farmland. The sight of it, with rows of greenhouses in the distance, was oddly peaceful. I parked near the entrance and left Bell in the backseat. She didn't sulk exactly, but the huff she let out as she laid down told me she wasn't thrilled about waiting.

Inside, I found Mr. Dapple, the senior supervisor, waiting for me in the front office. He agreed to speak with me after a brief introduction. Dapple looked to be in his sixties, a large man with his beige work jumpsuit rolled up at the sleeves. I couldn't help but notice the prison tattoos that decorated his forearms—crude drawings inked in blue, like they'd been done with a needle and pen ink.

Catching me glancing at them, he stretched out his arm and pointed to one of the more prominent tattoos, a cartoonish mermaid. "This was my first," he said with a chuckle. "Did ten years in Perryville. Picked up most of my art while I was there."

I didn't laugh at his use of the word *art*—he was clearly proud of the tattoos, and I didn't want to disrespect him. I also wasn't about to ask what he went away for. I needed him on my side, and pushing too far could shut him down. Instead, I decided to steer the conversation elsewhere.

"Did you work at the tomato plant during your time?" I asked, trying to keep things casual.

"Nah, Perryville's too far away," he said, shaking his head. "I worked on a seasonal corn farm when I wasn't in trouble. Learned a lot about olericulture, and that's how I found my calling. After moving up here, the tomato plant found me. Been a good partnership ever since."

"Olericulture?" I repeated, trying to make sure I got the word right.

"It's everything to do with growing and marketing vegetables," he explained. "I like being involved in the entire process." He gestured for me to follow him, and we walked out through a side door, down a narrow alleyway, and into a small trailer that served as his private office. Inside, it was sparse—a low-slung brown couch and a desk with a computer. I sat on the couch, which immediately swallowed me up. If I needed to get up quickly, it wouldn't be graceful.

I leaned forward to give him my full attention. "I'd like to ask about one of your employees. I'm hoping to determine if he's a suspect or not, and any insight you can provide would be valuable. Things like attendance, overall performance."

Mr. Dapple studied me for a moment, as if weighing whether or not I was the kind of cop he could talk to. It was always hit or miss with people who had done time, but after a few seconds, he gave me a small nod. I'd earned his trust, at least for now.

"Give me a name, and I'll help if I can."

"Beau Chaplin," I said, watching his reaction.

"Beau?" His brows furrowed slightly. "Yeah, I know Beau."

I pressed forward. "I'd like to know what kind of worker he is. His general demeanor around here."

Dapple scratched at his white-bearded chin, deep in thought. "Beau's a good employee. Shows up on time, doesn't call in sick. He's been gaining more responsibility, and if he sticks around, I can see him moving up the ranks pretty fast. One of the best employees I've got."

I let out a breath I didn't realize I'd been holding. "That's good to hear. What exactly does his job entail?"

Dapple's shoulders relaxed as he leaned back in his chair. "He's been working with our agricultural pest control specialist. Seems like he's found his niche there. People want organic produce now, and we've been moving toward a fully organic operation. Beau's been helping us with that, especially with hydroponics. He's eager to learn, even talked about going back to school to get a degree. We need more people like him—people who understand how to manage pest control without relying on pesticides."

I smiled, trying to appear relieved. "It sounds like he's doing well for himself. Has he had any issues with coworkers? Any confrontations?"

"None," Dapple said confidently. "Beau gets along with everyone. He's even taken some of the inmates under his wing, mentors them. A lot of these guys have never had jobs where they were respected, you know? We hire felons, give them a second chance. Workers like Beau, they're the ones we're trying to help. When we lift them up, they lift others. It's a good cycle."

I stood and extended my hand. "Thank you, Mr. Dapple. You've put my mind at ease. You've also taught me a lesson today."

He smiled, his face softening. "How so?"

"My job is to find the guilty and lock them up," I explained, shaking his hand. "We don't often think about what happens after they serve their time. It's good to see a place like this, giving people a second chance."

Dapple grinned, and we said our goodbyes as he walked me back to the front office.

Back in the car, Bell gave a small yip as I climbed into the driver's seat. "I hear you," I muttered, pulling over a short distance from the plant to let her out. She was quick, darting around for a minute before hopping back into the car, her mood improved. I had just enough time to drop her off at the police department before heading to Jennifer's house. If there was poison involved, I wasn't taking any chances. Bell would stay safely out of the way.

At Jennifer's house, the rookie officer who'd been tasked with keeping an eye on things was waiting, standing near a white hazmat van parked at the curb. I greeted him briefly before turning my attention to the three members of the hazmat team—two men and a woman—who were waiting nearby.

We shook hands, and I quickly waved off the rookie, explaining what I'd learned at the tomato plant. Investigator Lott, the one in charge of the hazmat unit, nodded thoughtfully.

"If he has access to ordering supplies, there's a wide range of chemicals he could get his hands on," Lott said. "Our equipment checks for a lot of them. We'll scan the house to make sure it's safe for you to enter. Have you been inside at all?"

"No," I said, rubbing my hands together to shake off the cold creeping into my bones. "I want it safe before I step foot in there."

"We can suit you up and take you inside with us if you want," Lott offered.

I hadn't considered that, but I nodded, willing to do whatever was necessary. I handed over my warrant, and Lott quickly reviewed it before handing it back.

Gearing me up took a few minutes. They fitted me with a white hazmat suit, booties, gloves, and duct tape to secure everything in place. A small oxygen tank was strapped over my shoulder, with a hood attached, giving me a clear, albeit claustrophobic, view through the plastic face shield. I felt like I was starring in a Hollywood virus movie. Too bad no one was around to capture this on video—I could already imagine Gabe's amused reaction.

"Stay aware of your surroundings once we're inside," Lott instructed. "And steer clear of any sharp objects. We don't want your suit tearing."

Once we were fully suited up, I followed the hazmat crew into the house, my camera in hand. I snapped a few pictures before we even crossed the threshold, documenting the exterior of the house and the address, verifying everything in the warrant.

The interior of the suit made it hard to hear, and even with the oxygen tank, I felt like I was suffocating. I forced myself to slow my breathing, steadying the tightness in my chest as we stepped into the foyer. The sound of my own breathing echoed inside the mask, adding to the disorienting sense of isolation.

The house was clean, almost unnaturally so. I'd been in this safe house several times over the years, and each time it looked different, as if each woman passing through left her own small imprint on the space. There was a strange stillness to it, a sense of impermanence that tugged at me.

"Stick close to Sam," Lott instructed, pointing to the man holding a rectangular electronic device attached to a long metal wand. "He's going to scan each room."

Sam turned to me with a nod, explaining as we moved. "This is a gas chromatograph," he said, holding up the larger device. "And this—" he gestured with the wand—"is a mass spectrometer. If the light on the spectrometer turns red"—he pointed to the blinking green light—"you'll hear a series of beeps. That's when we know we've got something."

I followed Sam closely, my camera in hand, snapping pictures as we moved through each room. Despite the tension, the light remained green, the house appearing clean of toxins. That was, until we reached Jennifer's bedroom.

The room was tidy, like the rest of the house, and I couldn't help but feel a pang of familiarity. Growing up in foster homes, I always hated when the houses were messy or unkempt. Clean spaces gave me a sense of control, of order. Jennifer seemed to live the same way, or maybe it was just because this wasn't really *her* home. It was a safe house, a temporary refuge. I kept my condo meticulously clean for the same reason—it was mine, and I kept it simple. Most of the things inside were Bell's, anyway.

A sharp, continuous beep cut through my thoughts, jolting me back to the present. Sam had just stuck his head out of the closet, where the alarm had gone off. Investigator Lott and Carmen, the other hazmat tech, hurried into the room.

"The alert went off as soon as I stepped into the closet," Sam said. "I want to finish scanning the rest of the room before we proceed inside."

Carmen, who carried a large test kit similar to the drug kits we used, placed it on the bed while Sam ran the probe. With no additional alerts, Sam returned to the closet. After a few minutes, he called out again.

"We've got paraquat," Carmen announced after a moment, her voice rising with urgency.

Paraquat. The name clicked in my head. It was a powerful weed killer, highly toxic.

"No dye," Carmen added, stepping out of the closet with a small vial in hand.

"What does the dye have to do with it?" I asked, curiosity piqued.

Carmen shook the vial, revealing a reddish liquid. "Paraquat produced in the U.S. is dyed blue and has a strong odor, to prevent accidental ingestion. It also makes you vomit immediately if swallowed, giving you a chance to survive. This"—she gestured to the vial—"came from outside the country. No dye, no odor."

I thought of Jennifer, her confused ramblings about clothing. The pieces of the puzzle started to fall into place. I reached for my radio, but of course, it was in the car, along with my phone.

"If you're lucky, you'll be decontaminated in an hour," Investigator Lott said, handing me his phone. "Call the hospital."

I used his plastic-wrapped phone to contact dispatch and had them patch me through to the hospital. After a few moments, I got Dr. Timmons on the line and explained what we'd found.

"Her condition has worsened," Dr. Timmons said grimly. "She's been put on a ventilator, and dialysis started last night. If it's paraquat, all I can do is treat the symptoms. There's no antidote. The only good news is that if she'd ingested a large quantity, she'd already be dead."

I thanked him and hung up, relaying the news to the hazmat team.

"Do you have enough to arrest him?" Sam asked.

I shook my head, running through the facts in my mind. "It's all circumstantial for now. I'll need to write up a search warrant for Beau's house and the tomato plant. If they're using paraquat from outside the country, that's illegal, right?"

"It is," Sam confirmed.

I thought of Mr. Dapple and the work they were doing at the plant. I couldn't help but hope that it wasn't shut down because of this.

Chapter Forty-Two

I T TOOK TWO HOURS before I finished taking pictures and went through the decontamination procedures in the back of the hazmat van. Once it was finally safe to leave, I headed back to the police department to give Bell a much-needed break. She looked at me like I'd betrayed her by leaving her behind earlier, but a quick walk and some belly rubs seemed to smooth things over. After that, I got back to the endless task of writing more search warrants.

An hour into typing, my phone rang. Our secretary's voice came through, informing me that Stephanie Eaton was on line two. I picked up, and she wasted no time getting to the point.

"I just spoke to Jennifer's mom. If you haven't locked Beau up, I'm going after him."

I sighed, rubbing the bridge of my nose. My patience was thin, and the last thing I needed was Stephanie going rogue. "If you go after him, I'll have no choice but to arrest you for obstructing a felony investigation, which, if you didn't know, is a felony. I understand you're upset, but you *will* let me do my job. Am I clear?"

Stephanie's tough tone wavered as she began to cry, her voice softer when she finally spoke. "Don't let him get away with this."

"I have no intention of letting him get away with anything," I said, my voice steady. "This case is my number one priority, but I need time to build it correctly. The best way you can help is by letting me do my job and keeping town gossip to a minimum. Can you do that?"

There was a pause, followed by a few sniffles. "I'm trusting you, Detective Jolett. I can't lose my best friend."

A small crack formed in my heart for Stephanie. I glanced over at Bell, taking a deep breath. "I know what it feels like to lose your best friend." My voice softened. I didn't tell her that mine was a K9 named Suii, or that the pain of losing him still lingered, despite having Bell by my side now.

"Thank you, Detective," she whispered, before hanging up.

I took a moment, allowing the room to settle into silence before returning to my warrants. When they were finally ready, I hit a wall—there was no judge available to sign them. With a sigh, I pulled out the cell number Judge John Eship had given me years ago for moments like this.

"You bag 'em, I tag 'em," he answered with a chuckle.

"Judge Eship?" I asked, unsure if this was actually him or if I'd dialed a serial killer.

"I take it this is official?" he responded, still laughing.

"This is Detective Jolett. I need warrants signed, but there's no one available at the courthouse. Any chance I can bring them to you?"

"I'm hungry. Meet me at Mom's Diner in thirty."

He hung up before I could say anything else. I looked at Bell. "You bag 'em, I tag 'em? We could have a serial killer judge on our hands."

Bell thumped her tail against the floor in response.

"You just want a burger from Mom's, don't you?" I said with a smile.

Her tail wagged harder, and I knew we were both on the same page. A greasy burger sounded pretty good, and Bell was more than willing to endure whatever gastrointestinal consequences came with it. I, however, would probably regret this decision later when I had to deal with the aftereffects.

Mom's Diner was tucked away behind the drugstore in the center of town. It was the kind of place tourists stumbled upon during hot Arizona summers when they were looking for a break from the heat. But for locals, Mom's was an institution—a place that served the greasiest, most delicious burgers in town.

When we arrived, Bell and I snagged our usual back corner table, and we waited for the judge. The place wasn't crowded, and the faint clink of dishes and the murmur of conversations created a comfortable background hum. I ordered three waters, and just as they arrived, so did Judge Eship. He raised an eyebrow at the extra glasses.

"Bell gets thirsty after her burger," I explained.

He chuckled and gave Bell a solid scratch behind her ears. She barely acknowledged him, her eyes fixed on me, silently reminding me that she was still waiting for her burger.

"That dog has you trained," the judge said with amusement.

"If I don't give her what she wants, there'll be consequences," I deadpanned. "I'd suggest you sign the warrants and avoid giving her any side-eye."

He laughed again, then turned his attention to the paperwork. We both knew he couldn't buy my dinner, and I couldn't buy his, so we asked for separate checks. I placed my order after he chose the nightly special, and then he got to work reviewing the warrants. He read through all three carefully, occasionally grunting as he made his way through the pages. One of the warrants was for Jennifer's cell phone, and I wasn't sure if he'd question that, but after a few moments, he simply nodded and pulled out his pen, signing each one with a flourish.

"Make sure they're filed at the courthouse first thing in the morning," he advised. "Preferably before you serve them."

I nodded. We both knew the drill—warrants needed to be filed quickly to avoid any legal complications, but things didn't always go smoothly in the real world.

The waitress arrived with our food, and I tore Bell's burger into small pieces, knowing she'd inhale it in one bite if I didn't. She ate like a perfect lady, her eyes never leaving me. The judge and I didn't talk much while we ate, keeping the conversation light. If anyone asked, we could honestly say we didn't discuss the case at all.

When we left, Bell and I both had full stomachs, and I had three signed search warrants ready to go. Sitting in my car, I began making calls, starting with Sergeant Spence. He didn't answer, so I left him a detailed message, outlining everything I needed for tomorrow. Next, I called Gabe, hoping he'd be available.

"You're in luck," he said. "Where do you want me?"

"We'll need to serve the warrants at the same time. I'm concerned about Beau's house being contaminated, so hazmat will meet you there. Once we hit the plant, Beau will know we're onto him. If we don't find anything, I can't arrest him, so we need to stay in contact. I'll have an extra officer with me to keep an eye on Beau as long as possible. Someone tried to poison Bell last night, and it's no coincidence. Beau has access to poisons, and we need to be careful."

"We'll have him tomorrow," Gabe promised, his voice resolute. "And hopefully, he'll take a ride in my back seat."

"Just make sure he's in one piece when he gets there," I said, half-joking. "I'll sic Bell on you if he's not."

"If Bell wants to take a bite out of him, I'll hold him still for her," Gabe said, laughing and completely ignoring my warning.

I smiled, despite myself. "Meet me at six a.m. tomorrow at the department, and we'll go over the warrants. I'll have a team ready."

"Ten-four, Detective Jolett," Gabe replied, the laughter still in his voice.

"Ten-one hundred, Detective Macky," I shot back, teasing him as I hung up. Gabe was still laughing when the call ended. I'd just told him I was on a bathroom break.

Next, I called Leo. He didn't even let me finish explaining before he cut in. "I'm in. You left me dealing with old men, and I need some action. This case is for the birds."

"You want the house or the plant? I need officers at both locations."

"I'm with you. I'll stand by and look intimidating while you find what you need."

"Sure, because that's how we solve cases—by looking intimidating." My voice was dripping with sarcasm.

Leo, unaffected, just chuckled. "Don't worry, Jolett. I'll have honeyed words dripping from my lips while I intimidate everyone."

I was glad Bell was female. At least I wouldn't have to deal with testosterone-fueled banter all night. Shaking my head, I grinned and hung up.

The first hint of Bell's dinner started to make its presence known in the small confines of the car. It was time to get her home. Once we were there, I searched the backyard carefully before letting her out. Rat Cat wasn't around, and I was relieved for the moment. Bell did her business, then gave the yard a thorough inspection while I kept watch. It was going to be a while before I let her outside unsupervised again.

By the time I crawled into bed, the air in my room was thick with the aftermath of Bell's burger. My stomach growled in protest, but sleep eventually claimed me, despite the not-so-pleasant smell.

Chapter Forty-Three

D ISPATCH WOKE ME AT two a.m., and even before they patched Dr. Timmons through, my gut told me it was bad news.

"I tried everything I could. Nothing we did helped, and she died twenty minutes ago," he said stiffly, his usual calm voice strained with emotion. I could tell he was taking Jennifer's death hard.

"Have you informed her mother yet?" I asked, rubbing my tired eyes.

"No, I haven't made that call," he admitted.

I hesitated, thinking of the warrants I needed to serve in the morning. "Could you hold off until after eight? I'm serving a warrant on the suspect, and if her mother finds out too early, it could complicate things."

"Eight is stretching it," he said, sounding conflicted, "but if it'll help you get this guy, I'll do it. I'll let the nurses know in case she calls."

"Thank you, Doctor," I said quietly.

Our conversation ended, but the darkness around me seemed to deepen. I stared at the ceiling, my mind swirling with thoughts of Jennifer's mother and her best friend, Stephanie. There was no real comfort in knowing I'd done everything I could. The fact that this case hadn't started as a homicide made it harder. It felt like I'd let them down somehow.

Bell whined softly at the foot of the bed, sensing my unease. I reached over and gave her belly a rub. "It's the job, Bell," I murmured, trying to convince myself as much as her. "But it's easier when you come in after the death. I feel like there's more I could have done."

She licked my hand, offering her silent but reassuring comfort, and it helped. Eventually, I fell back asleep until the alarm dragged me back into the world.

The morning light brought no new surprises—thankfully, no poison waited in the backyard. Bell was able to give her usual low growl at Rat Cat while I got dressed. If anyone tossed something over the wall while Bell was out there, I was confident she'd alert me with more than just a growl.

At the courthouse, I dropped off the warrants to be officially stamped, grateful one of the clerks let me in early. I also handed over the return warrant information from yesterday. The old saying was true—police work involved a lot of paperwork. As a detective, it seemed to multiply.

My team for today included nine officers, along with myself, Sam, and Investigator Lott. Sam was coming with me to the plant, while Lott would head over to Beau's house with Gabe. Both men from hazmat had chromatographs and spectrometers to scan for any toxic substances. With any luck, we'd be taking Beau into custody today—and hopefully, it would be long-term.

Bell gave me the saddest look when I left her behind. I hated leaving her, especially not knowing what had been thrown over the fence the night before. In hindsight, I should have had the hazmat team examine the meat. Too late now.

We arrived at the plant five minutes before eight, pulling up in three unmarked cars. The door to the small front building was unlocked, so I stepped inside and asked the secretary for Mr. Dapple. The men stayed outside, but she could see them through the glass door. Her expression tightened when she noticed them—a flicker of anger in her eyes.

The hostility didn't surprise me. The plant employed prisoners, and the workers, even the secretary, were protective. I had no doubt the cops had hassled them before. Thankfully, the plant lay within the county, not the city. That would make things a little easier for me.

When Mr. Dapple arrived, the warmth from the day before was gone. He looked at me with cautious suspicion. "What can I do for you, Detective Jolett?" he asked, his tone laced with annoyance.

"I need to speak with you privately," I said firmly.

He led me back to his office without a word, his frustration clear. As soon as we were inside, he turned to face me. "Why are you hassling one of my employees, Detective?"

I didn't waste time. "Give me five minutes, and I'll explain everything. I need your help."

He stared at me for a moment, then reluctantly nodded. "No promises."

I quickly laid out the highlights of the case, including the paraquat we'd found at Jennifer's home. "This is now a homicide investigation," I explained, handing him the search warrant for the plant.

He sighed, his expression hardening as reality sank in. "Beau orders items from time to time," he admitted. "We don't use paraquat here, but he would have had access to ordering it."

My chest tightened. Dapple was going to help me. "What time does Beau start work?" I asked.

"He starts at eight, but he's always early," Dapple said, glancing at his watch. "He should be in his office right now." He turned to his computer and started typing. "Let me check the invoices. We do have one supplier outside the U.S. that could be a possibility."

I moved closer as he scrolled through the invoices. When one caught his eye, he zoomed in and highlighted a word, then Googled it. The results were gibberish until he added *paraquat* to the search. *Bingo.* Dapple read aloud from the information on the screen and pointed to an image of a product listed under an unfamiliar name. "This paraquat is illegal in the U.S.," he said grimly. "Beau ordered it two months ago, and that is not my signature on the purchase order."

"Can you print the order for me? If there's a hard copy, I'll need that as evidence."

"I understand." He looked dejected but didn't hesitate to help. I respected him for that. Dapple had done hard time at Perryville, and he had no interest in doing more. His life had changed for the better, and he was proof that change was possible.

"I've got officers outside ready to assist with the warrant," I told him. "I'll need one of them to accompany us to Beau's office, along with a hazmat specialist."

Dapple scratched his cheek, deep in thought. "Call them in. I can't believe Beau's ruined his life this way. He was a solid employee, just like I told you yesterday." He shook his head sadly. "That poor woman."

I called Leo while Dapple notified the secretary. Once the team was assembled, Dapple led us through the plant's indoor greenhouse. The workers turned to stare, their eyes cold and wary. It wasn't a welcoming environment for cops, and I felt the tension in the air. It was the kind of situation that made me wish Bell was with us.

We moved through the outdoor garden section, which was surrounded by small buildings. Dapple stopped at one of the doors and tried the handle, but it was locked.

"Strange," he muttered, pulling out his keys to unlock it.

The light inside was off, and Dapple called out, "Beau, are you in there?"

Silence.

I put a hand on his arm before he could step inside. "The office needs to be checked by hazmat first."

Sam stepped forward, already in his protective gear, and entered the office with his chromatograph and spectrometer. I hung back, watching from the doorway.

Leo stood beside me, watching in silence. I could tell he was disappointed he hadn't had the chance to place handcuffs on Beau, but he'd survive.

Five minutes later, Sam poked his head out the door. "There's paraquat in his desk. It's still in the original container, and I'm removing it now. He even left the label on. I'll finish checking the office, but there's a small storage room in the back that I need to look at."

I turned to Dapple. "Can you find out if Beau came to work today?"

He nodded and made a call, while the rest of the crew kept a watchful eye on the plant workers, who were still glaring at us from a distance.

Sam emerged from the office holding a small, black, plastic-covered container, about six inches long. My mind immediately jumped to Officer Conners handling the poisoned meat in my backyard. I cursed under my breath, realizing I hadn't told him to get checked out. Quickly, I sent Conners a text, urging him to see a doctor. The fact that Rat Cat was still alive gave me hope that it hadn't been paraquat in my backyard, but I couldn't be sure.

My heart pounded as I finally entered Beau's office, glancing around.

"I took photos," Sam said. "I'll send you copies."

"Thank you," I replied, grateful for his thoroughness.

Dapple's voice broke the silence. "Beau hasn't shown up for work, and he hasn't called in sick. He knows something's up."

I immediately called Gabe. "We've got paraquat in Beau's office, and he didn't show up for work."

"He's not at his house either," Gabe informed me. "We've checked everywhere."

"I'm putting out an ATL on him," I said. "As soon as we're done here, I'll get an arrest warrant from the judge."

"We haven't found anything at the house so far. Hazmat went through with their fancy machines, but all we've turned up is a little marijuana."

"Call the drug task force and see if they want to pursue a separate search warrant for that," I suggested. "For now, a little weed isn't my priority."

"Gotcha, Detective."

"Thanks, Gabe. Keep me posted if anything changes."

Our conversation ended, and I turned back to Dapple. "I need to speak with Beau's friends here at the plant. Someone might know where he is."

Dapple shook his head. "I'm not sure they'll help, but you can try. I need to notify the owners about what's going on. Will this hurt the plant?"

"You've cooperated fully," I assured him. "At this point, I don't have anything that implicates the plant itself. This looks like Beau's doing, but I still need to talk to the other employees."

"I'll do what I can to help."

Despite Dapple's support, none of Beau's coworkers had anything helpful to say. It was like hitting a brick wall. Leo, annoyed that the warrant had turned out to be more routine than action-packed, grumbled as he and the other officers loaded up to leave.

I couldn't blame him—no one got to put the cuffs on Beau today. As he drove off, still complaining about running a "rosy warrant," I couldn't help but think about where Beau might be hiding.

And how soon we could bring him in.

Chapter Forty-Four

T HE FOLLOWING MORNING, I asked Gabe to join me in Sergeant Spence's office. Gabe looked tired—par for the course in detective work—but still solid, like someone who'd been fed well by his wife of forty years. He was in decent shape for his age and far too young to retire, though I knew he'd earned it if he wanted to.

"I've got a nationwide warrant out for Beau's arrest," I began, addressing both Gabe and the sergeant. "I even did some fast talking at the county attorney's office to get them to guarantee funds for extradition."

"Why'd the county give you trouble over extradition?" Gabe asked, grimacing. It was exactly the kind of bureaucratic nonsense that drove us all crazy.

"They figure Beau's dangerous, sure, but the person he's most dangerous to is already deceased, so they didn't see the threat as 'imminent.' Basically, they're worried about the budget and say funds are tight."

Gabe rolled his eyes, already familiar with those excuses. "Conners called me this morning. We got a positive result back on the poison thrown over my fence. It was rat poison, the kind you can pick up just about anywhere."

Gabe let out a short laugh. "Figures. I confiscated some from his house, just in case."

I smiled. "We'll test it to see if the batches match. I should also have Jennifer's text messages and phone calls in the next day or so."

Sergeant Spence leaned back in his chair, watching us carefully. "Any idea where Beau's hiding?"

I shrugged. "That's the million-dollar question. His friends at the plant aren't talking, and they might not know anything anyway. Jennifer's mother has no clue, and her best friend would kill him if she found him first. I was hoping for suggestions."

"He'll crawl out of his hole eventually," Gabe said, leaning forward. He was confident, though we both knew time wasn't on our side.

"My reports are written, the case is solid. I just need an arrest," I said, a bit more frustration creeping into my voice. "Until then, I need another homicide. I'm tired of dealing with old men who haven't kicked the bucket yet." I batted my eyes dramatically at the sergeant. "I'll do almost anything."

Sergeant Spence chuckled. "You sound like Conners. He's been begging for a detective spot again."

That surprised me. "He thinks JD is leaving. I asked JD, and he said he isn't going anywhere."

"That explains why Conners has been in my office five times a day kissing my butt," Spence said with a sigh. "I'll give the chief a heads-up that Councilman Conners may be paying him a visit soon."

I hesitated, then spoke up. "He did a competent job on Bell's attempted poisoning. He was professional."

"Can I get that in writing?" Gabe asked with a grin.

"Truth is truth," I said, rolling my eyes. "Even when it feels like swallowing glass."

Spence ignored Gabe's jab and turned to me. "You're back on homicide indefinitely, Jolett. I cleared it with the chief. You can help Gabe with his case if nothing comes up for you in the next week or so."

I flashed Gabe a wide smile. "I'm all yours. Bell may need some convincing, though."

"She's easy," Gabe said, smirking. "A belly scratch and she'll be eating out of my hands."

"I require a steak dinner, but the outcome would be the same," I shot back.

"Children," Spence interrupted, shaking his head at us.

"Yes?" Gabe asked, both of us grinning like we were back in school.

"Get out of my office and do some actual detective work. Good job on the case, Jolett. Your suspect will show up."

Gabe invited Bell and me to lunch, and we ended up at Mom's again for another round of greasy hamburgers. Bell wasn't complaining, and neither was I, though I knew I'd regret it later. We spent the meal going over Gabe's current case, bouncing ideas off each other. It was rare that we got to tag-team a case due to the usual cutbacks, but when we did, it reminded me of working with Tony. My heart skipped a beat at the memory before I forced myself to focus on the conversation.

I got home a little after six. With dinner taken care of, I decided it was time for some exercise—both for Bell and for me. After all, we'd just inhaled enough food for the whole day. I put on my jogging clothes, clipped Bell's regular lead on, and we set out for a run.

A mile in, Bell was having the time of her life, bounding ahead while I struggled to keep up, huffing and puffing. "You need to get me out more, Bell. I'm losing my endurance," I muttered, cutting our run short by looping around the next block.

Bell didn't seem to care that our run had been halved, and she definitely didn't have the same urge to toss her hamburger like I did. "Good job, Bell," I panted. "Maybe we'll try this again tomorrow."

She shot me a skeptical look, her "yeah, right" face clear as day. "Or not," I added, hanging up her leash when we got home.

Bell whined at the back door, so I followed her outside. Sure enough, Rat Cat was waiting on his usual perch, taunting Bell like he did every day. Leaving her inside for now, I took a quick walk around the yard, searching for anything unusual. I kicked through a pile of leaves in the corner, just in case, then went back inside as the doorbell rang.

"Hold on, Bell," I called out. "You can go be antagonized by the cat in a minute. I need to see who's at the door first."

I checked the peephole. The old man standing there was familiar—Jeb Garland—but the woman with him was not. I sighed. Small towns. People thought they could come to an officer's home whenever they pleased. It had happened before, but once I explained protocol, it usually didn't happen again.

I opened the door just a crack. "Let me put Bell in the backyard, and I'll be right with you."

"Sure thing," the woman said in a chipper voice.

Once Bell was occupied with Rat Cat, I returned to the door. "May I help you?" I asked, trying to keep my tone polite, though curiosity was starting to rise. There was something about the woman that reminded me of one of the few foster mothers I'd liked as a child.

The woman, who had soft laugh lines around her eyes and mouth, turned to Jeb and gave him a glare that could melt steel. His damp hair and lack of his usual stink suggested she'd made him clean up. She turned back to me with a warm smile and held out her hand. "I'm Mrs. Garland, the unfortunate woman married to this old reprobate."

I shook her hand, still half in shock. She wasn't done.

"I heard from my quilting group that my husband was disrespectful to you. After speaking with him, he's decided to apologize." Her eyes narrowed as she turned her death stare back to her husband.

Jeb stared at his boots, missing the glare that could have set his pants on fire. "Sorry," he muttered, his voice gruff.

Mrs. Garland wasn't having it. "That's not good enough. Look at her and show respect."

I was in awe. I wanted to be Mrs. Garland when I grew up.

Jeb reluctantly lifted his head and met my gaze. "I'm truly sorry, Detective Jolett."

Mrs. Garland growled, causing Jeb to flinch. "That's *Detective* Jolett, you dipweed. You can't even get her title right, but you will before we leave."

"Detective Jolett," he corrected quickly.

Mrs. Garland smiled at me, her eyes soft again. "My quilting group thinks you're the bomb. If you ever want to speak to the women in this community, let me know. We'd love to host you—and your amazing dog too. Is there anything else you need from my husband before we leave?"

I couldn't help myself. If I didn't say something intelligent, I was going to burst into laughter. "Actually, yes. I'd like to know who shot Lucky's window."

Jeb scuffed his boot against the porch. "I don't know," he muttered, glancing nervously at his wife.

Mrs. Garland smacked him on the side of the head, and I suddenly found myself witnessing a domestic assault, unsure of how to react.

"Give the woman a name, or so help me, you'll never set foot in Lucky's again, and you won't stay married to me either."

Jeb let out a defeated sigh. "It was Leroy. He was drunk and knows it was stupid."

"Thank you," I said, a little more sympathy in my voice. I wouldn't want to go home with Mrs. Garland if I were him.

"We'll get out of your hair now, sweetie," she said, her voice back to its chipper tone. "If my husband or any of the other old coots in town give you trouble, just let me know. The men think we don't know what they're up to, but they're wrong."

"Uh, thanks," I squeaked, still trying to process what I'd just witnessed.

Mrs. Garland grabbed Jeb by the arm and marched him back to their car, but not before calling out, "They're cheating Larry out of coffee refills at Lucky's, by the way. They fill their cups more than once."

"Maud!" Jeb whined, sounding exactly like Bell when Rat Cat was just out of reach.

The door clicked shut, and I couldn't help but laugh. I had no idea what to do with all of that. Should I laugh or call an officer to check on Jeb?

I walked into the kitchen and filled a glass of water, trying to shake off the absurdity. But before I could sit down, the doorbell rang again. This time, I sighed. *Mrs. Garland must not be done with me*, I thought as I headed for the door.

I didn't bother checking the peephole, expecting more of Jeb and Maud's domestic saga, but when I cracked the door, Bell slammed into the back door with a ferocious growl. A split second later, the door was shoved open, and I was thrown back.

My instincts kicked in immediately. Lifting my arm, I blocked the incoming blow just before the bat connected with my head. Pain exploded in my arm, momentarily numbing my brain. I barely had time to register Beau's sweaty, twisted face before he grabbed a fistful of my hair and dragged me away from the door.

Fear for my life should have been front and center, but all I could think about was Bell. If I didn't survive this, she'd be next. Beau's face was contorted with rage, his spittle flying as he snarled at me. He was completely unhinged.

He slammed my head into the floor, making me dizzy as he reached back to close the door. But he wasn't quick enough. Eighty pounds of K9 fury launched herself at Beau, sinking her teeth into his shoulder. I had no idea how Bell got inside, but I was beyond grateful.

Beau screamed as he raised the knife, ready to stab Bell. "No, you don't!" I shouted, kicking at his hand. The knife flew out of his grip and skittered across the floor. Bell dug in deeper, her growls muffled as she clung to Beau like a teething ring. I kicked the knife farther away, my broken arm throbbing in agony, but I was still in the fight.

Over the chaos, I saw my neighbor Bill standing in the doorway, his face pale with shock. "Call 9-1-1!" I shouted, praying that help would arrive in time.

Beau collapsed to the ground, screaming in pain. I scissored my legs around his, trapping him while Bell held on tight. "Get him off, get him off!" he shrieked.

"It's a *her*, you idiot," I snapped back. Stupid to correct him, but I was running on adrenaline. My legs kept him locked down while Bell maintained her grip, causing him more agony. Sirens wailed in the distance, and Bill stepped back into the room, pressing his boot against Beau's head.

"Don't bite me, doggie," Bill said to Bell. "I'm one of the good guys."

Scratch what I'd thought earlier—I was glad to have Bill as my neighbor. A minute later, the room was filled with police officers. "Bell, release!" I commanded.

With a final growl and a snap of her jaws, Bell let go and backed off. Conners grabbed Beau, rolling him onto his stomach and pressing a knee into his back while slapping the handcuffs on him. Beau groaned, but the fight had left him.

"The knife's in the kitchen," I told Conners, still cradling my throbbing arm.

Bell licked my face, her warm tongue offering comfort as I wrapped my good arm around her. Shock was setting in, and I could feel my fingers trembling.

"Laci," Gabe's voice said softly from somewhere nearby. "I called an ambulance for you. Where are you hurt? Did he get you with the knife?"

"No," I mumbled. "My arm. It's broken. The rest of me is fine."

"I'll let the paramedics decide when they get here," he said, relief in his voice.

Conners returned after securing Beau in the patrol car. "I called a second ambulance for him; you get first care. He's got a few teeth punctures, but nothing fatal. I've got everything I need for the arrest charges tonight, not to mention Jennifer's murder. Take care of yourself."

As he walked away, Gabe leaned closer. "Was that Conners, actually doing his job without whining?"

"You're dreaming," I muttered, too exhausted to care.

"That's what I thought. Stress hallucinations."

The paramedics arrived, and despite my protests, they insisted I ride in the ambulance. Gabe threatened to bypass Sergeant Spence and call the chief if I didn't behave. The only concession I got was bringing Bell with me. I wasn't letting her out of my sight—she'd saved my life.

Sergeant Spence arrived at the hospital fifteen minutes after we did, refusing to leave despite my assurances that I was fine.

"You staying the night?" Gabe asked, his tone sarcastic.

"No," I shot back, just as stubborn.

"And how do you plan on getting home?"

"Uber."

"Over my dead body." He glanced at Bell. "Neither of us will let her get away with this."

"You've got the sergeant on your side," Spence agreed, arms crossed.

I sighed. "Just let me sleep for a week, then we can talk."

They both laughed, but I was dead serious. Whatever they'd given me for the pain in the ambulance was working, though unfortunately not well enough for what came next. The doctor reset my arm, and the pain ripped through me like fire. I cried out, and Bell growled low in her throat.

"Are we going to have a problem?" the doctor asked, eyeing Bell warily.

"Only if you reset my arm again," I muttered through gritted teeth.

"Just a brace until the swelling goes down," he said, sizing it for me. "Anything else hurt?"

I didn't mention the pounding headache from where Beau had slammed my head into the floor. "More pain meds would be great."

"Coming right up." He eyed Bell again. "She going to bite me if I give you a shot?"

"Bell, bite the doctor," I commanded, deadpan.

She wagged her tail.

The doctor chuckled. "I see she's a softy."

"A softy who saved my life. You'll be treating the guy she attacked shortly."

"I already did. He's here, crying like a baby, but he'll live. No permanent damage."

I didn't care much about Beau's recovery, but I had to ask. "Will he have any lasting injuries?"

"Doubtful. Your dog turned his shoulder into hamburger, but I'm a wizard. He'll be fine."

If I wasn't in so much pain, I might have appreciated the humor. Instead, I let the meds work their magic as he finished putting my arm in the brace.

Two hours later, after much grumbling and complaints, I was released.

Chapter Forty-Five

T HREE DAYS LATER, I found myself at Jennifer's funeral, my arm still wrapped in the brace the ER physician had put on. I hadn't bothered to get it replaced with a cast; a visit to the doctor felt unnecessary. As long as I was careful, no one would be the wiser.

Funerals were never my favorite part of the job. I wouldn't have come if Jennifer's mom hadn't asked me personally. I wasn't good with condolences or small talk. Without Bell by my side, I felt even more out of place. This was the first time we'd been apart since my hospital visit, and her absence was unsettling.

I still hadn't figured out how Bell managed to get to the front door during the attack. If she could jump the wall, surely the cat would have been history by now. Unless I saw her do it, I might never know.

Marge, Jennifer's mother, stood in the condolence line, waiting to greet me. When it was my turn, she reached out for a handshake but then pulled me in for a hug. I wasn't much for hugging, but I accepted because, honestly, what else could I do?

"Thank you," I said softly when she released me. "I'm so sorry about your daughter."

Marge sniffed and dabbed at her eyes. "I never understood why she loved him," she said, her voice cracking. "I would give anything to have her back, but she also holds some blame.

That's the hardest part for me. I would've done anything to help her, but she didn't deserve this."

"No, she didn't," I said sincerely.

The next person in line was Stephanie, her eyes red and swollen from crying. She didn't hug me, but she offered a small apology as we shook hands. "I was upset when I spoke to you. I'm glad you got him, though. I don't know what I would've done if you hadn't."

"I'm glad, too," I said.

"Please come by Marge's house after the service," Stephanie added, echoing Marge's earlier invitation. Now I knew there was no escaping it, so I nodded in agreement.

After the graveside service, I followed the line of cars to Marge's small duplex on the west side of town. Inside, the place was packed, every surface covered with food dishes brought by ladies from her church. One of them made sure to tell me that in case I missed the obvious.

"Thank you for catching Jennifer's killer. You're the town's hero," one of the women said as I tried, unsuccessfully, to find a corner to hide in.

I froze. I had no idea how to respond. Hero? I was just doing my job. Thankfully, Stephanie swooped in like a savior.

"She took a beating to do it, too," Stephanie said, nodding toward my arm. She smiled a little. "Her dog is my personal hero, though. Bell took a chunk out of Beau's shoulder. Too bad it wasn't his face."

I forced a smile, ignoring the comment about his face. "Bell's the real hero."

"I was hoping to see you here," said a familiar voice behind me.

I turned to find Mrs. Garland, her presence both unexpected and—considering her reputation—slightly concerning. At least Jeb's body hadn't turned up anywhere, so I could feel comfortable saying hello.

"Mary," Mrs. Garland addressed the woman who had called me a hero. "This is the detective I told you about. She agreed to speak to our quilting group. She's bringing her dog, and we'll get all the inside details on catching that horrible man."

I blinked, feeling trapped. When had I agreed to that? I hated public speaking, especially to groups. Bell was the only one I enjoyed talking to. Well, maybe Jack, too. But now, with Mrs. Garland locking me into this, there was no escape.

As I desperately searched for a way out, Stephanie caught my eye, winked, and then walked off, leaving me to my fate. She really didn't like me. It took another hour of awkward small talk before I finally made it to the door.

My phone rang just as I was about to drive off. I checked the screen—Jack. I answered, grateful for the distraction.

"Hello," I said.

"Are you home?" Jack asked, his voice cheerful.

"I will be in fifteen minutes," I replied, curious.

"Perfect. I've got lunch for three, and I'll be at your place in about twenty."

"You're in town?" My heart rate picked up a little at the thought.

"I am," he confirmed. "And the food will be warm, don't worry."

"I'm starving," I admitted, feeling more than a little suspicious.

"I'll see you in a few," Jack said before hanging up.

Nervous energy buzzed in my stomach. I barely had time to change out of my funeral clothes and into jeans and a t-shirt before Jack knocked on the door. Of course, I checked the peephole first—lesson learned.

Jack stood there with a bouquet of red roses in one hand and a bag of food in the other. He grinned as he thrust the flowers at me. "For your injury in the line of duty," he said, then pulled a chew stick out of his back pocket and handed it to Bell, who was wagging her entire backside in excitement. "And an antler for her heroism."

"Roses and an antler. How romantic," I said before I could stop myself. My face immediately heated up, and I cursed my inability to filter my thoughts.

Jack laughed, though there was a sadness in his eyes. "His Majesty went to his new home," he said quietly. "I was feeling a little down and thought maybe you were still on leave for your injury. Figured I'd try my luck."

Now *he* was blushing.

We made quite the pair, and I wasn't about to read too much into his statement. Both of us struggled with small talk, so the best course of action was to let the awkwardness slide.

"You gonna invite me in?" Jack asked after a moment.

"Only if I can pretend this is a date," I shot back, my new-found bravado surprising even me.

Jack wiped his forehead in an exaggerated gesture. "Good to know. Asking someone out on a second date is so much easier."

We sat down to eat, and for once, talking came easy. It felt natural, not forced, like we'd been doing this for years. For a first date, if that's what it was, it was the best I'd ever had. I even told him about Mrs. Garland's quilting group invitation, hoping for some sympathy.

Instead, he gave me a straight face. "Talking to a ladies' group? That's community policing at its best."

"I'd rather face a firing squad, and I thought you, of all people, would understand."

"I do," he said, his face still serious. "But I have a secret that helps every time."

"What's that?"

"Just pretend they're naked dogs."

I almost choked on my drink. "Wait, what? I thought the trick was to imagine them naked, not *with fur.*"

He grinned. "My way works better. Trust me."

We spent the afternoon together, talking and laughing like I'd always imagined normal people did on dates. I even took him out back to show him the wall where Bell had made her escape during the attack.

"She staggered her jump," Jack said, inspecting the corner where the block walls met. "Hit this wall, then the other. It's something she's trained to do."

"Then why didn't she ever eat the cat?"

Jack chuckled. "Maybe she likes cats more than we do. Or maybe she's just picky."

"She's not picky," I retorted. "She eats hamburgers and ice cream."

Jack raised an eyebrow. "She *shouldn't.*"

I held up my injured arm. "She saved me. If she wants burgers and ice cream, she's getting them."

He laughed and shook his head, letting the argument go. We spent the rest of the afternoon enjoying each other's company, and I finally asked him about not having a dog at home.

"I had one," he said, his voice softening. "He died of old age a few years ago. Now, I bring home dogs that need extra training. It's easier without a personal pet at home."

"The man needs a dog," I said, more to myself than to him.

Jack didn't kiss me when he left, but before he went, he asked, "How about that second date?"

"Yes," I replied, my heart skipping a beat.

"I've got a week off next month. Maybe we could meet up and continue today's conversation?"

"I'd like that."

He grinned, and I felt a thrill run through me as I watched him drive away. Bell looked as sad as I felt once he was gone.

After straightening up the house, I called Gabe to check in. He filled me in on the upcoming court dates for Beau. I'd missed the arraignment, but Gabe had gone for me. "Pretrial is next Wednesday, but it won't be much. The real stuff starts when we hit superior court."

Gabe also mentioned that Jennifer's phone records had come in—hundreds of calls and texts between her and Beau. "Expect a plea deal," he said. Beau had lawyered up immediately after his arrest, and we still didn't know his motive. We had pieced together some of Jennifer's cryptic ramblings, though. Beau had rubbed paraquat into her clothes—clothes that had been left at his place since before the divorce. She'd asked if she could have them and now she was dead.

Jennifer deserved better.

After hanging up with Gabe, I called Leo.

"You still milking that injury?" Leo answered instead of greeting me like a gentleman.

"I would be at work if the chief didn't threaten to fire me if I showed up," I shot back.

"Uh-huh. We all know you're just milking it."

"Do you want me to hang up?"

Leo chuckled. "What do you need?"

I filled him in on the Garlands' visit after my hospital stay. "Any update on your case of senility?"

"I should get a promotion for this one," he said, laughing.

"You don't *want* a promotion, remember?"

"Leroy confessed before I even had a chance to rough him up behind the gas station. Apparently, he was worried I'd knock out his false teeth."

"You're all heart, Leo."

"Yeah, well, I have a soft spot for old men with bad dental work."

We both laughed, and it felt good. I had friends, a job I loved, and the best K9 partner in the world. What more could I ask for?

As we were about to hang up, Bell started whining at the back door. Jack had brought her a cupcake from a fancy dog treat shop, but apparently, her stomach wasn't agreeing with it. I opened the back door, expecting her to dart outside, but something caught my eye.

In the corner of the yard, in the pile of leaves I'd kicked through earlier, was Rat Cat—and she wasn't alone.

I stepped outside, closing the door behind me. Bell nosed her way out, too, just as I realized what was happening. Rat Cat had a kitten. And judging by her movements, she was having another one.

"Bell," I said, staring in disbelief. "We need towels and hot water."

Bell gave me a confused look before trotting over to sniff at the tiny newborn kitten.

"Okay, maybe not the hot water," I muttered, running back inside to grab towels. By the time I returned, a second kitten had arrived, and Rat Cat was cleaning it up. Over the next hour, two more kittens made their appearance—one a black-and-white mix, and another an orange tabby like their mother.

I had no idea what to do with them.

After making sure Rat Cat was settled with her new family, I found a box and gently moved them inside, carrying the whole bundle into my condo. I didn't have any cat food and had no idea how to care for a mother cat and her kittens.

There was only one thing to do.

I dialed Jack. He answered on the second ring.

"If this is to cancel our second date, I didn't hear you," he said, teasing.

"No," I replied, glancing over at the box of kittens. "You need to get back here. I've had kittens."

Chapter Forty-Six

J ACK DIDN'T RETURN, BUT his laughter echoed in my mind, a haunting melody that reminded me of how alone I truly was. His voice rang loud and clear in my memory, teasing me, "You're on your own." He wasn't wrong. The next six weeks unraveled in a chaotic blur, leaving me to navigate the mess that was my life.

I carefully placed the kittens, their tiny, fragile bodies squirming against the softness of the towels, into an old laundry basket. It wasn't the most glamorous setup, but it would do. I tucked the basket into the dark recesses of my closet, leaving the door cracked just enough for Rat Cat—because, honestly, what else could I call her?—to slip in and out as she pleased. The arrangement meant hauling a litter box, food dishes, and water into my room, turning it into a makeshift nursery for the tiny creatures I never asked for but couldn't turn away.

No, I hadn't wanted a cat. Not at all. But those kittens? They were adorable. Their wide, curious eyes, barely able to focus, and their squeaky meows chipped away at my resolve. And despite Bell's intimidating size and her predator instincts, she never once acted like she might hurt them. Quite the opposite—Bell was smitten. She cleaned them whenever their mom wandered off and guarded them like they were her own. As much as I tried to ignore it, a strange domestic harmony had settled over the chaos in my home. But if I was being honest, my life was still a mess.

Throughout both the police and sheriff's departments, I became the unofficial adoption agent. One by one, the kittens disappeared, placed in homes as soon as they were weaned. Soon, only Rat Cat remained, prowling the apartment like a lost soul, as forlorn as Bell when she realized her playmates were gone.

I found myself at the mercy of my neighbors, Bill and Molly. It was a long shot ,but I was desperate.

"I'm not a cat mom," I told them, waving a hand toward Bell, who sat watching from the porch, ears perked at the mention of the kittens. "And Bell doesn't need the distraction anymore. She's... protective." I paused, then, almost impulsively, blurted out, "But how about we share joint custody? Rat Cat can go between us." The words tumbled out before I could stop them.

Molly looked at Bill, a silent conversation passing between them. Her face lit up with a grin that stretched wide. "I'd love to take the cat off your hands. Permanently," she added, her eyes sparkling.

Relief surged through me, though I managed to hold back the urge to jump up and down. Instead, I offered a tight smile, trying to play it cool.

"There are two conditions," Molly continued, her tone businesslike. "I'll give her a proper name that fits her personality, and when Bill and I visit the grandkids, you'll check on her. We can leave enough food and water, but she'll need someone to make sure everything's okay every couple of days."

I wasn't much of a hugger, but at that moment, I nearly broke my own rule. "She can stay with me and Bell when you're out of town," I said, more composed now. "I'll give you everything I've bought for her, and she's scheduled to be spayed next week. It's all paid for."

Molly reached out her hand, and I shook it, sealing the deal. "When can I come to get her?" she asked, her voice full of excitement.

"Whenever you're ready," I replied, a weight lifting from my shoulders.

Molly wasted no time christening her new cat, naming her Sugarfire in honor of Sugarplum who I'd told her about. As I explained the daily routine, a strange feeling settled over me—part relief, part sadness. I would always worry about those kittens, but knowing Rat Cat—now Sugarfire—was just next door eased some of the burden. I explained it all to Bell, and though she whined at first, I could tell she would come around. Bell and Sugar fire's friendship couldn't bebroken now.

Life at home settled into a rhythm after that, quieter with just Bell and me. I missed Jack. His absence felt like a wound that hadn't fully healed. He'd had to cancel his vacation due to some unforeseen complications, and I had been looking forward to that second date. But life went on, and soon, things returned to what could be considered normal.

I was knee-deep in a new homicide investigation when my office phone rang, shattering my concentration.

"Detective Jollet?" A male voice crackled through the line, formal and direct.

"Yes, this is she. How can I help you?"

"I'm Detective Boling from the San Antonio Police Department. I've got a case that might connect with one of yours. Do you have time to talk?"

The mention of San Antonio sent a jolt through me, stirring memories I would have rather kept buried. I suddenly had a bad feeling about this.

"Of course. What's the case?"

"Gary Bender gave us your name," Boling said, his tone shifting, as though preparing to drop a bombshell.

My heart sank. I knew exactly where this was going.

"Carl Ledmen's girlfriend has died under mysterious circumstances," he said, his voice heavy with implication.

I felt sick. I'd always known he'd killed his wife, but I could never prove it. "How did she die?" I asked, dread creeping into my voice.

"Drug overdose," he replied, "but her friends and family swear she wasn't a user. Ledmen claims she took his deceased wife's pills because of some emotional issues, but her family says that's a lie. She wouldn't even take aspirin if she didn't have to."

I didn't hesitate. "He murdered her," I said bluntly. "Just like he killed his wife. I couldn't prove it then, but I'll have our clerk send over everything I've got on the case."

Boling and I spoke for a few more minutes before I transferred him to records. I sat there for a while after the call ended, staring blankly at my desk. Two weeks later, Boling called back. Ledmen had been arrested, and he suggested I revisit my case files. As if I hadn't been doing that every hour I could squeeze out. I released my anger. If I had a detective who hadn't solved a homicide and was now dealing with a murder because of it, I would recommend the same thing.

A woman had died, and I couldn't prove her husband did it. I'd had the county attorney's office go through it again to see if they could find anything to charge. It was a no go. That guilt weighed heavily on me, and that night, I found myself dialing Jack's number, desperate for a familiar voice.

When he picked up, his calm presence washed over me like a balm. "I don't talk about it much," he began, his voice soft, "but I lost three children on a SWAT raid. They tell you it's not your fault, but the guilt doesn't go away. I think about going back to SWAT sometimes, but I like where I am now. Sure, they tease me for working with dogs, but I don't mind."

His words sank in, and for a moment, I couldn't speak.

"Laci? "he asked after a pause.

My tears came, unbidden. Me, the woman who never cried.

"It'll be okay," Jack said, his voice soothing. "Sometimes, the criminals are smarter than us, but his arrogance caught up with him. Will you be okay?"

"Yes, "I managed through a sniffle. "For some reason, your story helps. Whether I ever get to charge him or not, he's going to spend the rest of his life in prison."

Jack's next words warmed my heart. "I've got the next couple of days off. How about that second date?"

A smile crept onto my face. "When?"

"Friday at six."

"I can't wait." There was warmth in my voice now.
****

As dates went, it was nothing short of perfect. Jack, ever the thoughtful planner, rented a hotel room and we went out two nights in a row. The chemistry between us was undeniable, growing stronger with every stolen glance and shared smile.

The next evening, just as magical, was more intimate. After dinner, I invited him in for coffee. It was an easy offer, one I didn't have to think twice about. And when I received my first Jack kiss, the world seemed to still around us. His lips, warm and soft, held a promise of something deeper. It wasn't just the kiss—it was everything that came with it. Trust. Understanding. A connection that went beyond the physical. My heart, hardened for so long, thawed even further.

From that moment on, my life shifted in ways I hadn't anticipated. We spent weekends together, each one more comfortable than the last, as if we had been doing this for years. There were moments of quiet, where just sitting next to him feltlike enough, and moments of laughter, where the sound of his voice felt like home. It wasn't long before Jack asked me to marry him. He wasn't flashy about it, not the type for grand gestures, but the sincerity in his eyes when he asked was all I needed.

Six months later, I was Laci Mallory, with all that came with it. The name change felt strange at first, like wearing someone else's skin, but soon it became part of me. Part of who I was becoming. Even before Tony's death, I wasn't exactly someone people gravitated toward. I was rough around the edges, too focused on my work, too driven. After Tony died, I was worse—a shell of a person who didn't know how to let anyone in. Suii saved me from that darkness. Then came Bell and now Jack, each of them filling the empty spaces in my life in ways I didn't know I needed.

Jack moved into my condo, transforming it from a solitary place into something warmer, more alive. His presence filled the rooms, his belongings merging with mine in a way that felt natural. He opened a private training and boarding facility, where he worked with the dogs he loved so much, pouring his heart into his passion. It wasn't just work for him—it was a calling. And as if that wasn't enough, he also signed on as a reserve officer at my department. He had a knack for fitting in wherever he went, and his calm, steady demeanor made him a valuable asset when we were short-staffed.

As for Mrs. Ledmen, the weight of her case would always sit heavy on my shoulders. I'd never stop feeling like I failed her, like I could have done more. But I refused to let that failure define me. It fueled me to be the best detective I could be, to fight harder for justice, to never let another case slip through the cracks. That was the only way I knew how to move forward.

It was strange to be loved by a man. Strange to feel the warmth of affection, the comfort of someone caring for me in ways I hadn't let myself dream of in years. Being married? That was an entirely different kind of strange. But the good kind. The kind that made me feel like maybe, just maybe, my best life was still in front of me. And for the first time in a long time, I couldn't wait to see where it would lead.

The End

9 781946 256515